MELTDOWN

LARS EMMERICH

MELTDOWN

PART I

SEATTLE, WASHINGTON

NOBODY LEAVES THIS LIFE UNSCATHED. THERE ARE plenty of scars to go around. That's what Domingo Mondragon's grandmother told him on the day he went to prison. Federal penitentiary. Three years ago, courtesy of the FBI. As in Freaking Bastards International, or Federal Bureau of I-hope-you-rot-in-hell.

Also, FBI as in Domingo Mondragon's current employer.

It's complicated.

Most people knew him as Sabot. Which is to say, most people didn't know him at all. Sabot was his hacker handle. If he'd been a little less prideful and a little more prudent, he'd never have done time. But Sabot wanted the world to know what he'd done, because he was proud of it.

He shut down a government. Just for a day, just for fun. It was a rat-bastard kind of government, one of those bullshit Middle Eastern places, long on oil and backwards religious dogma but tragically short on moral compunction and social responsibility.

Sabot fancied himself as comeuppance personified. From his Queens apartment, working at his kitchen table within earshot of his four live-in siblings and that infernal rattling refrigerator, Sabot organized the cyber attack that crashed every server they owned.

Practically, it meant very little. The servers were back up again in a day or so. There wasn't much lingering damage, except for a few exhausted techs who'd worked overtime in the bowels of the server farm to restore service.

But it sent a message. Screw The Man. Fight the power. Thinking about the attack still gave Sabot a charge.

And he'd had a lot of time to think about it. A little over a year, after the judge suspended most of his sentence to account for all of his cooperation.

It was the cooperation that took the biggest toll. In exchange for years of his own life, Sabot turned rat. The conviction count stood at seventeen, with four more trials in various stages of completion.

Twenty-one in all. It was a lot of friends to sell down the river. Enough to make Sabot look over his shoulder every once in a while. Most of those people were nerdy high school kids and twenty-something maladroits. But Sabot figured at least one or two had friends who knew how to fire a gun. So he kept his eyes open.

The betrayals had been easy enough. "Just be yourself and do what you do," Special Agent Adkins had told him as soon as he signed the plea bargain. "Just pretend we never met. And if you warn anybody of what you're doing, the deal's off. Not to be dramatic, but without a deal, you'll probably die in prison. Just so you know where we're coming from."

Compelling.

Sabot behaved.

While the FBI action hadn't exactly devastated the ranks of the loosely-affiliated quasi-network of hackers known as Anonymous, the arrests had certainly sent a message. One might have the power to shut down an entire country's computer network while watching old Tom and Jerry reruns, but karma might just shove itself right up your ass.

Sabot missed New York, missed the intensity of a rebel's life, missed the seedy low-rent neighborhood that was home, and missed the camaraderie of being a digital outlaw.

More than that, he hated being owned. And he especially hated being owned by the organization he used to publicly taunt. That was tough on his pride.

But the pay was pretty freaking good, especially for a man from the projects. Relative affluence had softened Sabot a bit. The cash buffed a few rough edges off of his personality. He realized there was a reason the middle class rarely revolted. Life just wasn't that bad.

Sabot hadn't ever imagined himself as a Seattle resident. He was New York like baseball and fuck-you. But he was a supervised ex-convict employee of the Federal Bureau of Investigations' West Coast Cyber Task Force. Pretty sweet deal, all told.

There was just one problem. The Bureau had taken away all of his computers. He wasn't even allowed to own a smart phone. His handlers printed out reams of server logs and chat room conversations for him to pore over, using his exquisite knowledge of computer code and the seedy side of the internet to search for evidence of cybercrime, but he wasn't allowed to do his own research, or even sit in front of a computer monitor.

Managing temptation, the boss said. You could take the kid out of the projects, but you really couldn't take the projects out of the kid. At least that's what the Bureau suits thought.

They probably weren't wrong. Sabot had met a few bastards since his release whose lives he'd have loved to jack up. It had been very tempting, and it was remarkably easy to do. In less time than it took to watch a single Seinfeld rerun, Sabot could steal an unlucky mark's bank account, credit card, email, and Facebook passwords. Most people didn't know how truly screwed they'd be if someone locked them out of their own accounts, but Sabot knew. He'd done it to dozens of posers, pricks, and fellow perpetrators, back in the day.

But those days were over. It wasn't like the jail sentence ever went away. It was just suspended. They let him out early so The Man could benefit from his unique talents. If they ever decided he wasn't playing ball, or if he got caught indulging his darker side, Sabot would find himself right back in the big house, fighting to avoid more prison sex.

He stepped from his apartment stoop out into the Seattle drizzle. *Always with the damned rain.* And what was with all the coffee shops in this town? Maybe the caffeine kept people's spirits artificially elevated, preventing them from going bat shit crazy on account of the relentless drear. *Maybe I should drink more coffee.* He sometimes worried that he might be losing his marbles.

Wasn't much he could do about it. He wasn't in a cage, but he wasn't exactly free, either. The Bureau had him by the balls. Permanently.

He opened his umbrella and rounded the corner, nearly running smack into the back of a long queue of people standing on the sidewalk.

Strange.

He stood on his toes to compensate for his diminutive stature, and peered toward the front of the gaggle. The line was apparently for the coffee shop. It was always busy, but Sabot had never seen it *that* busy.

He sidestepped the line and walked past the coffee shop to catch his bus. Half a block later, he looked up from the pavement in front of his feet to see a similar situation outside the local breakfast cafe. People were stacked like cordwood, waiting for their morning muffin and pumpkin spice latte, or whatever the neo-yuppies ate for breakfast.

"What's going on?" he asked a put-upon lady in a black dress and oversized white sneakers.

"Someone said something about the cash register being down," she said.

He grunted and moved on. Didn't want to miss his bus.

He needn't have worried. He arrived at his stop in plenty of time, but was chagrined to discover another flock of angry commuters. On a normal day, there were rarely more than a dozen people waiting at his stop. But today, there were upwards of fifty. They were loud, agitated, annoyed, and annoying.

Sabot sidled up to the fringe of the gaggle and asked a guy in a business suit why the bus stop was so crowded.

The man's reply was puzzling. Not only was Sabot's bus late, but the three preceding buses had also failed to show up.

Sabot wondered why.

"Haven't you heard, buddy?" the man replied with an aggravated look. "The whole damned world is melting down."

LOST MAN LAKE RANCH, COLORADO

THE SUN BARGED INTO THE WINDOW, WARMING
Protégé's face. He awoke. The clock said eight thirty.

Naked, stunning, and amazing, Allison snored softly next to him in
bed, the covers barely covering her hips, her breasts beckoning for more
indulgence. Despite the tingle in his loins, he decided to let her sleep. After
their midnight flight to Aspen in the old man's private Gulfstream jet, they'd
stumbled into bed a little more than three hours ago.

He slipped out of bed, still exhausted but too curious to sleep. He
tightened the curtains to seal out the sunlight, hoping to guarantee Allison
a few more hours of uninterrupted rest, then padded quietly into the next
room.

He smelled coffee. A fresh pot had brewed itself, and Protégé helped
himself to a cup.

He hadn't brought any clothes, but he figured it probably wouldn't be a
problem. The old man tended to think of everything.

Protégé opened the closet door in the suite's anteroom. It was full of
clothes. His size. He put on a pair of cargo pants and a flannel shirt. Not really
his style. He swore by Armani and power ties. Up until yesterday, anyway.

5

oit different now.

outtoned-down CEO, promoted well ahead of his peers
e division of one of the world's most powerful companies.
y ago – really, just a few hours – but it may as well have been
ady, Protégé found himself thinking of his job as being part of
. of a world that probably no longer existed.

ired a cup of coffee, opened the sliding glass door to the balcony,
ped out into the crisp mountain air, taken aback once again by the
iding enormity of the peak that loomed large across the stark valley.
ir was thin, cold, and invigorating. It felt like possibility, with a dash
anger.

He'd had his fill of the latter. Life behind a big oak desk, with legions
of kowtowing underlings at one's beck and call, wasn't entirely disagreeable,
and Protégé's recent foray into a far more physical, visceral, and unforgiving
world had left him wondering about the wisdom of his decision to come along
on Archive's ride.

Crazy old bastard. Protégé had half expected the plan to fail, and Archive
himself freely admitted their odds were just a smidge better than even.

He'd played his part, preserving his status with the wizened old tycoon,
a billionaire multiple times over in various disparate industries, but a large
part of Protégé had *hoped* the plan would fail. That way, they'd have avoided
what was bound to be a very painful aftermath.

Speaking of which.

Protégé freshened his coffee, buttoned his shirt, slipped quietly from the
room, and made his way to the vast sitting room on the lodge's first floor.

It was time to see just how successful they'd been, and to discover just
how painful the aftermath might be.

"My friend, it appears that we've summoned the kraken." Though he hadn't
slept, not a hair on Archive's ghost-white mane was out of place, and his
signature goatee narrowed to a razor sharp point at its tip. He wore a perfectly
tailored suit, also a signature item, and twirled his silver-topped walking cane

absently as he sat in a plush leather armchair before a giant wall of televis
each tuned to a different news station.

Protégé felt dazzled and overwhelmed by all of the information in fr
of him, unintelligible text scrolling by like a giant ant army, and wonder
how the old man didn't have a seizure from all of the photonic stimulation.

Protégé took a breath and settled his eyes on a single TV screen, slowly
digesting the news loop's import. "Oh, shit," he said. "I guess we've made a
bit of a mess. Chernobyl meets Wall Street."

"Precisely as we predicted," Archive said with a small, satisfied smile.
"Don't tell anyone I'm pleased, though. I've ostensibly lost billions, and
millions more by the second."

"Something tells me you'll squeak by."

The old man chuckled. "Quite so." He pushed a button on a remote
control, and all of the screens coalesced to a single news station, the giant,
panicked talking head cast larger than life on the ostentatious liquid crystal
monolith hung on the wall.

"Devastation," the on-scene reporter said, the stately New York Stock
Exchange building in view behind him. "Absolute devastation. For the first
time since the terror attacks on 9/11, every American exchange is closed.
Tokyo's in free fall. The FTSE's been nuked. I don't even want to look at the
dollar—"

"Freefall is a great way to describe the dollar, too," the anchor interjected.
"I'm stunned. This is just… unbelievable."

"Unbelievable is right, Maria. Do we even have the mechanism to
calculate the losses the US economy is experiencing right now? We might be
a Third World country by noon."

Motion stirred behind the reporter, and the cameraman zoomed in on
the main entrance to the exchange, where traders suddenly billowed out like
well-tailored smoke from the doorway, in a mad dash to be somewhere else.

"It looks like something's happening behind you, Jim," the anchor said.

"I'm getting word here, Maria… I'm getting word that… Can this be
correct? Can we confirm this before I announce it on national television,
people?" The reporter's eyes fixed on someone off-camera, and he put his
finger to his earpiece.

ons,

at

d

e said a second later. "Oh, my. Oh, my God."

d to charge out of the exchange, hailing cabs and running ubway stations.

s face turned ashen, and he took several breaths before aria, I think I'm getting an idea of where those traders are ting word here that the Federal Reserve Bank is, uh… well, I'm e Fed, all twelve banks, is completely *closed!*"

ews anchor was agape, speechless. "I can't begin to fathom what that nean," she finally said. "The Federal Reserve Bank system lends cash member banks for daily operation. Without that short term cash…"

"It's unbelievable. I can't believe this is happening," the field reporter said.

"Ladies and gentlemen," the anchor said, "this is truly a grave development. I just urge you to remain calm…" More panicked stock brokers dashed from the exchange, spilling out into the streets, charging headlong into traffic. "… and I'm sure we'll get a better idea of what's going on before too long…"

Archive pushed the power button, and the giant screen died. "It begins."

"Still pleased as punch?"

Archive mulled. He sighed. "A tad concerned now, to be terribly honest."

Protégé nodded. "It does seem to have a bit of an apocalyptic vibe about it."

VETERAN'S HOSPITAL, WASHINGTON, DC

SPECIAL AGENT SAM JAMESON LAID HER HEAD ON AIR Force Colonel Brock James' chest, letting her blazing red hair fall over his body, hearing his heartbeat through the hospital linens, inhaling his scent, feeling the familiar warmth and contentment his being brought to hers. "I thought I'd lost you," she said.

"You damn near did," he said, repositioning the intravenous line taped to his arm. "I thought that guy with those crazy wolf eyes was going to snap me in half, or put a bullet between my eyes."

"I'm glad he didn't."

"I'm glad you saved the day," he said.

"Aw, shucks." She nibbled his earlobe, heard his sigh, felt him nudge closer to her.

The nurse walked in. "I'm supposed to check your vitals and kick you out," she said.

"Was it something we said?" Brock asked, stopping his hand's southerly migration on Sam's midriff.

"Hardly. We did such a good job putting you back together that you no longer need us."

9

ne monitor. "Heart rate's a little high," she said, the
g smile on her face.

d.

'A little twitterpation is good for the soul."

iled. "Looks like you're healthy enough to contemplate
vities. But can you walk?"

Brock said. "And I whine a lot."

e laughed. "It'll hurt for a while. But I think you're in good shape
o go back out into the wild." She scribbled something, tore off the
paper, and handed it to Sam. "My number," she said. "In case you
er need… anything." She blushed again, and left the room.

am and Brock dressed. The news channel prattled on in the background
ow volume, reporters muttering apocalyptic words and phrases in
unned awe.

Brock walked gingerly toward the hospital lobby, Sam in tow, carrying a
bag of bloody clothes and bandages, remnants of the previous weekend's
nightmarish encounter with a brood of very disagreeable bastards.

They rounded the corner and groaned. A crowd of patients queued at
the front desk. "I hate lines," Sam said, pulling out her Homeland badge and
holding it up in the air. She walked to the front of the gaggle and addressed
the admissions nurse. "Did your help call in sick?"

The nurse laughed. "I wish. This crazy computer's acting up. Something's
wrong with the billing system, so I can't check anybody out. I'm having to
write everything down on a piece of paper."

Sam grimaced. "Related to that news story?"

"There's a news story?"

"Never mind. Can I fill out a form to save some time?"

The nurse handed her a ream of paperwork. "Don't know if it's going to
save any time, but here you go."

"Thanks," Sam said. Then, under her breath, "I'll mail it in when I'm

finished." She returned to Brock, grabbed his hand, and walked o
door.

It took a full ten minutes to reach the car, and Brock struggle
battered frame and wounded leg into Sam's Porsche. He groaned as sh
her way around the parking garage exit ramp. "Sorry, love," she said

"You won't hear me complain. Your driving skills saved my ass las

Indeed they had. Sam had chased down one of the world's bigges
commandeered his vehicle, and blasted away a kneecap with her .45
had served as sufficient motivation for the goon to make the call to let
go, ending a three-day kidnapping adventure that would undoubtedly r
them in their nightmares for years to come.

Not a second too soon, either, Sam thought. The doctors had said
were lucky. Brock had gone into shock, and there wasn't much time to spa

Brock flipped on the radio. None of the satellite stations were workin
"Strange."

He twisted the knob until a terrestrial news station came on. Mor
financial gloom and doom.

"This sounds like a big deal," Sam said, pointing at the radio.

Brock nodded. "And I thought you were crazy for not owning stock," he
said. "I'm glad you talked some sense into me. I'd be penniless right about
now otherwise."

"Brokers are going to start leaping from tall buildings."

"Probably already have."

"In a related story," a grave-sounding newscaster said, "all of the trains
are empty today in the nation's capital. That's because a glitch in the payment
system has prevented commuters from purchasing tickets at automated
kiosks, and there aren't enough human attendants to meet the demand.
Passenger lines at some of the busiest subway stations are said to extend all
the way up the stairs and out onto the sidewalks. There's speculation that
this payment malfunction is related to the banking anomaly that's been
reported on the financial networks, but the Federal Reserve has so far not
issued a statement."

"Holy shit," Brock said. "This is turning into quite a party."

ut the front

d to fit his
he wound

night."
thugs,
. That
Brock
evisit

hey
re.
ng.

e

d at it, groaned, and answered. "Boss, I
 from last night," she said.

n the other end of the line. "I know, Sam.
 good boss, mostly because he stayed out of
asn't a bad thing in a stifling bureaucracy like
d Security.

ndoffishness might be attributable to the fact that
ied violent deaths while on the job. It had taken a
l the vacancy after the second guy met an untimely

need you to come in as soon as you can," McClane said.

. couldn't ruin someone else's day?"
k if it wasn't important. See you soon?"
you first."

SOMEWHERE ON THE EAST COAST
OF THE UNITED STATES

IT WAS OFTEN SAID THAT THE PRESIDENCY OF THE UNITED States was the most powerful office on the planet. There may have been a time when that was true, but it had to have been a long, long time ago.

Nearly a century, by the Facilitator's reckoning. Maybe even longer. It was impossible to know for certain. There was no archive of previous Facilitators and their deeds, for obvious reasons, so he couldn't be precisely sure about the time when the Presidency became a pro forma office in service of the Consultancy's interests.

Often, that knowledge – that he was the most powerful living human – pleased the Facilitator, a god among men. At his bidding, kings and titans rose and fell.

Quietly, of course. True power moved in whispers and shadows. If clamor was unavoidable, it was carefully arranged so that it never led back to the Consultancy. And it never, *ever* pointed to the Facilitator himself. The spotlight was for amateurs and bit players. Prime movers were more than content to pull the levers, then watch from a distance as the world conformed to their inexorable will.

Heady stuff. Oil, gold, diamonds, rare earth metals, government agencies, heavy industry, financial services of all ilk – they made the world go around, and they all orbited the Facilitator, captive to his massive gravity, a social and financial singularity as powerful as any black hole.

It was the way of things. The principle of cumulative advantage. More power inevitably accrued to the powerful, and more riches to the rich. Sure, occasional revolution was inevitable, but it was generally harmless, if managed well, and there were layers upon layers of more likely targets to absorb any negative consequences, insulating the truly elite from the morass.

Usually.

All of the power, wealth, and control normally gave the Facilitator a deep sense of satisfaction, the feeling of meaningful accomplishment, of having attained the loftiest heights of man, anonymous though he was in all but the tiniest of circles.

But not today.

Today, it just felt like weight. Something had shifted. The world had tilted on its axis. The same sun shone in the sky, but today it portended menace, a mask of hate-filled fusion hurling the worst of all evils: change.

The Facilitator's eyes returned to the silent television set.

Complete and total meltdown. It was a disaster of unfathomable proportions, probably unrecoverable.

An alarm sounded on his desk. Time for his heart medicine. *Getting too old for this. Time to find a successor?*

Folly, he knew. Being the Facilitator was a job for life. One didn't retire from it, though more than one Facilitator had certainly *been* retired. The sword of Damocles swung dangerously above his head, but he had grown accustomed to its presence. He was an old man, and death no longer fazed him.

But a stock market crash certainly did.

And now, it appeared, the worst imaginable calamity had also happened.

There was no contingency plan.

If he wielded the hammer of the gods, the very fabric of its essence, and the very ether through which it sliced, was surely made of dollars.

And the dollar was dying.

Lesser men would have been ossified long ago by an entrenchment as royal as the Facilitator's. But not him. He had not won his post atop the

Consultancy by accident. He was brilliant, resourceful, determined, and utterly without compunction. A man of decision and action.

An hour ago, seconds after learning of his trusted deputy's arrest, he had given the order to end the man's life. Thirty years of friendship and exceptionally profitable business association, but the Facilitator hadn't flinched, hadn't even thought about it, had barely registered the enormity.

He just did what needed doing.

That's what he would do now.

Without question, the game had changed. But he was still its most powerful player.

He picked up the phone. He had work to do.

SEATTLE, WASHINGTON

SABOT CALLED HIS SUPERVISOR'S NUMBER AT THE regional Bureau office, but nobody answered. He wasn't allowed to be late, even a little bit, and the bus situation was a problem.

He didn't own a car. Had never learned to drive, really. Driving in Queens was like running underwater. Terribly inefficient and seriously aggravating, and he'd never seen the point.

Seattle was agreeably walkable, and public transportation was usually reliable, so he'd never bothered with a car after moving out west, either.

But he owned a bike.

He cursed under his breath as he trudged back home through the rain, already soaked despite the umbrella. The prospect of pedaling through the rain-soaked streets all the way to the regional Bureau office had put him in a foul mood.

That was probably why he never noticed the guy on his apartment stoop, lurking in the shadows, or the other guy, the one who had been following him for the last two blocks.

Sabot shoved his hand into his pocket, pulled out the key, and reached for the lock.

But he never got there. A gloved hand pressed hard over his mouth and neck, pulling him backwards, his legs blocked by something or someone behind him. He felt his head snap backwards, and feared that his neck might break.

The pissed off hackers had finally gotten to him, he thought.

The pavement came up to meet him, cold and soaked, and he felt wetness seep instantly through his clothing. Something sharp jabbed into his shoulder, a burning sensation in its wake, and he suddenly felt overwhelmingly dizzy, as if he might throw up. But he didn't stay awake long enough for his stomach to follow through on its threat.

He had a crushing headache, and he wanted to keep sleeping, but that voice wouldn't shut the hell up. It kept calling his name.

And the motion. His head kept jerking around, accompanied by a loud slapping noise each time, but he didn't know what that was all about. He was sure that he could figure it all out if he opened his eyes, but Sabot really didn't want to open his eyes. He just wanted to sleep.

Something forced his right eye open, and a vicious light stormed the breach, making his headache even louder and more insistent. "What the hell!" he heard himself say, but it sounded far away and slow and muffled.

Someone sat him upright, and Sabot immediately tried to lay down again. *Can't sleep sitting up.*

Smack. Something hit his face with a vengeance, clearing the cobwebs. He opened his eyes. "Who the hell are you?"

Hard eyes searched him. A square jaw, blonde hair, big shoulders, and big teeth. "A friend." Smoker's voice. Smoker's breath, too.

"Don't seem too friendly to me."

"Sorry about that. It'll make sense before too long."

"Really, man, what is this? I've got places to be. I can't be screwing around, man. I'm on parole."

The hard eyes softened into a near-smile. "We know, Sabot."

"Who's *we?*"

"Trust me. It'll all become clear before too long."

Sabot stood. He remained vertical for a fraction of a second before the narcotic aftereffects took their toll. Then he fell to the floor in a pile.

"You bastards messed me up, man."

The guy laughed. Sabot heard more laughing coming from somewhere else in the room, but he didn't see who it came from.

"Maybe it's best if you just stayed seated, Sabot." Strong hands lifted him onto a nearby sofa. "We'll explain our offer, you'll agree, and we'll all be on our way in time for The Price is Right."

Sabot looked carefully at the blonde haired man with the big square jaw and the hard eyes. "How the hell do you know about The Price is Right?"

Another near-grin. "Sabot, we know a great deal about you. Down to your strangely juvenile mid-morning television break."

"What's your handle?"

"We're not hackers," the man said. "I'm Smith. That's Jones." He nodded toward a tall, thick oak of a man standing silently in the corner. Sabot hadn't seen him before.

"Right," Sabot said. "And I'm Yankee Freakin' Doodle."

"Hardly. I'd say you're Bronx beaner, through and through."

"Queens."

"Same thing."

"The hell it is. What do you want with me?"

"Nothing."

"Then why am I here?"

"Because a very powerful man wants something from you."

"I'm not interested," Sabot said. "I gotta stay straight, man. I can't go back in the can."

"You miss it, don't you?"

"Prison?"

"Hacking."

Sabot snorted. "Naw, man, I don't miss it. What the hell do you think I'm going to say? I'm stayin' straight, and that's that. Now let me out of here."

"When's the last time you heard from your little brother? Miguel, is it? The one just out of rehab?"

Sabot hardened his stare. "What are you playin' at, man? You don't mess with a man's family. You know who I work for?"

Smith's square jaw flexed. "As a matter of fact, we do. You report to Special Agent Adkins. Your boss and babysitter."

Jones handed Smith a phone. Smith handed it to Sabot. "Go on. Say hi."

It was Special Agent Adkins. "Sorry, man. This showed up with a lot of momentum," he said. "Don't know who's pulling the strings, but they're powerful tugs and big strings. You'll report to these guys until they're done with you."

Sabot handed the phone back.

Smith smiled that hard smile again. "Congratulations. You've just been hired." He threw a set of keys on the desk and walked out, Jones in tow.

Sabot rose. His legs were still shaky from the drug they'd used to knock him out. *Kidnapped, then hired?* Had to be some kind of joke.

If so, then Adkins was in on it, too. *Bastard. Must have been hiding a sense of humor all this time.* Special Agent Adkins was as buttoned-down Bureau as anyone on the planet. He talked about *leveraging* capabilities – whatever the hell that meant – and everybody who had something to say about a particular topic was a *stakeholder.*

Nobody talked like that in Queens. Leverage was what you used to dislocate someone's pinky, and if a *vato* needed to know something, you just told him straight up. No fancy words to make shit sound more complicated than it was, to make people think you were smart. Smart *did*. Smart didn't talk about it. *Nothin' but the realzz in the hood, yo.*

But that was a long time ago and an entire continent away, and in the interstitial eon, Sabot had become accustomed to Adkins' particular brand of stilted colloquialism and bone-dry personality. *Like an ashtray.* Didn't make sense that Adkins would be in on any kind of scheme. His voice on the phone certainly lent legitimacy to what was otherwise a pretty sketchy show. *Freaking kidnapped.* That was a new one. What would Angie think about that?

Thinking about her reminded Sabot he had someplace to be. Lunch. He looked at his watch and cursed, then made for the door.

Locked.

So was the other door.

He swiped the keys off the table. There were two doors in the room, and the keychain held two keys. Seemed like simple math. He tried the door that Smith and Jones had exited moments earlier. Neither key worked.

"What are you playin' at, assholes?" Sabot shouted. He didn't like being locked up. In his experience, it led to unwanted advances from large men.

He tried the first key in the second door. More bad luck.

But the second key and the second lock were made for each other, and the knob twisted with little effort. Good thing, too. Sabot's blood was up, and he was prepared to get a bit medieval. *Lock me up? Bitches got no idea.*

He stepped through the door. Dark room, cheap furniture, no windows, no other door, no sign of life. Small, close, warm, humid. *A little cramped for a broom closet,* Sabot thought, annoyed.

He inhaled.

He smelled a computer.

A *new* computer. It smelled like home, like possibility, like the world getting ready to lie down at his feet.

It smelled like forbidden fruit. Like a parole violation. Like incarceration. *But damn, it smelled* good.

It sat on a small desk, otherwise empty, which faced the door. A new laptop. He could shut down a continent with it. Overthrow kings and douchebags, for no apparent reason.

The blinking light of a cable modem on the floor caught his eye. Like the computer, it beckoned.

They gotta know how hard they're messing with me right now.

Sabot turned to leave, but something bronze reflected the light on the edge of the desk. One of those fancy name tags, the kind you see on the suits' desks at the Bureau.

He read the writing: DOMINGO MONDRAGON, BITCOIN COLLECTOR.

What gives? Some kind of mindscrew?

A phone rang, unnecessarily loud in the tiny space, startling him. It was an old-school phone, hanging up on the wall, and it wouldn't stop ringing.

Finally, sick of the noise, he picked it up. He listened.

"Sabot?"

He recognized the voice. "Adkins?"

"Yeah. Confused yet?"

Very. But Sabot didn't say anything. He felt like he was being manipulated. He didn't like the feeling.

"I'm supposed to tell you to google Satoshi," Adkins said.

"Sa-what?"

"Satoshi." Adkins spelled it.

"Adkins, are you saying you want me to use this computer?"

"No. But *they* want you to use that computer. No holds barred. And I've been informed that *I* want what *they* want." A small chuckle. "Don't jizz yourself."

The line went dead.

THE TEXAS PANHANDLE

MIKE CHARLES DROVE NORTH INTO THE WARM TEXOMA afternoon. He was known as Boomer in his retired fighter pilot circles. But in the most important circle, he was known as Stalwart.

Mesquite, dust, barbed wire, and an occasional ranch animal moved through his vision. He drove a tiny rental car, barely large enough to accommodate his tall, athletic frame. He chose it for the gas mileage. The trunk was full not of luggage, but of gasoline. Four ten-gallon cans of the stuff. The fumes seeped through the backseat and assaulted Stalwart's nostrils, and he was occasionally forced to roll down a window. The gas and the wind noise took turns annoying him. *The price of revolution.* He chuckled to himself.

Forty gallons should more than cover the long trip north to Colorado. Lost Man Lake Ranch was a very long day's drive away, and Stalwart expected difficulty filling up. Gas stations wanted money in exchange for fuel, after all, and the money thing was going to be a problem for a while.

Until people figured things out, that is.

Stalwart hoped it didn't take too long. In fact, he was betting on it.

He turned on the radio. The satellite stations weren't operating, of course, but that was to be expected. He'd played a substantial role in that particular condition. *Large enough to be locked away for a very long time,* he thought. He hoped things didn't break that way.

But they certainly could. His not-so-little role had started with one of the most outrageous larcenies in history. He helped steal the machine that ushered in the current chaos.

Stalwart's brilliant friend used that machine to smoke three communications satellites, two massive fiber optic cable relay stations, the New York Stock Exchange, and the Chicago Board of Trade.

Big day.

Now, Stalwart was left hoping his assumptions about human nature weren't too far off.

The power isn't in the symbol. The power is in the agreement. He repeated these words to himself like a mantra.

He hoped the masses would realize it before they tore each other to shreds.

A strident voice brought his mind back to the present. "Stand by for the President of the United States," the radio announcer said.

"My fellow Americans," a familiar, stentorian voice began. *He sounds like a president,* Stalwart thought. *Even if he's a shithead.*

"These cherished United States have been the victim of a vicious attack on our liberty, on our values, on our morals, and on our freedom itself." *Overplayed. Predictable.*

"Early this morning, terrorists disabled key elements of our communications infrastructure," the President said. *Terrorist. Hmm. Never thought of myself that way,* Stalwart thought.

"We believe this attack was carried out within our borders," the president continued, "by religious extremists." *Religion?* Stalwart laughed out loud.

"Today, for the first time since those dark days following the horrific attacks of 9/11..." The President's voice droned on.

Stalwart sighed audibly. He knew the comparison was inevitable. But it was manipulative. It was a good case in point for why he had chosen to participate in the scheme in the first place. *Because we grovel at the feet of the people we empower, begging them with our blind stupidity, indifference, and ignorance, to lie to us and steal from us.*

The president's voice rose. "I have not yet ruled out military action against these pernicious individuals and the organizations that back them. Today, I issue a stern warning to those responsible for this barbarism: The United States of America will hunt you down. We will find you in your dark caves and your desert training grounds. We will punish those nations that harbor and shelter you. We will leave no stone unturned. We will bring you to justice."

Stalwart chuckled, shaking his head. *Always fighting the last war. They really have no clue, do they?*

"Today," the president continued, "is indeed a dark day for our nation and its allies. Our trade has been halted. Our banks have suffered setbacks. Important communications assets have been damaged."

Not damaged. Destroyed. Stalwart smiled.

"But these setbacks are temporary," POTUS intoned. "They are superficial. In the long run, they are meaningless. The strength of our nation is our people, our resiliency, our resourcefulness, our industry, our intelligence, our education. And, above all, our moral rectitude and our core values of integrity, ingenuity, and industry. We shall stand together, and together we shall rise from this setback."

He's half right. The symbols were, indeed, meaningless in and of themselves. Rather, Stalwart thought, they were meaningless when separated from what they represented, which was really the important thing. *The agreement between humans.* The exchange of value, of life energy, of items of need. This was what really separated humanity from the animals, Stalwart figured. The uniquely human capacity for cooperation.

Currency was the omnipresent symbol of that all-important capacity. It was the life blood of commerce, of society.

And it needed to die. It had been twisted beyond recognition, distorted by those in power into an instrument of oppression. None are more hopelessly enslaved than those who falsely believe they are free. Plato? Goethe? Stalwart couldn't remember who said it. But truer words were never spoken, he figured.

Insidiously, the shackles weren't overt. Really, the whole thing was beautifully and elegantly conceived, and flawlessly executed, Stalwart thought. And it probably wasn't even designed to screw over almost everyone else on the planet. It was probably just designed to enrich a few already-rich old men.

The Fed. The root of all modern evil. At least in Archive's view. Stalwart tended to agree. How could one make ephemeral the assets that individuals held safe and dear? Quite easily. Just dilute them. Make them common. Print more. Every new dollar made every old dollar less valuable. You could hide a nickel under your pillow for a few years, but the dark magic of inflation would eventually turn it into a penny.

And the whole world was infected. At the moment, the world's most valuable commodity was oil. And oil was traded exclusively using dollars. Greenbacks. No other currency would buy you a barrel of oil, on any exchange in the world. George Washington's face made the world go 'round. No two ways about it.

So every nation on earth had been co-opted into replacing their own blood with the blood of the beast. Rather, this blood *was* the beast. The dollar was a carcinogen, a virus, the delivery vector for ever-more strident, increasingly thorough oppression.

"Rest assured that while the short-term will be uncertain and uncomfortable," the president said, "in the long run, nothing has changed."

Half right again. The short-term would certainly be uncertain and uncomfortable.

But *everything* had changed.

At least, Stalwart hoped it had.

He crossed the Red River, and with that crossing, he found himself in Oklahoma. He checked his gas gauge. Half full. His plan was to keep his tank above that mark at all times. It was only prudent.

Stalwart decided to stop at the next rest stop to refuel. There was no use even trying a gas station. They would undoubtedly all look like they looked during the gas crisis of the early 1970's: cars lined up for blocks, motorists alternating between a grim collegiality and bare-knuckled hostility, depending on how desperately they needed the gas.

Best to stiff-arm that entire scene, he thought.

But he wasn't prepared for what awaited as he rounded the bend and exited the highway.

Something was wrong. There were a few dozen cars in the parking lot, but the red brick building housing the restrooms appeared nearly abandoned. Nobody milled about. It was alarmingly still.

Stalwart popped the trunk and the refueling door as he stepped out of the tiny rental car. He made his way around to the back of the car and reached for a gas can.

"Hey, buddy," a distant voice said. Stalwart looked up. Fat man in overalls, walking around from the back of the brick building, big smile on his face. "Over here, buddy," the man said, waving.

It felt strange. Where was everyone else? There were way too many cars in the parking lot for just one person to be visible.

Something else was off, too. This part of the country was known for its unabashed friendliness, but the fat guy seemed *too* friendly. He was trying a bit too hard.

Stalwart closed the trunk, slapped the gas flap shut, and climbed back into the rental car, twisting the ignition key as he pulled the door closed. He locked the doors, backed out of the parking spot and turned north, toward the rest stop exit.

He glanced at the redneck in overalls on his way past. The man was speaking into a walkie-talkie.

This is not good, Stalwart decided. He reached beneath his seat to remove a small black case, glancing out the window occasionally to keep the car pointed in the right direction as he accelerated through the parking lot.

The case's handle caught on the seat adjustment lever, and Stalwart cursed. He resolved that he'd keep the .45 pistol in a far more accessible location in the future. He tried various combinations of brute force and finesse to remove the case.

Finally, it yielded, and Stalwart threw the case onto the passenger seat. He looked forward.

Sonuvabitch. He slammed on the brakes, feeling the chintzy car's antilock system hammering away, feeling his body thrown forward into the shoulder strap. Shock and disbelief crossed his face. *This can't be happening.*

The car came to a lurching stop a handful of inches from another very large man in flannel and overalls.

Wielding a shotgun.

Stalwart slammed the car into reverse and stepped on the gas, only to hear a bowel-shaking blast from behind him. He felt the unmistakable sensation of a tire flattening. A third redneck flashed across his rearview mirror, his hand working the slide on a twelve-gauge Remington.

Redneck Number Two leveled his shotgun at Stalwart's face.

The driver's side window shattered, a gloved fist propelling shards of glass into Stalwart's face. The hand reached in and opened the door from the inside.

Stalwart reached for the case on the passenger's seat containing the .45, and frantically fumbled with the latches.

"I wouldn't do that, friend," a gruff voice said, the sentence punctuated by the sound of a shotgun shell racking into place in the chamber.

Stalwart turned his head to face the nearest assailant, who motioned him out of the car. "Ya'll move real slow-like, y'hear?" Youngish. Face oddly misshapen. Stupid-sounding. Dangerous.

"Are you sure about this?" Stalwart asked. "I mean, the police are bound to stop by any moment, don't you think?"

The three men laughed, harsh and cackling. One spoke into a radio. "Clem, this here city boy says the po-lice are coming. What do you think?"

Motion near the brick house. Stalwart turned. A man walked through the grass toward Stalwart's stopped car, dressed in black, large Smokey hat on his head, sporting a big utility belt full of police stuff. He had the unhurried stride of a man in charge. He spat tobacco juice every dozen steps or so.

Stalwart felt a gun barrel in his back, nudging him forward toward the cop. Highway patrolman, he realized as the distance between them shrank.

Not so much a patrolman. More like highwayman.

"Not from around here, are you, boy?"

Stalwart bristled. A decorated combat veteran, he didn't take kindly to being called a boy, no matter how many guns were pointed at him to emphasize the point. "This is how you treat your visitors, *boy?*" he asked.

The shotgun butt landed with a dull thud, digging into the small of his back, the pain of his instantly-bruised kidney bringing him to his knees on the hard gravel.

"Come on, now," the cop said, his face wearing the smile of a man accustomed to wielding power capriciously. "No need for bad blood. Best you make nice. Ain't it, Jimbo?" He nodded toward the fat man in overalls, who had finally made his way over to Stalwart's car.

"S'right Clem," Jimbo said, somehow stretching the cop's name into two syllables. He waddled up to Stalwart, still on his knees in the gravel, grimacing in pain.

The big man clamped a rough, weathered hand hard around Stalwart's jaw and lifted his face to look him in the eye, lips parting in a malicious grin, revealing a messed-up grille with a smattering of brown teeth peppered with tobacco remnants. "You gon' be here for a while, I reckon."

DEPARTMENT OF HOMELAND SECURITY
HEADQUARTERS, WASHINGTON, DC

DAN GABLE POUNDED AWAY ON THE KEYBOARD OF HIS office computer. Sam realized it was representative of how she most often thought of him, as the eminently capable guy behind the scenes, gaining access and marshaling resources.

But that wasn't entirely accurate. Her deputy had certainly seen his share of field action. He'd saved her life on more occasions than she could count.

Last night was one of them.

And on one particularly memorable occasion, it could be argued that Dan had brought Sam *back* to life.

Dan was Sam's singular exception to the golden rule of counterespionage investigation: trust no one. Trust was risk. Trust was vulnerability. Trust was blindness.

Sam trusted Dan implicitly. He'd simply proven himself too valuable to be anything but her right-hand man, and despite the rugged cavalier-ness and pleasingly frontier-esque individualism inherent in the spy catcher's mantra, the world was simply too big, too powerful, and too screwed up to tackle alone. Every Sam needed a Dan.

If he ever turned on her, she knew it would be catastrophic. But he probably wouldn't turn on her. She didn't think it was in his nature.

Plus, they loved each other like siblings, even though Dan worked for Sam. Their relationship was informal but always professional, collegial but all business. They hung out together on weekends, but that was only because the job demanded they work weekends. Bastards needed catching, and that rarely happened on a convenient, predictable schedule.

"So what's this all about?" she asked.

"Something weird has gone down," Dan said, looking up from his computer monitor.

"Sounded that way. We saw the news ticker on in Brock's hospital room, and caught a little bit of the radio news on the way home."

"What station?"

"Some local thing," Sam said. "My XM channels weren't working."

"That checks. XM rides on the same birds that carry bank transactions."

"Birds?"

"Satellites," Dan explained. "Someone fried a few of them. And the terrestrial cable switching trunks, too. Mason McClane called a while ago, panties all in a wad over some call his boss got from Sec Treas. Everyone was wondering how the hell the most connected country in the world could somehow end up with its banking system cut off entirely from all communications."

"So how'd you figure it out?"

"I didn't," Dan said. "I just called an NSA buddy when I got to work. He sent me a SIGINT file. I was just starting to play with it when you walked in."

"Quick thinking. I hadn't made the signals intelligence connection."

"Yep. Not a single cell phone can fart without the NSA catching a whiff."

"Creepy."

"Handy, in this case," Dan said. He imported a page full of numbers and symbols into some other program. Seconds later, a map appeared.

"Looks like Virginia," Sam observed.

Dan zoomed in. "Hampton, to be precise." He whistled. "Someone threw a ton of energy skyward. Looks like they did it a few times, separated by just a few seconds."

Sam shook her head. She thought about how many satellites orbited the earth, and how dependent the global economy had become on satellite communications. Because they were so far away and so difficult to damage while in orbit, satellites had enjoyed relative sanctuary from the innumerable skirmishes that punctuated the human soap opera every day.

Until last night, apparently.

"I think the game has just changed in a big way," she said.

Dan nodded. "Yeah. This is a big deal. And the fact that they took out the transoceanic fiber-optic relay stations means they knew exactly what they were doing."

"I thought at first that it was some sort of brute force thing," Sam said, "but this is starting to feel very strategic. Surgical, even."

Dan's phone rang. He answered, listened for a second, then said, "She's right here."

Sam took the phone. Mason McClane sounded tired. *There's a lot of that going around today.* "Hi Mace," Sam said to her boss.

"Sam, sorry to drag you into this. You've had a helluva weekend. I'm relieved and happy you got Brock back in good shape, and you seriously cracked some skulls in the process."

"Thanks, Mace. All's well that ends well, I suppose."

"Things have gone to shit. Can you come upstairs?"

McClane's office wasn't posh by any stretch, but it was comfortable, and the view was even better than Sam's. Looking east, Sam saw the Capitol building, and the Washington Monument stood tall, stark, and beautiful to the west. She recalled a very memorable midnight chase a few years ago that had ended in a bitter, bloody struggle at the foot of the monument. Wasn't the kind of thing a girl could forget.

"Sam?" McClane was looking at her. "You with us?"

"Yeah. Sorry. What did you say?"

"I was just saying, this is exceptionally sensitive stuff. Eyes only."

Sam nodded. *Usually is.*

"It wasn't just an attack against the communication nodes used by the banking industry," McClane said. "It looks like there's much more. All twelve regional Federal Reserve banks were hacked."

"There are twelve Federal Reserve banks?" Sam asked. "I thought there was just one."

McClane shook his head. "I thought the same thing, but I've gotten a civics lesson this morning. The Fed banks are not really federal, and they're not really reserve banks. But yes, there are twelve of them. Or there were. Today, there are effectively *none*."

"Come again?" Dan said.

"Completely crushed. Some kind of a cyber attack. None of the system administrators at any of the banks can even log in."

Sam looked puzzled. "So they can't ignore their email or play solitaire. What's the big deal?"

McClane laughed. "That's what I thought, too, until Treasury explained it to the Director and me this morning. Here's the rub. There is almost no money in the country's banking system. Almost every bank borrows its daily supply of money, then lends it out at a higher rate. They make money on the spread."

"And you're saying that the daily money supply comes from those twelve non-federal, non-reserve banks?"

"Exactly. In the form of new loans. The federal banks exist to make the money supply 'elastic.'" McClane made quotation marks in the air with his hands. "Even if there's a run on a local bank, that bank can borrow as much cash as it needs, in order to avoid a panic."

"Except, now they can't," Dan said.

Sam considered for a moment. "We're totally screwed," she concluded.

McClane nodded. "Pretty much."

"Has the herd stampeded yet?"

"CNBC was on-air live at the stock exchange this morning when the brokers all figured out what happened. They ran out of the building like it was on fire, scrambling to withdraw their own funds before the local banks ran out of cash."

Sam shook her head.

"We've asked the news stations not to broadcast this," McClane continued, turning his computer monitor so Dan and Sam could see it. He clicked on a video, and expanded it to full-screen size.

Absolute bedlam. It looked like a Third World war zone. The video showed a parking lot full of cars, and full of crazed, rioting people bludgeoning each other and hurling things through the windows of a building. The sign in the corner of the parking lot said First National Bank of Reston.

"Jesus," Sam said. "Where are we, Mozambique?"

McClane nodded grimly. "May as well be. It's a little-known paradox that as a currency melts down, that currency's cash suddenly becomes extremely scarce. People scramble to get as much of it as they can, and spend it to buy food and water before the currency inflates so far they can't afford to buy anything with it."

Weird. "So much for a few days of relaxation," Sam said.

But she was prepared. She had a hardened shelter in her basement full of food, water, guns, and even gold. She'd installed it after a particularly grisly case left her more than a little paranoid. Seemed like it would come in handy right about now.

"Right. We think there's something else going on, though," McClane said. "Like I mentioned, there was that computer virus that filleted the Fed."

"Some would say they had it coming," Sam said.

"Maybe so. But this virus went miles beyond a mere denial of service. From what they can tell, the virus actually overwrote all of the account information. For *every* account."

"Wow," Dan said. "So it's not just that the money isn't available. Nobody knows how much money each account holder *should* have available."

"Right," McClane said.

"This is going to make Paris in 1789 look like a vacation," Sam said.

"And Russia in 1917," Dan said.

"You don't know the half of it," McClane said. "The DNI called FBI and DHS this morning. There's preliminary evidence to suggest that the virus that decimated the Fed came from *inside the NSA*."

Sam let out a low whistle. "I'm sure nobody's spun up about that at all," she said sardonically.

"Not at all," McClane responded in kind. "Now you know why this is eyes-only."

"Yeah," Sam said. "We wouldn't want the masses to know they were right."

Dan laughed. "How do you work for a government you don't trust?"

"Keep your enemies close," Sam said darkly. *Honestly, it's a damn good question,* she thought.

"So here's the deal," McClane said. "We have two angles to chase down here. One is the giant electromagnetic emission that came out of Hampton. I think Dan filled you in on that."

Sam nodded.

"The other angle is the NSA breach. Obviously, we need to tread very lightly there." McClane looked sternly at Sam.

"Lightly is not really in my repertoire," Sam said.

Dan agreed. "Ask the guy whose kneecap she blew apart last night."

"Then learn," McClane said. "But at the end of the day, we need to figure out what the hell is going on."

Sam nodded. "I agree. Big as this was, it could be the beginning of something much bigger. Who else have you talked to about this?"

McClane shook his head. "You undoubtedly noticed how empty the building was. It's been tough to get ahold of anyone."

"Strange," Sam said with a wry smile. "Maybe they suddenly had something more important to do than sit in meetings." Like trying to keep their houses from being looted.

Or maybe they were out doing the looting themselves.

"Anyway, I smell a road trip," Sam said. "Dan, I think you're probably better suited for the NSA thing. I can't even spell 'virus.' I'll head south to Hampton to chase down the satellite thing."

McClane nodded. "Keep me in the loop," he said.

Sam and Dan stood up to leave. McClane held up his hand. "I almost forgot," he said. "A national security watch item was stolen last night. It popped up on the classified network this morning and the watch officer reported it to the director."

"They finally got their hands on that rocket-powered dildo?"

"Very funny." McClane didn't always appreciate Sam's sense of humor. "Actually, somebody walked off from Langston Marlin's Fort Worth facility with a half-ton beam director."

"Beam director? As in, the business end of a laser?"

McClane nodded. "Or other directed-energy weapon, yes."

"Like the kind you could use to fry a satellite?"

"Precisely."

Dan looked at Sam. "I hear Texas is nice this time of year."

"But how do we get there? Payment systems are all down."

"I'll leave those kinds of details to you two experts," McClane said.

"That's bureaucrat for 'I don't know what the hell to do, either,'" Sam said.

McClane smiled. "You saw right through me."

WASHINGTON, DC

SAM DROVE SOUTH INTO THE GROWING DARKNESS. SHE
had taken a government vehicle from the DHS motor pool and filled it with
gas at the vehicle farm. The gas pumps provided for official government
use didn't require a payment method, because the government had already
bought the gas. The pumps just required a key fob, which Sam checked out
along with the keys. As long as she could continue hopping between federal
installations, she'd be fine.

Running out of gas could be more than a little inconvenient, she reckoned.
She had the feeling from her conversation with McClane that the payment
problem wasn't going to sort itself out for a long, long time. *Bet we just end
up scrapping the whole thing and starting over,* she thought.

On second thought, maybe not. She figured there would be significant
pressure from the people at the top of the current system to restore it to its
former state. They'd probably prefer not to start all over again with zero
dollars on the ledger, since they'd had billions just a day ago. *I'd probably feel
the same way.*

She patted the pancake holster and her trusty Kimber .45. She loved that
gun. Indirectly, it had saved Brock's life a day earlier. *More like twelve hours*

36

ago, she realized, looking at her watch. It had been one hell of a weekend. And the week wasn't shaping up too well, either.

She checked the hastily-packed duffel bag she'd thrown together before leaving home. Six full magazines of ammo, plus a .40 FNX backup weapon and more ammunition.

Sam had the feeling they would come in handy. When people lacked important things like food, water, and gas, they tended toward violence. She was pretty sure her Homeland badge would give any would-be opportunists pause, but she was even more sure that her Zombie Killer hollow-point ammunition would encourage circumspection.

Six gallons of water slid around on the passenger side floorboard, and a backpack full of freeze-dried food made her among the most self-sufficient humans on the continent at the moment. Six days, if she was smart about it. After that, all bets were off.

It better not last that long, she thought to herself. She'd barely had time to become carnally reacquainted with Brock after his harrowing kidnapping had ended. *Two days. That's it. After that, come hell or high water, I'm going home to ride that magnificent meat stick of his.* The world could save itself. Or not. She didn't really care either way, she told herself, though she knew it was a lie.

Traffic snarled in the usual place, just a few miles south of DC, where I-95 necked down from four lanes to three. It was one of Sam's least favorite spots on the planet.

But it was worse today than she'd ever seen it. Some drivers had been smart enough to pull their cars over to the shoulder, or even onto the grass beside the shoulder, before their tanks ran empty.

Other drivers, the maddeningly stupid ones, had simply sat in traffic and run out of gas. The only way around the stalled cars was to weave between them, an infuriating exercise that required her to drive everywhere between the shoulder and the median, picking her way past loitering motorists, who were wandering around while they awaited help that Sam was certain wasn't coming.

People gravitated toward her car as she drove past. *These people think I'm going to whisk them away to safety,* she realized. *I knew better than to take an*

37

official-looking car. She locked the doors, turned on the emergency lights, put on her sunglasses, and didn't make eye contact with anyone as she drove past.

This is going to get extremely ugly, she realized. It was only a matter of time before people started knifing each other over candy bars, and shooting each other over siphon hoses to steal gas from parked cars. *Guess we'll see exactly how First-World we are, won't we?*

It took just over an hour to cover the next three miles to the Triangle exit. As she drove past the overpass, she saw the exit ramp on both sides completely packed with cars. The surface street was a parking lot, and lines of stagnant cars all seemed to originate at one of the three gas stations within view from the interstate. *Figures. Live by car, die by car.*

She drove past a stalled food truck, its driver throwing packages out to a crowd of stranded motorists. Sam applauded the philanthropic gesture, but then she realized it was probably entirely pragmatic. Wouldn't do any good for the food to rot on the truck, and the driver probably just wanted to unload it all before it started stinking to high heaven.

After the Triangle exit, the southbound lanes opened up considerably, and she started making better time.

She turned on the radio for company. "Fed Chairman Arnold Goldblum today denied reports that the nation's money supply is in jeopardy," the reporter said.

The newscast cut to Goldblum's familiar, patronizing voice. "The fundamentals of our economy and our monetary system are no different today than they were yesterday," he said in patrician tones. "The dollar remains fully supported and backed by the full faith and credit of the United States government, and the United States economy. Rest assured, we will quickly put this anomalous event behind us, and our systems will soon return to their normal, smooth operation."

Somebody should show him a picture of I-95.

"Other reports are not quite as optimistic," the reporter said.

A man's voice came on, pitch elevated, speaking in quick, clipped New York sentences: "There's no communication between banks, and nobody knows what anybody's account balances are. It's not like the money got stolen, or misplaced someplace. That money is just *gone*. It simply ceased to exist."

It's going to be a long week, Sam thought.

NEAR ARDMORE, OKLAHOMA

STALWART WALKED SLOWLY INTO THE BRICK REST STOP
building, Jimbo's shotgun pressed into the small of his back. Fat, slovenly,
smelly Jimbo appeared to be the second-in-command behind Clem, the
policeman-turned-highwayman. Stalwart wasn't sure where the kid with the
rat's face, who flanked the procession and giggled occasionally when nothing
was funny, fit in the pecking order. Village idiot maybe. Or the community
fluffer.

"Shoes off," Jimbo commanded.

"If it's all the same, I'll keep them on," Stalwart said.

Rat Face's rifle butt caught him in the ribs. He doubled over in pain.

"It ain't. Shoes off. And your shirt."

Stalwart knew from his Air Force training that the best chance of
escape was during capture. Once they locked you up, your odds decreased
dramatically. From the Great War on, the vast majority of hostages and
prisoners of war who got thrown into a concentration camp either died in
captivity or had to await the cavalry. From the sound of things, Stalwart
didn't think the cavalry was coming – especially with a cop at the top of the
vagabond pecking order.

He stayed doubled over longer than necessary, feigning pain even after the pain had subsided, using the time to assess the situation, evaluate alternatives, calculate his odds.

Pretty shitty odds.

There were two shotguns and a pistol trained on him. He wasn't a ninja.

He took his shoes off, then his shirt. Rat Face snatched the shirt, held it up, produced a lighter, and set it aflame. *Not a good sign.* The kid then disappeared outside with Stalwart's shoes in one hand and burning shirt in the other.

Stalwart heard two loud shotgun reports, interspersed with a feral cackle. Rat Face returned to the building holding the remnants of Stalwart's shoes, the fine leather shredded by buck shot. Stalwart felt his spirits sagging. *Doesn't look like it's going to be a short stay.* "What do you want from me?" he asked.

Jimbo smiled a wicked, dirty smile by way of reply.

"You've already taken the car. Let me go."

"Nah." Jimbo spat on the floor. "Reckon we'll keep y'all a spell."

"Why?"

Another blow to the ribs from Rat Face. And more cackling. As he recovered from the strike, Stalwart noticed a set of double doors in front of him, secured by a chain wrapped through both handles.

As he stood back up, he watched Jimbo produce a key from the front pocket of his overalls, unlock the padlock, and unwrap the chain from around the door handle.

"Yer new home," Jimbo said, opening the door. "Play nice with yer new friends."

The stench hit him first. The chamber was full of people, shirtless and shoeless, sweating in unventilated semi-darkness. Their heads turned as one to look at him.

A hard shove in the small of his back vaulted him into the room. He stumbled over a small child seated on the hard tile floor. The door slammed shut behind him, and he heard the chain snake its way through the handles on the other side.

As he surveyed the room full of people, he couldn't help but wonder whether he had just experienced the iron fist of instant karma.

SEATTLE, WASHINGTON

SABOT HAD MISSED HIS LUNCH DATE. THE TIME HAD come and gone in a flash, and he was oblivious to its passing until it was too late.

Angie would be pissed. Probably mad enough to freeze him out for a couple of nights, whip him real good by denying that sweet thang of hers, get him running back to her on his best behavior.

He didn't mind. He was sitting at a computer for the first time in years. He was *back*. No Bureau overlords breathing down his neck. At least none that he knew of.

Satoshi. It was a weird name, kind of a random thing to have to search for. It was linked to someone called Satoshi Nakamoto.

Wikipedia:

Satoshi Nakamoto (中本 哲史 *Nakamoto Satoshi*) is a person or group of people who created the Bitcoin protocol and reference software, Bitcoin Core. In 2008, Nakamoto published a paper on The Cryptography Mailing list describing the Bitcoin digital currency. In 2009, he released the first Bitcoin software that launched the network and the first units of the Bitcoin currency, called *bitcoins.*

Nakamoto is said to have continued to contribute to his Bitcoin software release with other developers until contact with his team and the community gradually began to fade in mid-2010. Around this same time, he handed over control of the Bitcoin.org domain and several other domains to various prominent members of the Bitcoin community.

Nakamoto is believed to be in possession of roughly one million bitcoins. At one point in December 2013, this was the equivalent of US$ 1.1 billion. Nakamoto's true identity remains unknown, and has been the subject of much speculation. It is not known whether the name "Satoshi Nakamoto" is real or a pseudonym, or whether the name represents one person or a group of people.

Sabot read the passage again. He'd read about Bitcoin before, ironically in a newspaper article, but his exile from all things digital had prevented him from learning much more about it.

A billion freakin' Georges, man. That was a lot of money. With a sum that large, a *vato* could completely rearrange his life. Might even be able to slip away from the FBI. Get a little place on a little island, maybe. And a big damned boat. Maybe then Angie wouldn't be afraid to settle down with him, squeeze out a *niño* or two.

All I gotta do is invent some new money, then hoard it like crazy. He chuckled. Sabot had no idea why they'd asked him to look up Satoshi and his crazy crypto coin, but he'd wasted enough time on it. It was time for some fun. *Sabot's back, baby.*

Fingers trembling and heart pounding, he started to type in the address to an exceptionally obscure site whose complicated web address he could still recite in his sleep.

He had but a few characters left to type when the computer dinged and an instant message window popped open. Someone named Balzzack011 had somehow sent him a message: "The dollar is worthless now. Suddenly everyone's a libertarian."

Sabot had no idea what that might have meant. Something to do with politics, which he couldn't care less about. As a felon, he wasn't even allowed to vote.

"??" he typed. He noticed that the instant messaging program automatically listed his name as Sabot. That was a problem he'd have to fix immediately, if not sooner. Anonymity was everything. The internet was no place to be yourself. He'd learned that the hard way.

"12,769,500 Bitcoins in circulation," Balzzack011 replied. "I want ten percent of them by the weekend."

Sabot shook his head. *I knew it. Entrapment.* "Get them yourself."

"Not open for discussion."

Sabot fumed. "Not going down for theft."

"Then you're going down for parole violation."

"No way. I'm legit. Special Agent Adkins' orders."

"Who? Is he the one who launched that DDoS from your computer this morning?"

Sabot's heart lurched. Distributed denial of service attacks were felony offenses. Of the ninety years of jail time still hanging over his head, sixty-five of them were for orchestrating and engineering DDoS attacks.

"Go to hell, man," he pounded. "I'm clean."

The reply came quickly "Fingerprints say you slammed a credit card company. I hear they get pissed when their transactions don't go through. They like to press charges."

Sabot sat, shaking his head, clenching his jaw.

The phone rang again.

Adkins again.

Sabot laid into him.

"You finished?" Adkins asked when Sabot paused for breath.

"Damn right I am. I'm walking. Right now. This is over."

"Calm down, Sabot. I don't know all of the details, but this is absolutely legitimate. It comes from extremely high up. They just called me again, and told me you were having some trouble coming to grips with things. They asked if I could maybe help you understand their bona fides."

"Bone what?"

"They also wanted me to tell you something. They said to tell you that you should think of Miguel, how happy he was when he got the Subaru running again. They said you would understand."

Loud and clear. *Owned again.*

"Who are these people?" Sabot asked.

"I don't know," Adkins said. "And I sure as hell am not going to ask. But the Deputy Director is the one who gave me the message, if that helps."

Another fine predicament you've managed to land yourself in.

Sabot hung up.

He sat back down at the computer. It dinged. Balzzack011: "Attitude adjusted?"

"Hardly," Sabot typed. "WIIFM?" What's in it for me?

"LOL," Balzzack011 typed. "You liked prison?"

"Who are you?"

"An employee. Just like you."

Sabot fumed.

The computer dinged again. "You get 0.5% of assets collected."

Sabot snorted. Didn't seem like too much upside, given all of the risk.

"If you're not anxious to get to work, you're obviously not doing the math right," Balzzack011's next message said. "Show of good faith: Click on the 'wallet' icon."

Sabot looked at the computer's desktop and found a Bitcoin Wallet application. He opened it. "Synchronizing with the network," it announced. Twelve small transactions registered.

He stared at the strange nomenclature, then cross-referenced one of the Bitcoin websites he'd found earlier, struggling to decipher the meaning of the ledger transactions.

"You just sent me 10 BTC?" he typed to Balzzack011.

"You're welcome."

Sabot huffed. He thought he might be able to buy a beer with ten Bitcoin, but little else. He googled the exchange rate to be sure.

The exchange rate chart looked strange. Either the figures were wrong, or something crazy was happening.

If the chart was right, you could have bought one Bitcoin yesterday for a hundred bucks.

But today, one Bitcoin cost two *thousand*.

And climbing.

Sabot whistled. *They just threw twenty large at me?* A compelling show of faith, he reckoned. He'd never seen that much money at once.

He picked up the wall phone and dialed Angie's number. Voicemail. "Sorry, babe, but something's come up at work. Something big. Don't worry. And please don't wait up."

LOST MAN LAKE RANCH, COLORADO

ALL WAS SILENCE. THERE WERE NO GENERATORS humming, no forced-air climate control systems blowing, and no voices. Archive, Protégé, and Allison sat on the balcony off of the lodge's exquisite dining room, enjoying an evening constitutional. The cool mountain air was well on its way to frosty, and the timberline breeze had the beginnings of a nasty bite.

"Helluva place to pick for a cult camp," Protégé joked.

Archive chuckled, exhaled a ring of smoke from a cigar rolled on the thighs of virgins somewhere in the Third World, and patted Protégé on the leg with an affectionate, avuncular air. "Kool Aid service begins at nine sharp."

Theirs was a somewhat unlikely friendship. Archive was a multi-time winner in the tycoon games, captaining giant banking and business empires. His wasn't nearly as flashy or public a persona as some of his contemporaries and friends, but Archive was significantly more accomplished than all but the world's richest men.

To the extent that a billionaire could grow disillusioned, Archive had. Rather than buying a few dozen politicians to legislate higher margins for his various enterprises, as was the norm in his tax bracket, Archive and a few like-minded pals had decided the whole oligarchical system had to go.

Protégé had helped. Throughout his years-long friendship with the old tycoon, Protégé had always had the feeling he was being groomed, molded for something specific. As it turned out, he was right.

He'd risen quickly through the General Electronics Government Services Division ranks to run the division, plucked from the crowd of capable managers in the company's stable. Protégé had always wondered whether his meteoric rise hadn't had something to do with his acquaintance with the old gray fox, but his vanity didn't permit him too much rumination in that direction. Clearly, his success was due to his unique combination of skills. Two standard deviations above average. Top two percent. Those were his common headlines, anyway.

Truth be told, it probably didn't hurt that he was well connected, thought it was through no doing of his own. Archive had chosen him, not the other way around.

They'd had innumerable lengthy philosophical discussions in the old man's lavish mansion on the outskirts of DC. Archive's style was often collegial, occasionally didactic, but sometimes downright patronizing. Protégé endured the annoying times in the way an heir endures the more tiresome elements of an eccentric patriarch's ways.

But those times were rare enough that they didn't grate on the young executive's nerves too badly, and he certainly felt that he'd gained much more than he'd given to the relationship. Not everyone got the chance to study at the feet of one of the world's richest and most accomplished men.

But Protégé was troubled. "We've uncorked quite a genie. I'm concerned about what's happening."

Allison nodded her assent, curling up against Protégé's chest for shelter against the growing chill, gazing out at the lingering colors of a nearly-spent sunset. He caught her scent, enjoying the stir it caused within him despite the troubling topic on his mind.

Archive cocked his head upward, exhaling. More expensive cigar smoke mingled with the smell of the mountain. "I am too. I'm afraid we'll see the darker side of our nature for a while."

"They'll fillet us if they figure out we're responsible."

"*When.*" There was a twinkle in the old man's eye. "It's inevitable. Entropy demands that they figure it out. It's not a question of if, but when."

"So you've signed us all up for martyrdom?"

The old man laughed. "Of course not. To the extent that anyone among us has 'signed up,' the rules of our little coterie demanded that we did so of our own volition."

He took a long drag of his cigar. Straight to the lungs, Protégé noticed.

"But I don't think we'll be massacred or hung at dawn," Archive said. "It's all about the narrative."

"Which you'll control exactly how?"

An amused smile, a twinkle, and a puff of cigar, then, "Inconceivable as it may seem as we sit here together right now, I'm not altogether unaccustomed to giving public sentiment a helpful nudge in the right direction."

"Clearly. But this is a bit of a doozy."

Archive nodded, eyes still twinkling. "Acquiring skills is amusing and entertaining in and of itself, but I fail to see the point if one doesn't draw upon one's unique talents when history affords one the opportunity."

That was the annoying Archive that Protégé occasionally endured. He did so with silence. Spiritual exercise.

A quiet electric motor whirred nearby, drawing the automatic windows shut. The dwelling controlled its own climate, but not by brute force. It regulated the amount of breeze and sun it allowed inside at various times during the day. The thick brick construction absorbed the sun's daytime energy and radiated it into the building at night, and the louvered windows opened and shut of their own accord to prevent the building from becoming too warm. Sure, the mountain climate demanded they burn fuel on occasion to keep sufficiently warm, but the efficiency numbers were through the roof. The sounds of the self-regulating building reminded Protégé that they were in perhaps the best place on the planet to weather the coming storm.

The current storm, he corrected himself.

Archive's phone rang. Vivaldi ringtone. "Art, my scoundrel of a partner in crime," Archive answered jovially. "When will you grace us with your presence?"

Protégé thought of the previous evening. He'd spent a portion of it inside a dilapidated wind tunnel on a former NASA research facility, now an air force base in Hampton Roads, Virginia. Protégé had delivered the hardware he'd stolen from his own company in DC, and Art Levitow, brilliant quantum physicist and government employee turned conspirator, mated those stolen goods with another stolen article flown in hastily from Fort Worth, Texas.

Thus, from a grand jury's perspective, there wasn't much separation between Protégé and the current worldwide crisis. In fact, Protégé mused darkly, one could argue that a very clear cause-and-effect relationship existed between the way he'd spent the previous evening, and the way the world was spending *this* particular evening: broke, broken, and panicked.

"Are the reports of atavism true?" Archive asked into the phone.

Atavism? Strange word, Protégé thought. *You mean, has the herd gone completely nuts?*

"Okay, Art, thank you. Please take care of yourself. I'll work on provisioning your return trip. And congratulations again on all you've accomplished. It is an important day, thanks to your brilliance." The call ended.

Protégé asked a question with his eyebrows, and Archive answered: "Stuck on the East Coast. He has plenty of cash, which the jet service company is still accepting, but the company's distribution system is apparently linked directly to its billing system, which is floating face-down at the moment, for obvious reasons."

"So he's stuck?"

"For the moment. The Gulfstream can easily round-trip without refueling, so I'll have the crew go fetch him."

Archive rose. "I hate to interrupt the moment, but it's time for us to provide that nudge we spoke of earlier. Art says the rioting rumors are quite true, which is a little unfortunate. But certainly accommodated in our planning."

"Meet Trojan," Archive said.

Protégé shook hands with a small, slight, bookish man in his early thirties. Trojan didn't make much eye contact, and his grip was a little too dead-fish for

Protégé's taste. "Nice to meet you," Trojan said to the floor, which reminded Protégé of the joke about the extroverted computer scientist: he talks to *your* shoes instead of his own.

"Don't let his unassuming manner fool you," Archive beamed. "Trojan is a lion."

The lion blushed and shuffled his feet nervously.

"Did you build the virus?" Protégé asked.

"Did the nickname give it away?"

Protégé smiled. He liked a little sarcasm. Evidence of the spark of life, he always thought.

"As you're undoubtedly aware," Archive said, "there was more going on over the weekend than I told you about explicitly."

Protégé nodded. "Clearly."

"Trojan built the virus that delivered the decryption algorithm."

"Who built the algorithm?"

Archive's eyes twinkled again. "Big Brother. At least, they contracted to have it built. I'm sure they didn't envision their little pet project ever being used to hobble the banking system."

Protégé shook his head. "I don't even want to know the rest."

Archive looked at Trojan. "Rested? Ready for more fun?"

"Sure," the skinny hacker said. "My nerves aren't frazzled enough. Any chance they're on to us?"

Archive laughed. "Of course. Only a matter of time. But what they do with us when they figure it out is what's important. That's where you come in."

Trojan sat down at a desktop computer and started clicking keys. Protégé saw a number of ugly black windows with green lettering open up on the monitor, cursors blinking as if to mark the time.

"How big is the botnet today?" Archive asked.

"The what?" Protégé asked.

"Botnet. Robot network," Trojan said. "Slave computers, taken over by the virus. Looks like it's around two hundred and seventy million."

Protégé looked confused.

"Trojan's virus spreads in innocuous communications, then hijacks the computer's processor," Archive explained. "Makes the user's computer run a bit more slowly, but not noticeably so, and there are really no overt indications that one's computer is engaged in a bit of a dalliance. In this case, all of that extra processing power has been marshaled to run the decryption algorithm."

Protégé shook his head. "So who controls them all?"

Trojan smiled. "Some guy I know real well."

"How?"

"You're looking at it," Trojan said, typing a command into one of the old-school computer terminal windows.

"From right here?"

Trojan laughed. "Where else did you expect?"

"Some roomful of computers somewhere, I guess."

Archive clapped Protégé on the shoulder. "It's a world I don't understand well, either," he said. "But I'm glad Trojan does."

Trojan's computer chirped. "We're in."

"In where?" Protégé asked.

Archive beamed. "Now that banking has ceased, Trojan has invited himself into the most powerful place remaining on the planet."

Protégé felt bewildered again.

"Hearts and minds, my boy," Archive patronized cryptically. "Hearts and minds."

He turned to Trojan. "Proceed, if you please."

OFFICE OF THE COMMANDER, USAF AIR COMBAT COMMAND, HAMPTON, VIRGINIA

SAM SAT AT A LARGE CONFERENCE TABLE IN A GIANT office. A huge mahogany desk dominated one end, a conference table stood in the middle, and a sitting area occupied the remaining third of the space. Had to be eight hundred square feet. A large flat-screen TV hung from the wall, and a muted 24/7 news station banged away silently.

A large piece of glass topped the conference table, and beneath it, unit insignia representing hundreds of different military organizations were arrayed neatly in rows. "All yours?" Sam asked, pointing at the display.

General Mark Hajek nodded. "Just shy of a hundred and forty thousand souls."

"Heady stuff," Sam said.

The general shook his head. "Not if you're worth a shit."

"Point taken. Anyway, thanks for your hospitality."

"Happy to help." Sam got the distinct impression that the general was anything but.

The trip south from DC had been brutal. All told, it had taken nine hours, three times the normal commute. Sam had once again become acquainted with the stupider, darker side of humanity, the side that lets fear replace

52

thought. How easily we forget, she thought dozens of times as she witnessed one rage-filled automotive near-assault after another, that cooperation is humankind's best – and only – survival mechanism.

Sam cut to the chase. "So my guys tell me that the beam that disabled the satellites came from this area."

"My guys told me you were direct."

"There's a satellite downlink station here, isn't there?"

The four-star nodded. "There is. I had the same thought. But no, the energy didn't originate from there. No way it could produce that kind of juice. It's built to receive faint signals from satellites in orbit."

"But the dishes are large enough to produce that kind of a beam, aren't they?"

"Sure are," Hajek said. "And you're asking all the right questions. I asked them of my people earlier today. But the power sources aren't strong enough to propagate that kind of waveform. Or control it. Thermal bloom is a problem, according to my chief scientist."

A colonel came into the room to refresh the general's coffee. Sam politely demurred the offer for a top-off. It was a little after ten p.m. She was going to have to sleep soon, and the last thing she needed was a caffeine buzz.

"Something else, too," Hajek offered. "The satellite facility on base is a mile away, on the other side of the runway. The coordinates we got from NSA don't resolve to that side of the installation."

Sam's eyebrows arched. She waited for the general to answer the implicit question.

"Across the street," Hajek said.

"Those old wind tunnels?" Sam asked.

The general nodded. "And there's a marina over there, too."

Sam thought for a second. "So maybe they motored into the marina, zapped a few birds, then cracked a beer and chugged away down the bay."

"Maybe," Hajek said.

"Your security people don't patrol that area?"

The general's jaw twitched. "They do. No reports of suspicious boating activity."

"So they drove the device on and off base?"

"That appears to be the other alternative."

Sam shook her head. "*One* other alternative. There is also a runway here. Are you sure they didn't fly it in?"

The general gave her a hard look. "Good question, Miss."

"Special Agent."

"I'm sorry?"

"Special Agent Jameson. Many men your age resort to chauvinism when they feel a little bit threatened by a woman my age and in my position. But you should tread lightly in my case. I can be a raging bitch. I'd like to see the flight logs and manifests for all of your traffic over the past five days."

Hajek shook his head. "Sorry. Classified."

"Bullshit," Sam said. "You know I'm cleared." Her eyes narrowed a bit. "They told me you were copied on the note between Homeland and Defense. True?"

Hajek eyed her.

"Look, whatever happened here, we're going to figure it out eventually anyway," she said. "So you might consider how you'd like to be perceived when that happens. Right now, you smell a lot like part of the problem."

The four-star considered. He didn't strike Sam as stupid, which meant that he was testing her with his recalcitrance. Maybe he'd have been able to intimidate a different kind of investigator with his rank, but Sam didn't usually feel much in the way of deference for rank and power. She gravitated more toward the bull-in-a-china-shop approach in those circumstances. Maybe slightly scorched-earth on occasion, she realized, thinking of the kneecap she'd blown away a little less than twenty-four hours earlier.

Hajek pushed a button on his phone. The colonel reappeared. "Show the *special agent* to base operations, please. Relay my approval for her to review all the flight logs."

Sam stood up and shook the general's hand. "Thanks," she said. "As a courtesy, I'll let you know what I find."

As she followed the seeing-eye colonel out of the giant office, something strange caught her eye. The newscast had been replaced by a still picture, a cartoon. It was one she recognized, but she couldn't think of where she'd seen it before.

"Please change the channel on your way out," Hajek called to the colonel. "Looks like the damn leftist newsies went on the fritz."

The colonel futzed with the remote, turning to the right-wing station. It showed the same picture, of an old man with a large mustache, wearing a tuxedo and a large top hat, carrying bags full of money. He was winking.

Sam finally figured out where she'd seen the cartoon before. *That's Monopoly Man.* The character adorned the box of the most popular board game in history.

The colonel switched channels again, this time settling on a local news station, with the same result. He tried a few more, but Monopoly man's mischievous grin greeted them at each stop.

Suddenly the cartoon started moving. He danced around, dollar bills flying out of the moneybags. "Turn the sound up," Hajek commanded.

Music was playing. Sam recognized it instantly. The Entertainer, the familiar tune made famous by the con movie, The Sting. One of her favorites.

The music quieted. Monopoly Man stopped dancing, stood square, dropped his sacks full of cash, and placed his hands on his hips. Then he wagged a finger at the camera, and spoke in a comical old-man voice. "Silly. So silly. So much silliness going on out there right now. Silly, silly, silly." The cartoon figure's head shook back and forth.

"We've lost our way, haven't we?" the figure asked rhetorically. The video had the aesthetic of a 1960's US propaganda piece, extolling the virtues of Thalidomide, lead paint, and other modern miracles.

Sam glanced at the general, who watched silently, transfixed.

"We've come to believe that money is something," Monopoly Man said. "But money, currency, cash… it's actually *nothing*. Nothing at all. Zip. Zilch. Money is just a symbol. It symbolizes an agreement between us. That's what's important. The agreement."

The character shifted, and put on a frown. "The old money had been corrupted and turned against us. So it needed to go. You probably didn't realize it, but you were trapped."

The cartoon figure put on a wide smile. "But now, today, you're free." He spread his arms wide and danced a little jig. "You can thank me later." He winked.

Abruptly, he frowned again, and wagged his finger. "But you need to stop misbehaving, and act your age instead of your shoe size."

He paused for an affected chuckle before continuing. "Before you steal from your neighbor or throw a rock through your bank's window, ask yourself a question: Because money is not a real thing, and because it's just the symbol of an agreement between us, couldn't we just use a different symbol for the same agreement?"

The music started to play again quietly in the background, and the mischievous smile returned to Monopoly Man's face. "I'll leave you all to ponder. But I shall return." He winked, then danced away.

Hajek fumed. "God help them if I ever catch them. Those bastards are taunting us."

Sam wasn't so certain. She preferred to follow the facts. "Flight logs, please," she reminded them gently.

"Of course," the general said. Sam caught the uncharitable note, and smiled sweetly in reply, as if to say *screw you right back.*

NEAR ARDMORE, OKLAHOMA

STALWART SAT IN THE WARM, DARKENING ANTEROOM OF the rest stop lavatory building, surveying the situation. He'd seen neither hide nor hair of the captors for the better part of two hours.

He observed the roomful of worried people carefully. Children cried occasionally, shushed quickly and with varying degrees of success by anxious parents. Noise was apparently a great way to draw unwanted attention from the band of slack-jawed rednecks who'd corralled them like animals.

Stalwart was an alpha male. He didn't take well to having his time wasted, much less to being detained. He was accustomed to captains of industry listening to his direction.

He was a big deal in the Department of Defense. Until yesterday, anyway. His family knew him as Mike, and to his old fighter pilot buddies, he was Buster, remnant of the time when his youthful exuberance had led him to exceed the sound barrier far too close to civilization and all of its breakable windows.

The previous morning, before he abetted a spectacular and, some might argue, earth-shaking theft, Stalwart had been in charge of an important multi-billion-dollar acquisition program for the Department.

He was pretty sure he wouldn't be welcome back at the Pentagon today, however. It might be just as well that he was locked up in some brick shithouse in Nowhere, Oklahoma, or wherever he happened to be. At least there was some slim chance of escaping this particular predicament. But if the Feds remained organized and effective long enough to catch up with him, he was certain there'd be no escaping. They'd throw away the key, maybe even pursue the death penalty for espionage.

Hope Archive has his shit together, he thought.

Everything that happened after Zero Hour had fallen squarely in the "not my department" category. Stalwart had had his hands full carrying out his own responsibilities, and he didn't have a great deal of mental bandwidth available to dive too far into the plan for how to handle the inevitable chaos their efforts would produce.

But he now wished he'd carved out just a bit more headroom to better understand how Archive and his extremely distinguished group of reluctant oligarchs planned to perform the bit of alchemy that would be required to prevent the masses from pitchforking each other to death.

A crying baby nearby brought his attention back to the smelly, sweaty room full of highway hostages, all seated morosely on the hard tile floor, fidgeting frequently as each new body position rapidly became uncomfortable. The baby's mother looked at him apologetically.

Stalwart smiled. "Can I help?"

"I'd be grateful. My arms are about to fall off," she said. She was blonde, athletic, pretty. Two other small children orbited in close proximity.

"Looks like your hands are full."

She nodded.

"I'm Mike," Stalwart said as he reached to take the baby.

"Stephanie. Steph to my friends. Thank you so much. I won't burden you for long, I promise. I just need to let the blood start flowing in my arms again."

"Where are you guys from, Steph?" Stalwart held the child comfortably in the crook of his arm, resting the little boy's head on his shoulders. *Just like the grandkids,* he thought. *Hope they're okay.*

"Fort Worth, on our way up to Oklahoma City to visit their grandmother. We're traveling with my boyfriend and his daughter." She nodded to a muscular man sprawled on the tile, dozing, and a dangerously pretty raven-haired girl who looked to be about a sophomore in high school.

Stalwart noticed a middle-aged couple looking at him. He smiled. "I'm Mike," he said. The man looked at him distrustfully, and the wife seemed to wilt a bit under his gaze. He extended his hand, and the man took it reluctantly. "Nice to meet you. Bob and Betty Stevens."

Stalwart was doing much more than just whiling the time and making small talk. He had the sense that if they were to escape from the band of dim-witted thugs, it would require a great deal of trust and cooperation between them. Connection bred trust, so he set about connecting. "How long have you guys been here today?"

"Since mid-morning, I reckon," Bob drawled, his voice and accent far friendlier than his eyes. "I guess we were maybe the third or fourth set of folks they put in here."

"They were here when those people threw us in here," Steph said. "That was about ten this morning." Her face darkened. "What do you think they're going to do to us?"

Stalwart shook his head. "Hard to say. I think we need to stick together and keep our wits about us, though. Have they fed you?"

They shook their heads.

"Given you any water?"

"Naw," Bob said. "But the plumbing's still on in the bathrooms."

Good. "Has anyone looked around for an opening to get outside? A bathroom window or anything?"

Betty shook her head. "I was in the bathroom when one of them was welding the windows shut. The chubby one with all the bad teeth. He gave me the creepiest look when I shut the stall door. If I didn't have to go so bad, I'd 'a run out of there and got Bob to look after me."

"Men's room windows too, I suppose?" Stalwart asked.

Bob nodded.

"Have they asked you for anything? Made you do anything?"

Steph shook her head. "Took our car keys, wallets, shoes, and shirts. Pretty degrading. The skinny kid was giving Jenna the eye." She motioned toward the pretty black-haired girl.

"Creepy," Jenna said.

"Probably best if you lay low, then," Stalwart said. "Any idea where they took your clothes and shoes?"

Bob spoke up. "I reckon they turned left out the door with our stuff."

"Away from the parking lot?"

"Reckon so."

Stalwart considered. He tried to recall the scene as he'd been captured, but he'd been preoccupied with the sudden pain in his kidneys and the shotgun barrel pressed to his back.

He did remember one detail, though. "Isn't there an abandoned farmhouse over that way?"

"Ain't abandoned!" A new voice joined the conversation. Stalwart turned to see an old man leaning against the wall, wearing overalls similar to the ones worn by the kidnappers. "Been hangin' my hat there fer nigh on forty year."

Steph asked the obvious question. "How'd you end up here, then?"

"Them no-goods pounded on my door this mornin' early. Mebbe an hour or two after firs' light. Wavin' them guns at me. I'm callin' the law, I sez, but they jes' starts a'laughin'. The fat one sez they arready done that. That's when I noticed the blue an' red lights a'flashin'. I ain't done nothin', I sez, but they was havin' none of it. Got real nasty with me. Figger'd I'd best come along like they said."

So it was planned.

Was it a coincidence that it happened today? Rogue cop and shit-for-brains rednecks decide to play wild frontier on the same day the financial system melts down?

Probably not. Early morning here meant mid-morning on the east coast, so the world knew what was going on with the financial system. And the police department would likely be attuned to anything strange, like payment systems all over the country suddenly going belly-up, so Clem probably had a solid idea that anarchy would likely break out.

So the kidnappers were opportunists.

It meant they were making things up as they went along. It gave Stalwart hope for a relatively quick resolution. Hasty plans often made for bad plans.

A loud clanging noise sounded from outside the door. The people on the

had the passkey to gain access to a particular wallet, you controlled all the Bitcoins assigned to that wallet by the giant worldwide ledger.

It behaved like cash – users just sent Bitcoin amounts between themselves in exchange for goods or services – with an important difference. If you lost a dollar, you were just out one dollar. But if you lost the passkey for a particular Bitcoin wallet, you lost *everything* in that wallet.

When the currency first came out, and each coin was worth little more than a penny or two, some guy had stashed something like ten thousand coins on his computer, and had subsequently forgotten about them – the coins were worth maybe twenty bucks altogether at the time – and he eventually replaced the hard drive containing his passkey.

A few years later, when Bitcoin values went through the roof, that same guy realized his mistake. Sabot had read that the poor bastard had spent two full weeks sifting through a landfill, looking for the lost hard drive containing the password to unlock millions of dollars worth of Bitcoins. He finally gave up.

So when you get 'em, you gotta hang onto 'em.

But how do you get them? They apparently called the process "mining," but it really wasn't that at all. Sabot realized it was really just a sexy name given to a very unsexy problem that needed solving: someone had to do the bookkeeping for all of these transactions.

What made the Bitcoin system unique, and therefore, valuable and irreplaceable, was the fact that all of the bookkeeping was done publicly. The ledger *was* the currency, in effect. There really was no physical or digital *thing* floating around, other than the record of past transactions, encoded forever in what amounted to the currency's genome.

Transactions were a little weird. People didn't physically transfer any money when they bought things with Bitcoin. Rather, they simply broadcast coded messages to the entire world, saying something along the lines of, "I hereby pay Joe Bagodonuts 1.69 Bitcoins."

At least, that's how Sabot visualized the process. In reality, it was a bit more complicated, but he tried not to get hung up on the technical details. For the moment, he just wanted to know what the hell it was that he was going to be stealing for his new and very generous employers.

When people "mined" Bitcoin, they were really just verifying the validity of each transaction. It was really quite ingenious, Sabot thought. Each deal, large or small, was announced to the world using the internet. "Miners" competed to be the first to package and encrypt a record of that transaction, appending it to a "block chain" of previous transactions for posterity, and cementing the transaction into the permanent ledger. There was no welshing on a deal, because the whole world acted as witness.

Whenever a particular computer – an individual "miner" – won the worldwide competition to verify and encode the latest block of transactions, that computer would announce its victory to the world. Every other computer on the planet would then cease working on the now-obsolete problem, and start working to encode the new problem, appending newer transactions to the latest block chain that was just generated by the winning computer.

As a reward for the effort, the winning computer received 25 Bitcoins, which appeared out of nowhere, just as if they'd been dug up out of the ground like a hunk of gold or silver.

It hurt his head a little bit to think about the way it all fit together, but it slowly started to make sense. It seemed like the idea had caught on because nobody really had the ability to manipulate the currency. It wasn't owned by a central bank. People were basically free to decide between themselves what was a fair price to pay for things. It just used the power of the network and millions of people participating in the process to make the whole thing go.

There were countries on earth whose money couldn't be relied upon – his own now among them, Sabot realized – and this Bitcoin thing seemed like a nifty way to hedge your bets. It all seemed agreeably democratic, and it appealed to his hacker ethos.

Plus, cryptocurrency appeared to be pissing off the governments of the world. In general, anything that made governments unhappy tended to put a smile on Sabot's face.

He switched over to another window to start searching for ideas on how to steal Bitcoins when a headline on one of the search engine returns caught his eye: "Doomsday Predictions True?" Sabot clicked and skimmed.

Apparently, people had been arguing about "safe money" for quite a while. The whole thing sounded political, which wasn't his thing, and Sabot was about to click off the site when a phrase in the text jumped out at him: "What would you do if you couldn't withdraw money from your bank?"

Sonuvabitch! With everything going on, he hadn't thought to check his own bank account. He didn't have an online password, of course, but he had the bank's phone number memorized.

He got a recording. "We're sorry, but we are unable to provide account balances, or to accommodate transfer requests, money orders, payments, or withdrawals, at this time. ATM transactions are also not supported. Please visit our website for the latest information on this rapidly evolving situation."

This is serious shit, man. He had bills coming due. He couldn't be late with the rent again. The old hag would kick them out.

He navigated to his bank's website. "We regret that we are closed until further notice. Please check back frequently for updates."

Where's my damn money?

He opened the Bitcoin wallet again. *Twenty-seven thousand smackers.* For ten tiny little Bitcoins.

Of course, he realized that the number could have been a zillion dollars, and it wouldn't have mattered. He couldn't sell the Bitcoins for dollars, because nobody seemed to have access to dollars. And who would want dollars if Sabot *did* get his hands on some cash? The value was vanishing too quickly.

He realized that his ten Bitcoins weren't making him richer as the dollar's value kept falling in comparison. He just wasn't going to be quite as poor as everyone else.

Maybe he'd be able to use Bitcoins to buy food. There wasn't much in the pantry at home.

He suddenly had a much greater understanding of why his new employers had hired him to steal Bitcoins. There wasn't much else around to buy things with.

He thought of Balzzack011's payment terms. Sabot could keep 0.5% of all of the Bitcoins he collected.

I'm going to collect a lot of those little things, he resolved.

LANGLEY AIR FORCE BASE, VIRGINIA

SAM HANDED THE FLIGHT MANIFEST PRINTOUT BACK TO the desk sergeant at Langley's base operations center. If the manifest wasn't a smoking gun, it was damn close.

Her phone rang. *Wish those silly things would quit working, too,* she groused. *A little peace and quiet for a few days would be nice.* "Hi, Dan," she answered.

"What'd you think of the Monopoly Man show?"

"Strange. We're obviously dealing with someone extremely sophisticated. Any idea how they got into the system of every major news outlet in the country?"

"If I was a betting man," Dan said, "I'd bet it's somehow related to the way they hacked into every Federal Reserve branch in the country."

Sam considered this. While the banking industry's computer networks were among the most secure on the planet, the news media's systems weren't far behind. The reason was obvious: whoever controlled the narrative, controlled the world.

"I'll buy that. Both networks seem like they'd be ridiculously difficult to break into."

"You can't even imagine," Dan said. "Everyone here is stumped."

"You're still at NSA?"

"Yeah."

"They're just pretending to be stumped."

Dan laughed. "You're such a misanthrope."

"Learned, not inherited," Sam said. Then a thought struck. "Anyone there have any idea where the transmission originated?"

"It appears to have originated from everywhere and nowhere. I'd like to meet the guy who engineered this thing, because it's pure art. But near as the NSA people can tell, the video feed was parceled over millions of different computers. They all sent a piece of the cartoon into the network computer systems, where the virus compiled and played the video."

Sam shook her head. "Sounds pretty unbelievable."

"Next-level stuff, that's for sure. I mean, nobody's even heard of this kind of thing before."

Sam laughed. "At least that's what they're telling you, Mr. Outsider."

"Good point."

"Any speculation on where the virus itself came from?"

Dan's voice lowered conspiratorially. "Strange you should ask. A couple of mid-level people in the server farm brought something to management's attention this morning – nobody knows what, exactly – but they were apparently given the rest of the day off as a reward for their efforts."

"Strange."

"That's not all. There's something like eight thousand NSA employees who didn't make it into work today because of all the craziness in the district. They're calling every one of them, and making them come in."

Sam scrunched her face. "That's not all that unusual, really. Homeland is calling all of its employees too, making sure they're okay."

"This is more than just accountability, Sam. They're interviewing each one of them when they show up at the door. It's a little bit creepy."

"Keep an eye on things there and keep me posted."

"I'm running out of pretext to be here," Dan said. "They're getting less cooperative by the minute."

"I think the whole thing originated with NSA," Sam said. "They're running scared."

"Yeah. I can see why. They've been in the press a lot lately."

"Who knew spying on your own citizens was newsworthy?" Sam deadpanned.

"Can you imagine if that story broke? 'NSA brings down the entire global economy'?"

"That would be slightly more than embarrassing. Call McClane and get him to pull some strings. I think it's important that you stay plugged into whatever's going on up there."

"Will do," Dan said. "Where are you headed?"

"Turns out that someone flew a cargo aircraft to Langley Air Force Base last night with an incomplete manifest."

"Let me guess," Dan said. "From Fort Worth, right?"

"Exactly. So I'm headed west."

"You're thinking it's the stolen beam director?"

"No, I just want a good steak."

"Be careful, boss."

"You too."

BANFF, CANADA

THE FACILITATOR STEPPED FROM HIS PRIVATE JET AND into the chilly Canadian air. A limousine awaited, idling on the tarmac. Night fell with a vengeance in this part of the world, but the Facilitator liked the air's stark bite.

It felt like reality, clearing out the fog of repetitive, useless thoughts that occupied his mind for entirely too much of the time.

"Good evening, sir," the driver said. The Facilitator grunted his reply, and the large sedan powered off into the surrounding mountains.

He hadn't fled, exactly, but he hadn't precisely battened down the hatches at his US home, either. The Facilitator was far too old – and truth be told, far too frail – to be caught up in any of the hooliganism that had begun to spread like wildfire across the country. The Canadians were a more circumspect lot, in his experience. More polite. Had to be, to survive those winters, he theorized, sealed up in close proximity to each other for months on end.

He switched on the television in the back of the limousine. Riots dominated the news loop. The contagion had left the continent and spread to Tokyo, Beijing, Frankfurt, and even London. The major financial centers seemed to bear the brunt, undoubtedly because those closest to the big banks were first to realize what the dollar's implosion really meant.

It meant that he, the Facilitator, was losing billions by the day. Maybe even hundreds of billions. It was difficult to say.

At least, that's how it looked on paper. But he was well positioned to survive. Just because he'd spent most of his adult life subjugating most of the planet's population beneath mountains of meaningless paper "assets" and debt-laden financial constructs, didn't mean that he drank his own poison.

He had *real* things, useful things, the kinds of things that people would pay dearly in any surviving currency to use, and he owned them outright. Farms, apartments, hotels, airplanes, entire subdivisions. All his by the hundreds.

From a legal perspective, the ownership trail was convoluted, of course. It could be no other way, given the security demands of his position. But his operational control was anything but diluted. Without question, he called the shots.

One didn't hold the world's most powerful position any other way.

A day like today was inevitable, he felt. It had been for decades. It was simply a matter of mathematics. Fiat systems invariably ended this way.

But the end of *this* particular currency was far more than just an interesting side note in history. Dollars had spread like a virus around the globe, infecting every country on the planet. It was the financial equivalent of the Black Death.

Worse, today's meltdown had the very real potential to incite significant, substantive changes to the order of things.

The Facilitator resolved to prevent that at all costs.

There would be blood. Probably a great deal of it. He regretted that, in a vague sense, but didn't consider altering his course for a moment. Violence was a necessary ingredient.

Because even more than financial ruin, violence demanded a scapegoat.

It couldn't be a puppet regime somewhere, toppled under false pretext to take the fall for the real culprit.

It couldn't even be a person. The world would want much more definitive assurances than would be afforded by the head, served on a silver platter, of just a single man, or even a group of men. It was likely that not even the President of the United States and his entire cabinet would be a large enough sacrifice to appease the angry gods of Never Again.

It would have to be the whole thing. *The whole freaking enchilada.* And that would take some finesse.

The Facilitator sighed as he picked up the phone in the limousine's armrest. *It was a good run,* he thought as he dialed. *But it's time to slay the beast.*

The phone connected. A familiar voice answered: "Please hold for the President."

PART II

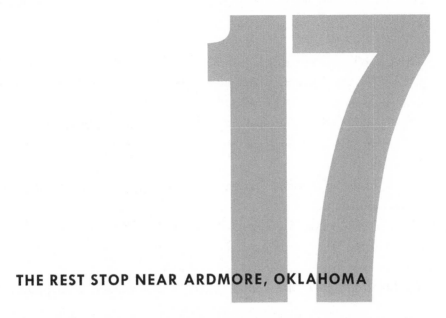

17

THE REST STOP NEAR ARDMORE, OKLAHOMA

STALWART HEARD THE CHAINS RATTLE THROUGH THE handles on the other side of the double doors.

They were coming back.

He stood. Better to be standing, he thought, to face whatever was coming through the door.

He had no idea what time it was. His expensive watch was now in the possession of a gap-toothed slob who smelled like a goat. Several hours after nightfall was as close an estimate as he could manage. Impossible to tell, really. It was one of those nondescript hours when only your innate sense of time could help, and his wasn't terribly innate.

Stalwart heard the chain fall into a heap on the floor beyond the doorway, and a door opened.

A small, slight figure stumbled into the dark room, tripping over other prisoners still sprawled shoeless and shirtless on the hard floor. The door slammed behind her, and the chain rattled loudly against the handles as their captors resealed the exit.

The stumbling person stopped and looked around, and Stalwart could see a girl's figure swaying unsteadily in the dim moonlight seeping in the high window above.

"Daddy?" she slurred.

Motion off to his left, then a gruff male voice. "Baby?"

"Daddy," the girl said, the word slow, exaggerated, unsteady. She stumbled toward the sound of her father's voice.

"Jenna, baby, what's happened?" The large, muscular man rose.

"They made me," Jenna said. She reached her father's arms, and he embraced her.

"They made me," she said, starting to sob softly. "They wouldn't stop."

"Are you drunk?"

"I'm so sorry, daddy." Her legs nearly gave out, and the large man caught her in his arms. "They sat on me and held my mouth open… I think they gave me too much… I don't feel very good, daddy…"

"Oh my God, baby, oh my God." Jenna's father held her, rocking back and forth.

Stalwart's heart sank. He thought of his own youngest daughter, fresh out of high school and making her way in college. He felt rage well within him.

And dread. He feared that he knew what was going to happen next.

"It hurts, daddy," Jenna said.

Her father pulled away and looked at her face. "What hurts, baby girl?"

"They pulled off my clothes…"

A father's anguished howl filled the room, echoed off the hard floor and the brick walls, reverberated in the hearts of every man in the room.

Jenna sank to the floor as her dad loosed his grip, bellowing in heart-rending agony, pacing, working himself into a frenzy.

Stalwart put a hand on his shoulder. "Don't do it. Bide your time. Now is not the time."

Jenna's father muscled him aside and made for the chained doors.

"Jeff! Please don't!" It was Stephanie's voice, high and pleading, fear breaking around the edges of her words.

Stalwart stepped in front of him. "Listen, man. Think about it!" he exhorted. "The time will come. But not now! Jenna needs you to keep your head. Think of Steph and the kids! Don't be stupid."

Hands like cinder blocks crushed the air from his chest, and Stalwart flew backwards, tripping over still-seated prisoners, landing across a prone woman, cracking his elbow painfully on the floor.

Jenna's father was all fists and flying feet, smashing the door with bone-jarring force, hollering and howling at the cowardly bastards who did this I'll kill you with my bare fucking hands so help me God open this damned door you damned cowards!

Above the din of a father's rage, Stalwart heard the rattling chain again, and the doglike calls of the hollering, drunken rednecks on the other side. He heard the chain drop to the floor once again.

It was already too late.

The door burst open, swinging inward with a vengeance, nearly clipping Jenna's father, who was poised for his attack. His fist connected with Rat Face's jaw. Stalwart heard it pop, heard something hard and plastic clatter on the floor, then heard a sickening thunk as Rat Face's misshapen skull pounded onto the tile, his comatose body half inside the chamber and half in the hallway outside.

Stalwart steeled himself for what he knew would come next, rising to his feet to help, knowing he would never make it in time.

He heard the slide of a shotgun rack a shell into place, saw the blur of Jimbo's big, slovenly frame jerking Rat Face's limp body out into the hallway, saw Jenna's father charge into the doorway, and saw the shotgun's flash light the room for a brief, horrific second, illuminating the crimson mist that erupted around Jenna's father's chest.

He fell, silent, dead.

The doors slammed shut. As the chain snaked its way through the handles on the other side, a wail of grief and terror rose, the sound tearing Stalwart's soul in half, a daughter's mourning cry for her father. Jenna ran awkwardly to her dad, dodging well-intentioned men intending to intercept her, and fell on the blood-slicked floor. She wrapped her arm around her father's body and buried her face in his bloody neck, her sobs muffled, joined by a sorrowful chorus of horrified onlookers.

Stalwart felt the tears flow, felt his chest constrict in painful sobs of his own. But his pain wasn't merely from the terrible things he'd just witnessed.

His was the agony of responsibility.

This is on me. I freed these demons.

He sank to the floor, his heart deflating along with his body. He slumped against the wall, and his hand fell to the floor.

And brushed against something familiar.

Through the fog of his emotions, his mind insisted he pay attention to what his fingers had discovered. He moved his hand around on the cold tiles, searching in the darkness for the familiar shape.

He found it. His hands closed around the object, feeling its lines, drinking in the salvation it represented.

Rat Face's cell phone.

SEATTLE, WASHINGTON

SABOT PRESSED THE PHONE TO HIS EAR, COUNTING THE rings. Six. Seven. A groggy voice answered: "Adkins."

"I need a ride. Can you come pick me up?" Sabot braced for what was bound to be an uncharitable response.

"Sabot, man, it's one in the morning and with all the noise in the streets, I just got the kids to go to bed."

"Sorry, bro. But this morning, see, I was fucking *kidnapped* by the people you're working with, and I've spent the day locked in some kind of a fake office somewhere working for them. And now I need to get home."

He heard Adkins sigh on the other end of the line. "First of all, they're not my people you're working with. And second, I understand they're offering more than a reasonable incentive, so it isn't like you're some kind of slave over there. Anyway, how the hell would I know where to find you?"

"You don't work for the Federal Bureau of Investigations, *culero*?"

Another sigh. "All right. Guess we did leave you a little high and dry."

"See you in a few, esé."

"You really should consider getting a car, Sabot," Adkins groused, turning left out of the warehouse parking lot.

"Really, esé? Would it have made my kidnapping this morning more convenient?"

Adkins frowned in the driver's seat. "Listen. Like I told you this morning, I had nothing to do with this, and I have absolutely no say in how it goes down. I'm here as your friend, giving you a ride in the middle of the night, but I'm no longer your supervisor. For the moment, anyway."

Sabot looked out the window, suddenly recognizing the neighborhood. "Wanna be more pissed off? I coulda walked."

Adkins chuckled. "That thought certainly crossed my mind. But it wouldn't have been a good idea. Do you know what's been going on?"

"Yeah, the dollar is falling, and shit like that."

Adkins whistled. "Man, they did have you locked down tight today, didn't they?"

"I had internet access, but I was busy working on something else."

Adkins filled him in. "Society is really devolving. The politicians are calling it a liquidity crisis, but there are some dissenting opinions who are making a pretty compelling case that it's much worse than that. It isn't just that the dollar is falling, it's that the dollar has been virtually erased from the US economy."

Sabot shook his head. "You're gonna have to start paying me in tortillas."

"That would be just as hard. People are breaking into grocery stores to steal food. They're running out of stuff in the pantry, but nobody has access to their money, or really even knows how much money they're supposed to have."

Sabot thought about his earlier attempt to access his bank account. Completely frozen, with no estimate of when things might be back up and running. "I hope they get this shit figured out soon, man. I got bills coming due."

"That's just the thing," Adkins said. "Some people think it's not ever going to get figured out. They think that the account information for the entire system has been wiped clean. Except for the cash floating around the system, which isn't much and is mostly held overseas, nobody has access to funds."

Sabot pondered. He'd seen similar economic forces at work, albeit on a much smaller scale and not nearly to the same extent, in the impoverished inner city neighborhoods of his childhood. "Gangs will be the next thing," he said.

"Absolutely right. That's why it wouldn't have been a good idea for you to walk home. But they're not the kind of gangs you're thinking of."

Sabot arched his eyebrows, and Adkins went on. "These gangs are made up of suburban people. They have suits and ties and minivans and lawnmowers. But they're roving around in each other's neighborhoods, looking for food and supplies."

"Violence?"

Adkins nodded. "Huge riot downtown. The local guys brought out the tear gas and water hoses."

"Did the soccer dads disperse?" Sabot asked with a chuckle.

"Sure did. It was a dumb move on the cops' part, really, because it just taught looters to move in smaller squads. That's what's happening now."

"So lemme guess," Sabot said. "They're going to call in the national guard, or something like that?"

"Rumor is they tried," Adkins said. "But most of the guardsmen stayed home. My hunch is they're standing guard over their refrigerators and gas tanks. But the governor has instituted a curfew, and temporarily outlawed guns."

Sabot shook his head. "How do you temporarily outlaw guns?"

"They have teams going to registered gun owners' homes, confiscating weapons."

"How many of them have been shot?"

Adkins smiled. "You aren't that far removed from the street, are you?"

Sabot shook his head. "Hacking probably kept me from dealing and pimping."

"You couldn't have just done your homework and gone to college? Anyway, yeah, there was quite a scene over in Beacon Hill. Four ATF guys were shot, before they burned the house down."

"Land of the free, esé."

"At least that's what the brochure says." Adkins pulled up next to Sabot's apartment.

"I bet the cops stop showing up for work."

"Look at you and your big brain. If you weren't a convicted felon, you'd have a future at the Bureau." Adkins smiled pointedly before continuing. "Only about a quarter of the cops are left on the job. The rest are at home defending their families, or running around with the gangs."

"Welcome to the new Third World, homes," Sabot said, getting out of the car. "Thanks for the ride." He slapped the roof and went inside.

None of the lights worked, and the apartment was eerily silent.

It had been over eighteen hours since he'd had anything to eat, and Sabot was starving. He figured he'd grab a bite, then snuggle in bed next to Angie and fill her in on their twenty-five-thousand-dollar windfall. Probably closer to thirty large, by now.

She'd probably still be pissed that he blew her off for lunch and stayed gone until the wee hours of the morning, but at least he had something positive to show for the time. It wasn't like he was at a strip club threading dollar bills into G-strings.

He walked into the kitchen. His shoes crunched on the linoleum floor. Broken glass lay everywhere.

He glanced over at the sliding glass door. Rather, at what used to be the sliding glass door. It was now just a frame. *Bastards.*

Then he panicked. *Angie!*

Sabot charged down the hall to their bedroom, stumbling over the low tea service table they used to store their keys and sundries. He found the room completely empty. The bed was still made.

Angie was gone.

His heart raced. He wished he hadn't let Adkins drive off. Adkins would know what to do. Sabot wanted to call him, but his cell phone was still missing, a lingering aftereffect of his kidnapping earlier in the day.

Sabot fumbled around in the dark, looking futilely for clues, then remembered the flashlight Angie insisted they keep in their underwear drawer. He fished among her fishnets and pulled out the big Maglite, switched it on, and cut swaths out of the darkness, not sure what he was looking for, but hoping something obvious would stand out.

The beam swept over his pillow on the bed, illuminating a familiar pink heart. It was a page from the heart-shaped notepad Angie kept by the bed. He charged over to retrieve it, relieved to see Angie's handwriting in darker pink ink.

Got your message, the note said, *and decided to head out to the burbs to take care of mom. She called several times, scared and confused. Hope you're safe! I'll be back in the morning, xoxox, Angie.*

Sabot breathed a sigh of relief. He wasn't sure what life would be like without Angie, but he was sure he never wanted to find out. She'd apparently left before the looters broke in.

He searched the remainder of the apartment, looking for anything out of place. They left the flat screen TV. Last year's model. *Guess everybody already has one of those,* he mused.

But the kitchen was cleaned out. The fridge was empty of everything except for a few aging condiment containers, left in the back of the fridge to allow their evolutionary experiments to continue unmolested.

The pantry was similarly bare. They'd taken anything and everything remotely consumable. They'd also taken candles, matches, and that stupid expensive German knife set, he noticed.

These people aren't looting, he realized. *They're surviving.*

He heard a noise, which found its way to his ears unimpeded through the hole where the door used to be. Sounded like it was coming from the back alley. Voices, harsh laughter, and breaking glass. *Was only a matter of time,* Sabot thought. The bastards always seemed to find each other in times like this.

He made up his mind quickly. One skinny beaner wasn't going to stop a band of roving jackasses. In fact, depending on the flavor of jackass, one skinny beaner might wind up being the entertainment. Roman style.

He made for the front door and slipped into the night.

There was never a question in Sabot's mind about where he would go. Back to the empty warehouse and its converted office, of course, with the glorious computer and its magical internet connection and its unfettered access to the world's information.

And the carte blanche to do whatever he wanted, as long as it produced Bitcoins for his new masters. *New partners,* he corrected himself. Sounded better, even if it was slightly delusional.

He opened the door to hacker's nirvana and sat back down at the desk. He'd found a styrofoam bowl of those nasty noodles he used to eat all the time when he was eyeballs deep in a hack, and he slurped a spoonful into his mouth. *Just like old times.*

Sabot got to work. Time was of the essence. If someone big and powerful enough to pull him free of the FBI had figured out that stealing Bitcoins was the way to become the top dog in the new world order, then about a billion other quasi-savvy mouth-breathers would have undoubtedly reached the same conclusion. It was likely to be the Wild West. While Americans were throwing rocks through each others' windows, the rest of the world was probably working its ass off to redistribute the cyberwealth. Competition would be fierce.

But Sabot liked a challenge.

The half-hour walk had given his mind time to churn on the koan-like problem: how do you steal a thing that doesn't exist? Bitcoins weren't really things. You couldn't put them in your pocket, and you couldn't even store them on a hard drive. They only existed as ledger entries out there in the great big Bitcoin universe. The whole world kept the ledger up to date; the ledger, in turn, kept track of the little messages that told everyone who was paying whom, and how much.

It was all about the accounts. Wallets, people were calling them, but that really wasn't an accurate description. They didn't store anything at all. If you held the cryptographic key that would unlock a particular account, then you could initiate transactions using the Bitcoins that had previously been "sent" to that account. If you didn't have the crypto key corresponding to a particular account, then you had nothing at all. It wouldn't help you to know how much was in the account, because you couldn't do anything with it.

If you had the account number and the key, then you could empty the wallet entirely, from anywhere in the world.

So keys are the key, he'd concluded, smiling at his own pith.

And how did you get your hands on the keys?

Easy. You got them from wherever in the universe they happened to be right now.

Bitcoin crypto keys were valuable things, which meant that somewhere, someone was aggregating them. Sabot was certain he knew at least a few places. There were Bitcoin exchanges all around the world, set up to allow people to buy and sell Bitcoins using the local currency of choice as the exchange medium. The exchanges would undoubtedly store people's account information.

It would be pretty easy to run a trace on a few thousand recent transactions. By the immutable law of the internet, a striking percentage of those users would undoubtedly have logged in using a computer that had been infected with key-logging spyware hidden on the hard drive. Sabot would just have to identify the computers (easy), then retrieve the key logger's records to steal the passwords (even easier).

So easy, in fact, that he could probably write a script to do it for him in a matter of minutes.

There was another problem to solve, however: what to do with the Bitcoins when he stole them. Because every transaction was recorded for all time, it wasn't really possible to disguise a theft. Stories were rampant on the internet of everyday Joes sleuthing out the wallet addresses of thieves who'd made off with millions worth of Bitcoins. It was still extremely difficult to recover stolen Bitcoins, but with enough motivation – which certainly existed, given the meteoric rise in Bitcoin value since the financial system came to a screeching halt – it was only a matter of time before an angry mob showed up at a thief's doorstep.

Thieves were caught because they moved large sums around all at once. Even "tumblers," or wallet-obscuring services that laundered Bitcoin transactions by dispersing them over a number of smaller wallets, couldn't disguise large influxes of currency. Investigators could simply watch the input and output transactions from known tumbler sites, and look for spikes in activity corresponding to inordinately large transactions.

Most of the world did business in sums much smaller than a single Bitcoin, so when someone suddenly started throwing around hundred-coin transactions, the entire world took notice.

Sabot's solution wasn't perfect, but it was pretty damn close, he figured. Instead of scooping all of the Bitcoins he stole into a few large wallets, he would create tens of thousands of individual accounts. Rather, another automated script would do that for him, and record the corresponding passwords.

He was planning to steal millions of Bitcoins, one tiny fraction at a time. That way, each of his transactions would look exactly like everyday, normal user interactions. His outrageous theft would be hidden below the clamor of daily market activity.

Not bad for a washed-up old Anonymous vet.

It felt good to be back in the game.

FORT WORTH, TEXAS

THE GULFSTREAM'S NOSE WHEEL SETTLED ONTO THE runway at the Naval Air Station Joint Reserve Base in Fort Worth, and the brakes and thrust reversers threw Sam and Brock's bodies into their seat belts.

They had the cabin to themselves, which facilitated a few intimate moments. She squeezed Brock's arm and smiled. "Thanks for the in-flight entertainment."

"We were already members of the Mile High club," Brock said with a wink.

"Yes, but never while riding in a government airplane. Makes me smile, for some perverse reason."

"Me too. I'm glad Landers threw me into the briar patch with you."

"Just another shitty boss looking for a scapegoat. I'm happy it worked in our favor, though."

When Brock told her of his orders to start the theft investigation in Fort Worth, Sam suggested they travel together. General Hajek had ultimately agreed, and the four-star had sent a helicopter from Langley to DC to fetch Brock for the airplane trip out West.

The door opened, and Brock whiffed the familiar Texas air. "Reminds me of flight school," he said.

"You trained here?"

"Wichita Falls. Couple hours north. Smells even more like cow shit."

A giant smile attached to a suit and tie walked aboard. On the man's lapel was a familiar stylized L that signified the bearer as a member of the Langston Marlin executive team. "Colonel James, great to see you!" the man boomed.

"Hiya Kit," Brock said, extending his hand. He started to introduce the LM exec to Sam, but he was several beats too late.

"Kit Farrel, Langston Marlin business development," the suit said garrulously, clasping Sam's hand in both of his own, his smile broadening improbably from its already overblown proportions.

"Sam Jameson. Spoken for."

Farrel blushed slightly, and Brock chuckled before rescuing Farrel. "Kit and I work together a bit on the anti-satellite weapon program," he told Sam. "LM does the assembly and final checkout here in Fort Worth."

Farrel nodded, motioning toward a door leading into a cavernous manufacturing facility. "We've been building aircraft at this plant almost continuously since World War Two, and it's a bit of a shift to be building a ground-based weapon here now." He shrugged. "But whatever the customer wants…"

Sam smiled. Farrel had an intelligent but personable air about him, with a tinge of a salesman's solicitousness. "We're the Eskimos," Brock said, "and Kit's the ice salesman."

"So I gathered," she said.

"It's been a rough week for us here in Fort Worth," Farrel said. "Our CEO was killed a few days ago, and then last night's theft."

Sam made sympathetic noises. From what she'd been told, the CEO's demise seemed much more like an assassination than just a vanilla murder. No theft had been reported, but Sam had her doubts. The LM entourage hadn't been visiting the Aberdeen Proving Grounds for tea and crumpets, and there was likely some classified information in play.

"I'm interested to hear what you've learned so far," Sam said as they stepped into the executive lobby of the colossal building.

Farrel filled her in. He seemed eager to relay that the security breach involved the access badge and passcode belonging to a senior DoD official named Mike Charles.

Holy shit, Sam thought. It was a name she'd heard very recently.

"The program co-lead?" Brock asked. Together with Major General Landers, Brock's direct boss, Mike Charles was in charge of the entire ASAT weapon development program. Langston Marlin was the prime contractor for the multi-billion dollar project. "He stole his own beam controller?"

Farrel shook his head. "No. The video feed showed conclusively that Mr. Charles didn't participate in the theft. But the team of thieves used his access badge and PIN."

Sam looked pensive. "Anyone hear from Charles lately?"

"He was actually here yesterday afternoon and evening," Farrel said. "Second time in four days. The Vice President had some concerns about one of the subsystems on the ASAT program, and Mr. Charles flew out here to take a closer look."

"What was he looking at?"

Farrel gave Sam a meaningful look. "The beam director."

Sam's eyes narrowed. *Strange.* "The same thing they stole?"

"That's right."

"I'm filing that in the 'more than a little bit interesting' category," Sam said.

Farrel winked. "You're not the first to make a similar remark. In fact, the engineers put together a demonstration especially for him, to prove we had made the progress we claimed."

"To be clear, I'm not accusing the government guy of stealing the government's property," Sam said. "It's entirely possible that someone extorted the access badge and code from him."

Brock nodded. "Buster's a pretty straight arrow, from everything I've seen."

"Buster?"

"Mr. Charles," Brock explained. "He used to fly F-16s with me, back when we were both much younger."

"That explains the sophomoric nickname," Sam teased.

Brock laughed. "I'd rather be a fighter pilot than a grown-up. Anyway, I wonder if anyone's heard from him since yesterday."

"To my knowledge, I was the last LM employee to speak with Mr. Charles," Farrel said. "He left here yesterday evening, and we haven't heard from him since then."

"Mr. Farrel, thanks for your time," Sam said.

Farrel looked surprised. "Don't you want to watch the surveillance footage?"

Sam shook her head. "I'm sure the locals will be plenty thorough. We've learned enough to guide our next steps."

"If you say so."

Sam extended her hand. "Thanks again, Kit. You've been extremely helpful."

"That's it?" he asked, shaking her hand. "Not even a cup of coffee?"

"Afraid not. Duty calls, as they say. But if you could arrange a ride to the rental car facility at the airport, I'd greatly appreciate it."

"Sure thing." Farrel disappeared down what Sam was certain had to be the world's longest hallway.

She caught Brock's incredulous stare. "We flew all the way out here for a two-minute conversation?" he asked.

Sam leaned in. "I learned something interesting earlier today," she said in a low tone. "An airplane with no cargo manifest took off from DFW and landed at Langley Air Force Base last night, a few hours before the satellites were zapped. Any guess as to which senior DoD official authorized the landing?"

Brock shook his head.

"Mike Charles."

"Get out!" Brock exclaimed. Then, in a lower voice, "I never would have suspected him of trying anything that crazy. He always seemed so perfectly buttoned-down."

"That's how it usually works," Sam said. "The good ones don't pack ninja stars or drive Aston Martins. You can almost never tell a spy by looking at him."

Sam dialed back to the DHS operations desk, hoping to get a trace on

Mike Charles' cell phone location. It rang a dozen times. *Your tax dollars at work.*

Finally, an exasperated operator answered, and informed Sam that none of the on-call investigative teams remained at work. "What are they doing?" she asked.

"Ma'am, I presume they're at home, fighting off the looters," the operator said in a barely civil tone.

"I see," Sam said. "In that case, what are you doing at work?"

"Not all of us have a life, ma'am."

"Sorry," Sam said, meaning it. "So there's nobody in the entire Department of Homeland Security who can run a phone trace for me?"

"Not tonight, ma'am. And honestly, I don't know when anybody's going to be in, either. The city's a mess right now. It's like a Third World country."

Sam cursed, thanked the operator, and hung up.

Aside from the personal inconvenience, she really didn't give a shit about someone ruining the day for a bunch of bankers. Sure, the world was in for a rough adjustment, and things would undoubtedly get a lot worse before they got any better, but Sam was confident humanity would work through it.

What did alarm her, however, was the prospect that there might be a deeper agenda at play. All of the chaos, panic, and mayhem smelled like a fantastic opportunity for someone to consolidate a shitload of power. There was a good chance that yesterday's strike against the financial infrastructure was just the preamble to something much more worrisome.

So as soon as she heard Mike Charles' name exit Kit Farrel's mouth, Sam had decided to let the local investigators do the legwork to track down the hunk of technojunk that someone had jacked from the LM plant. Sam was far more interested in learning about what else might be coming down the pike, and Mike Charles seemed like a pretty good guy to chat with to start answering that question. *Where are you, Buster, old boy?*

A thought struck. "Don't you guys have a central travel reservation management system?" she asked Brock.

He nodded. "Works like a charm, unless you want to travel somewhere. Then it licks goat balls."

Sam laughed. "If Charles flew out to Fort Worth on government business, would he have made reservations in the system?"

"No, but his secretary undoubtedly would have."

Sam looked at her watch. Around noon on the East Coast. "Any chance she's at work today?"

"Zero. They closed the program office to let people take care of their families."

Sam cursed.

"But I'm your huckleberry," he said. "I have access permissions to see everyone's reservations. I'll look it up on the laptop on the way."

Sam smiled. "You're so much more than just a big dick," she teased.

Farrel returned dangling a set of keys. "With our compliments," he said. "The EVP insisted you take a car from our motor pool."

"Thanks," Sam said. "But we'll have to insist on renting our own. Courts are funny about accepting favors from investigation subjects." Plus, she had an ulterior motive for going to the rental car facility at the outskirts of the airport.

Farrel smiled. "At your service," he said. "I'll drop you off."

Sam read the sign aloud: "Bottom Dollar Rental Car. You don't say." Adjacent rental car agencies sported neon signs and sharp-dressed personnel. Bottom Dollar's sign was plain blue lettering on white plastic. Nobody tended the desk. "You guys seriously travel like this?" she asked, incredulous.

Brock nodded. "Can't make it appear like we're getting over on the taxpayers. So we save a few pennies by renting at 'Bottom Feeder' while we waste billions on other silly shit."

Sam dinged the bell, with no visible effect.

A clerk manning a rival rental agency's counter leaned over and smiled. "I haven't seen them all day, ma'am."

"Thanks. Guess I'll help myself." She walked around behind the counter and shook the computer mouse, waking up the reservations system. It wasn't password protected, which Sam was certain was some kind of consumer protection violation. *Ralph Nader would be all over this.*

Brock handed her Mike Charles' car reservation number, which he'd retrieved from the government reservation system via remote VPN on the ride over to the airport, and Sam typed it into the computer.

Sam smiled. Her gamble paid off. Even Bottom Dollar paid for a vehicle tracking service. At Bottom Dollar's end of the market, theft and other disagreeable consumer behavior were probably a significant concern, so they squeezed a SatStar subscription into the operating budget. The computer summoned Charles' reservation details, and Sam copied down the vehicle identification number and the SatStar tracking code.

Then she followed the link to SatStar's tracking page.

Password required.

Brock cursed, but Sam smiled. "Big Brother to the rescue," she said, inserting a small device into the computer's USB port.

"Gift from the NSA?" Brock asked.

"Probably. Something Dan picked up. I didn't ask questions. But I'm sure there's a Constitutional problem of some sort associated with this little thing." It cracked the password in a handful of seconds, and the SatStar tracking page loaded.

A big red banner appeared across the top of the page. "Your payment method is invalid. Tracking for this vehicle was suspended twelve hours ago pending additional funds."

Sam shook her head. "Probably the same payment problem everyone else on the planet seems to be having." She scrolled down the screen, and was pleasantly surprised to discover a plot of the rental car's path, up until the time the Bottom Dollar account ran out of funds.

She zoomed in. "Looks like a rest stop, in… Ardmore, Oklahoma? Never heard of it."

"Ah, Ardmore," Brock said. "Conveniently located right next to absolutely nothing."

"That's what it looks like," Sam said. "But at least we know what direction he's moving."

"Probably staying out of the big cities to avoid the chaos."

"Road trip?" Sam asked.

"To Ardmore? Surely he's long gone by now."

"Undoubtedly. But we'll head up north to close some of the distance, and work on getting someone to help us locate his current position."

"How?"

"Don't know," Sam said. "But there's usually a way. Automatic tollways, RFID tags, stuff like that. Or, we might even be able to strong-arm SatStar into giving us account access."

Brock nodded, then his expression turned sour. "Sorry, I can't go along," he said.

"Why not?"

"I once vowed never to set foot in Oklahoma again."

"Not even if I sweeten the deal?" Sam asked.

He smiled that smile that always made her tingle. "What are we waiting for?"

Sam dialed the SatStar number, half expecting nobody to answer, but someone picked up on the second ring. *For the first time in my life, I'm thankful for offshore labor,* Sam thought. She explained the situation, read her DHS badge number to the SatStar agent, and waited while the SatStar system looked up her federal ID number in its internal law enforcement list.

"Madam Jameson, I am pleasing that you are authorized. Please to be waiting." She couldn't place the accent or the peculiar grammatical butchery.

Moments later, the operator read a string of numbers. Sam read the coordinates back to be sure she'd heard correctly, then typed them into the rental car's navigation system. She looked closely at where the red dot resolved on the display.

"Are you sure?" she asked the SatStar agent, squinting at the electronic map in the dashboard screen.

"Quite certain, madam."

"Because it's the same coordinates as twelve hours ago."

"Current as of the last refreshment cycling," the operator said. "Forty-five seconds ago merely. The car is not moving since many hours ago."

Sam thanked the operator and hung up. Half an hour, the navigation system said.

"Wonder if he shot himself in the rest stop parking lot," Brock mused.

Sam smiled and shook her head. "Always the optimist, eh?"

Brock laughed. "I should stop asking you about your workday. All the violence is seeping into my brain."

"Honestly, I thought the same thing you did. Either something's happened to him, or he's switched cars."

"Only one way to find out," Brock said.

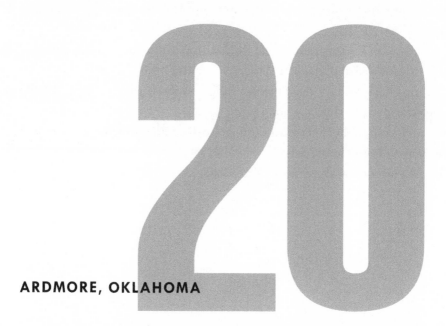

ARDMORE, OKLAHOMA

THE SICKLY SWEET STENCH OF WARM BLOOD PERMEATED the anteroom, and as the temperature in the rest stop building climbed with the morning sun, people were beginning to get sick.

Stalwart and a couple of reluctant volunteers had hauled the heavy corpse, belonging to the man who was Jenna's father and Stephanie's lover, into the men's room. It wasn't a good solution, as every male member of the group of prisoners had to view the bloody shape, now covered by paper towels, as they relieved themselves and slaked their thirst at the bathroom tap.

But it was better than staring at the body all day, Stalwart felt.

Jenna was inconsolable, sobbing and shaking in a corner. She was suffering from the aftereffects of the alcohol that the band of subhuman low-lives had forced down her throat, and suffering from the aftereffects of a brutal gang rape. And she was devastated by the loss of her father, who had met his bloody end defending her honor.

Stephanie, mother of two young boys and the fallen man's mate, sat in a daze, her young children not fully comprehending the situation, yet prescient enough to sense its severity.

Stalwart's anger had settled into a smoldering seethe. Revenge wasn't his to claim, but he possessed a keen sense of justice from his many years spent leading other people, and it led him to make a promise to himself. If the opportunity arose, he would rid the planet of the buck-toothed, slack-jawed scum who had committed the atrocities that hung like a pall over the roomful of rest stop prisoners.

He thought of the cell phone, the one that had fallen from Rat Face's pocket after Jenna's dad had knocked the half-wit unconscious with a flying fist. The phone was now buried under a day's accumulated trash in the men's room garbage can.

The battery had died long ago. Stalwart had been able to make just two phone calls.

The first was to a number he had memorized, but hoped he would never have occasion to use. It was a long shot, he figured, but it was worth it. When you trusted someone the way Stalwart trusted Archive, it only made sense to start there.

He had made the second call with a great deal of trepidation. It was an enormous gamble. The outcome was far from certain, and, by rights, he should have discussed it with his fellow prisoners. In the end, though, he had simply made the decision and acted on it, sitting in the cold bathroom stall, keeping his voice low.

The call could either have made their situation immeasurably better, or infinitely worse. He wasn't sure which outcome would win out, but he knew that inaction wasn't on the table.

So he had taken his chances, and dialed 911. It was a risk he couldn't *not* take. People had been raped and murdered, and he wasn't about to sit idly by while the shit-breathers in overalls – and one animal wearing a police uniform – continued to terrorize the group of half-naked prisoners huddled in the outhouse anteroom.

The robotic message had surprised him: "Please hold. If this is not an emergency, please hang up now. Due to excessive call volume, we will answer your emergency call in the order in which it was received. Please remain calm."

Then, "your approximate wait time is… forty-seven… minutes." *You've got to be kidding me.*

The battery had died before he'd spoken with an operator.

Stalwart was surprised by how much hope had built up in his heart. Despite the cold logic and the low odds – the 911 call might just have been routed to Clem, the tobacco-stained redneck of a police officer who seemed to be the ringleader of the highwaymen – his emotions had seized onto the hair-thin lifeline with surprising strength and quickness.

He had cried when the battery died. Stalwart didn't remember the last time tears had flowed from his eyes, but he had wept bitterly in that cold, dark bathroom stall, gripping the phone tightly enough to make the plastic creak, stifling the sound in the crook of his elbow.

He'd gotten rid of the evidence by wrapping the phone in paper towels and burying it deep in the trashcan. Something told him that after the emasculating experience of being knocked out cold, Rat Face would feel the need to save face. He would be dangerously angry, and Stalwart didn't want to give the little weasel an excuse to take his anger out on anyone. Far better to let him think he'd lost his phone in the brush somewhere.

Maybe the little coward would think it had fallen out while he was busy defiling Jenna.

He doesn't know it yet, but Rat Face is a dead man.

Stalwart heard footsteps beyond the double doors that held them captive. Adrenaline surged, and his heart rate doubled. As had become his custom when the tormentors appeared, Stalwart stood.

Jenna's sobs grew louder as the familiar sound of the chain retreating through the door handles rattled through the crowded, stench-filled anteroom.

Other men stood as well, fists flexing subconsciously.

The doors burst open. Rat Face and Jimbo stood in the entry, shotguns in hand, fat wads of tobacco stuffed in their faces. As Stalwart's eyes adjusted to the brightness, he made out Clem's shape, standing in the background, the picture of rectitude and civil authority in his state trooper's uniform. Stalwart fumed. *You die slowest, asshole.*

"We's goin' on a little trip," Jimbo announced with a wicked grin, tobacco grains stuck between his teeth.

Rat Face giggled and fidgeted with the excitement of a child. "Ever' body yup!" he yelled, his voice breaking up an octave. *A weak boy trying to earn his manhood at our expense,* Stalwart thought.

He assessed the situation. Rat Face's gun was strung across his shoulders, arms draped over the barrel and stock. He'd be easy to take out.

But Jimbo was another story. He held his weapon at low ready, Stalwart saw. There was obviously some military or law enforcement training in his background. And Jimbo had already demonstrated his willingness to end someone's life.

Jimbo would be a problem

Stalwart's eyes moved to Clem, standing out in the sunlight. His pistol was drawn. Stalwart couldn't see the round indicator or the safety lever from a distance, so he had to assume the weapon was ready to fire.

There was a fourth goon, too, Stalwart knew. He hadn't made an appearance since the initial abduction, but Stalwart had to assume was still lurking somewhere.

And there could be more of them.

He shook his head. *These odds suck.*

Stalwart looked over at another of the prisoners, an athletic thirty-something with a spark in his eye and a set to his jaw that Stalwart liked. The young man's eyes queried Stalwart. *Do we make a move?* he seemed to be asking.

Stalwart shook his head. Five casualties, minimum, if it went poorly. They would have to bide their time, look for an opportunity, plan their attack.

They marched single-file out into the day, shoeless and shirtless, prodded with shotgun barrels into the back of a rented moving truck. Jimbo's fat gut jiggled as he pulled the big overhead door shut, the noise deafening inside the truck. Stalwart heard a padlock snap into place, sealing them in.

The van lurched forward, throwing the prisoners onto each other.

Stalwart gritted his teeth. *Be patient,* he coached himself. *Make the smart play when the time comes.*

Brock waited for a moving van to exit the rest stop parking lot, then eased the rental car into the lot. The parking spaces were nearly all occupied, but there was no sign of life. No one milled about, no kids played in the grass, and there were no pet owners following their dogs with bags of crap.

"What is this, the rapture?" Brock asked.

"Seriously," Sam said. "Does this mean God hates us?"

"We're looking for a white Kia," Brock said. He read out the license plate number.

"Over there." Sam pointed.

"It has a flat," Brock said. "Left rear."

She got out of the car and took a closer look. She pointed to buckshot holes around the wheel well. "He probably didn't mark this on the inspection sheet," she deadpanned.

"Looks like someone changed his plans up for him."

Sam searched the car, but found nothing useful. She opened the trunk, and the smell of gasoline made her eyes water. There was an empty gas can lying on its side. "I wonder if he got rolled for his fuel and supplies."

"Looks like they cleaned him out. Not even a suitcase."

Sam nodded. She sat down on the curb to think things through.

"Gotta see a man about a horse," Brock said. He ambled across the grass to the brick building containing the restrooms.

Sam hadn't the slightest idea what to do next. She didn't know whether Charles had been coerced into handing over his access badge, and was lying in a ditch somewhere, or if he was somehow involved in the theft.

But she knew from the SatStar tracking readout of the rental car's history over the last day that Mike Charles, or whoever was driving his rental car, had driven away from Fort Worth the morning *after* the beam controller was stolen from the Langston Marlin plant. So whatever misfortune had befallen the car and its driver – the kind of misfortune that had involved a shotgun blast to the rear tire, at a minimum – may or may not have been related to the theft itself.

I hate it when more evidence makes things less clear.

Brock returned and sat next to Sam, hands shaking.

She looked at his face. White as a sheet. "What's up, baby?"

"Found something in the men's room," he said, showing her the soles of his shoes.

They were covered in blood.

21

LOST MAN LAKE RANCH, COLORADO

PROTÉGÉ LOOKED AT THE NOTEPAD ON HIS LAP, FILLED with the old man's distinctive scrawl. It was a remarkable plan. Thorough, well-examined, and with the brutal, cold logic of a man accustomed to making decisions of enormous import on the basis of incomplete information.

It was the way of things. The hacks who taught executive decision-making had never made a real decision in their lives. It was obvious by the way they espoused "gathering all the relevant facts," which was an impossibility by definition. Making decisions was inevitably about shaping future outcomes. The future was messy and chaotic, nothing like the orderly figments of the gurus' imaginations. And as a rule, the future never lifted its skirt. You never knew until you got there.

So at its core, everything of consequence in life was a gamble, and setbacks paved the road to success. Few understood this as deeply as the old man, Protégé thought. Archive had failed his way to fortune many times over.

But never on this scale. Archive and his distinguished group of like-minded tycoons and captains of industry – Protégé included – had played what could only be regarded as one of the riskiest poker hands in human history.

And it wasn't going nearly as smoothly as they had hoped. Hence the notepad, outlining a few details of the contingency plan Archive and the group of distinguished illuminati had enacted.

Members of the group had been arriving via various means at the largely self-sustaining enclave at Lost Man Lake Ranch in a steady stream since the wee hours of Tuesday morning, and the large ranch house – more a resort than anything else, elegantly appointed in addition to its self-sufficiency – now supported more than two dozen members and their families.

They hadn't all agreed on the best course of action right away, of course. There had been lively debate, as would be expected among a crowd of self-made millionaires and internationally recognized personalities. But they had eventually wound up in vehement agreement with each other on the best way forward.

And despite the disconcerting news about the way society was reacting, they stuck by their earlier decision to destroy the financial juggernaut. The choice had been based on what Art Levitow, the brilliant quantum physicist whose device had disabled the computers and satellites that ran the banking system, termed a "mathematical inevitability." Debt-fueled self-dealing always ends in bloody revolution, he'd claimed.

After Levitow rattled off a long list of countries whose fiat economies had collapsed spectacularly over the past century, Protégé wasn't inclined to argue, and Levitow's logic had formed the basis of Protégé's decision to participate in the "bloodless devolution" they'd hoped to pull off.

But there was blood.

Protégé shook his head, images of street rioting and bloodied, hungry, frightened citizens flashing through his mind. True, the casualties were small in an absolute sense. The news channels were reporting just shy of a thousand deaths nationwide. Roughly a normal month's worth of automobile accident fatalities. Not an epidemic, by any stretch, but Protégé couldn't help feeling a sense of responsibility.

But much better than your average revolution, he thought, turning back to the page of Archive's notes.

The phone rang. Archive answered, and put it on speakerphone. "General Williamson," he said.

"Hello, old man," a deep African American voice intoned. "I'd never have signed up for this if I realized how much work I was creating for myself."

Archive laughed his easy, mirth-filled laugh. "But you're well-staffed, I trust. After all, you are charged with ensuring the safety and security of the entire North American continent."

"That I am," said the commander of Northern Command, or NORTHCOM in military parlance, the joint organization comprised of units from all four military branches. "I must say I'm more than a little apprehensive about my ability to fulfill my charter, though. Things appear to be on an uncomfortable vector at the moment."

Archive chuckled. "Is that four-star speak for 'going to hell in a hand-basket?'"

"Sure is."

"So you've made the call to embed the counterinsurgency teams?"

"Absolutely. Moving out from Norfolk and San Diego, mostly."

Protégé listened intently, studying the flow chart block containing the words "Spec Ops COIN Units," written by Archive's ridiculously expensive Montblanc pen just minutes ago.

"So you're using the SEAL teams, then?" Archive asked.

"Primarily, yes," Williamson answered. "Special Operations Command is heavily committed overseas at the moment, and the bulk of them won't be back home for another forty-eight hours."

"And you're confident they'll make the adjustment to operating in American society?"

"I am," Williamson said. "Though there will undoubtedly be problems. You can't send twenty year-old kids overseas to live with Afghani tribesmen for a year and then expect them to assimilate seamlessly into a group of fragmented American gangs who are all trying to fill the power vacuum."

Archive exhaled, a concerned look on his face.

"But they will figure it out," the general said. "They're good at what they do."

"Do we have an idea of which gangs are emerging as regionally dominant?"

"It will probably come as no surprise that the gangs best positioned to prosper during the financial freeze ended up being the ones with an existing infrastructure. So the drug cartels are branching out, and starting to take over food delivery and other services."

Archive nodded. "Makes good business sense."

"And it's a great way to gain social legitimacy," Williamson said. "My orders to the special operators were to support and amplify those kinds of efforts, while doing their best to avoid participating in the more negative behaviors endemic to the particular groups they're infiltrating."

"Well said. Won't the local gangs be suspicious of newcomers?" Archive asked.

"Certainly. But they're the only real functioning social structure at the moment, and they're recruiting like mad. Less than a quarter of our law enforcement officers and firefighters are on the job, because they're all at home trying to take care of their families. So there's nobody else to deal with problems as they crop up, and the gangs are starting to provide basic necessities, using their existing underground networks to move those goods around. We're also seeing the suburban middle class take on a labor role in support of the infrastructure effort."

Archive smiled. "What an amazing juxtaposition."

"Absolutely," Williamson said. "And I'm relieved to learn that the kind of spontaneous organization we hoped for is actually taking place."

"But there's a bit more bloodshed than we'd hoped. Can we fix that?"

"Not quickly. I'm afraid the casualty numbers will continue to climb. My special operators will be able to reduce the violence to some degree, but I only have so many of them, and it's a big country. My strategy is to focus on the big population centers, to keep them from erupting in open conflict while people organize themselves to meet their own needs."

Archive considered. "I think it actually helps that most law enforcement officers are at home. That makes them less visible to the gangs, who are habituated to viewing authority as enemies."

"Concur," Williamson said. "Make no mistake, though. There are some really bad people in those gangs. We need to be very careful about how we approach this situation. It's extremely tenuous."

"What are your marching orders from the top?"

Williamson snorted. "Disastrous."

"He hasn't."

"I'm afraid he has. It won't be announced for a few hours, and I'm stalling for more time. But the President has issued a verbal order for me to institute martial law. We're activating the National Guard."

Archive's expression turned sour. He shook his head. "That may be unrecoverable."

"I don't think so," Williamson disagreed. "I'd say we'll get ahold of half of our guardsmen in the next forty-eight hours, and not even half of *them* will report for duty within the next couple of days after that. And due to some inherent inefficiencies in the congressionally-mandated structure of my command, which I won't make any real effort to mitigate, actually getting them deployed in numbers could take me up to a week."

"I thought they were supposed to be anywhere in the world in seventy-two hours," Archive said.

Williamson laughed. "That's what the Guard Bureau wants us to think. Truth is, we'd be hard-pressed to send them anywhere inside a month, and that's without trying to get them to leave their spouses and children at home in the middle of a social meltdown."

Archive smiled. "Sounds like it's not quite a straightforward proposition."

"Which works to our advantage at the moment," NORTHCOM said. "Besides, I don't have any food reserves to hand out to civilians, so my soldiers would just be milling about on street corners, making a spectacle of themselves."

Archive pondered. "All things considered, it sounds like we're actually in decent shape. You have things well in hand, General."

"I wouldn't go that far," Williamson said. "But I think we're moving quickly in the right direction, and I plan to move extremely slowly in the wrong one."

Archive laughed. "I'm glad you're on the job to walk such a fine line."

"I won't last forever. If the President survives the crisis, I'm sure my head will be one of the first to roll."

"You're always welcome at the Ranch," Archive said.

Protégé nudged the old man and handed him a small slip of paper torn from the notepad, on which he had scrawled a single word: *Stalwart.*

"Heavens me, I'd nearly forgotten," the old man said. "General, we've got one of our own in a dire situation in rural Oklahoma. He called us late last night. He was captured by a local band of toughs, and they're murdering people. Is there any chance we can send help?"

"I'm afraid not," Williamson said. "If he was in a major city, I'd be able to send someone. But I can't afford to divert my men from the urban areas out into the sticks. It's just too touch-and-go in the cities right now."

Archive nodded. "I understand. We'll hope for the best." He thanked the general and signed off.

Protégé let out a breath. "Sounds like this thing could go either way."

Archive agreed. "I hope this doesn't turn into Rwanda."

"That would be one way to solve the overpopulation problem," Protégé said grimly.

"But not one I would want to be responsible for."

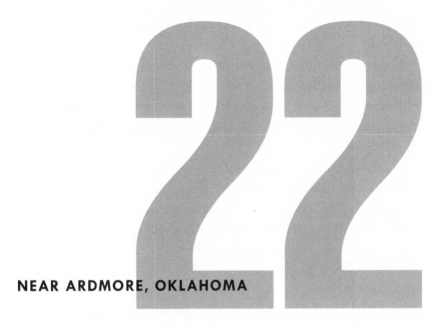

NEAR ARDMORE, OKLAHOMA

"I THINK I'M GOING TO PUKE," BROCK SAID, STEPPING away from the corpse in the rest stop men's room.

Sam lifted the paper towel covering the dead man's face. "Is this Mike Charles?" she asked.

Brock shook his head, lifting his shirt to shield his mouth and nose from the powerful stench. "Definitely not."

Sam peeled away a shard of blood-soaked paper towel covering the man's chest, revealing a gaping wound where his innards once were. "Twelve-gauge, I'd guess," She said, shaking her head. "Shot from up close, judging by how tight the pattern looks."

"Looks like it did the trick."

Sam searched the corpse for a wallet or a set of keys, but found nothing she could use to identify the body, or provide a clue as to why the man might have been killed.

She looked at the floor. It was covered in bloody footprints of all shapes and sizes, just like the larger anteroom. *Who murders a man and then walks around barefoot in his blood?* It was macabre. And it went against basic human nature. "I count at least a dozen different footprints around here," she said.

"This is creeping me out."

Sam nodded. "Either it was some ritual cult killing, or there's something else going on."

"My money's on 'something else,'" Brock said. "I don't think rest stops are big cult gathering locations."

"All the empty cars in the parking lot are bothering me, as are the barefoot footprints. I think a bunch of people were locked in here with the corpse."

Brock shivered.

Sam followed a string of partial footprints out the door of the anteroom, across the narrow sidewalk, and into the dry grass of the rest stop. All of the footprints crossed the sidewalk and headed into the grass at roughly the same point. "Looks like they all headed out into the field," she said, following the faint impressions remaining in the dry grass.

The trail stopped abruptly, just a few feet in front of a set of tire tracks.

Holy shit!

Sam thought she'd figured out what happened to all the people.

She straightened up and stared at the rest stop entrance. "Brock, do you remember that rental truck that was leaving as we arrived? What direction did it turn on the frontage road?"

"Turned right," he answered. "Why?"

"I think it was full of people."

Sam matted the accelerator and peeled around the corner leading out of the rest stop parking lot and onto the frontage road, then angled toward the highway on-ramp. She didn't have any idea how much time had elapsed since they'd passed the rental truck on their way into the parking lot, but she was grateful for the dearth of highway exits in the rural section of I-35. There was still a chance they'd be able to catch up to the truck despite its head start.

Traffic was agreeably sparse. It wasn't like the city people were fleeing to the barren plains to meet their suddenly-urgent need for food and water, but there were still a few cars about, driving at a far more Oklahoma-esque pace than Sam could tolerate at the moment. She used the horn, the lights, and the shoulder to work her way northbound around the annoyingly slow rural drivers.

Engine whining, the small rental car crested a promontory and rounded a gentle curve in the highway, heading toward an underpass. "There!" Brock pointed out the passenger window. A UHaul truck was making its way up the exit ramp toward the cross-street.

"Dammit!" Sam had already passed the exit. She recalled having read a road sign a mile ago informing her that the next off-ramp wouldn't appear for another five miles.

That wasn't going to work for her. She checked her mirror, slammed on the brakes, and turned hard to the left, bouncing and jolting over the shoulder and across the dusty median. Brock barked as the jerks and bumps jostled his wounded thigh.

The tires chirped as they regained their grip on the pavement on the southbound side of the highway. Sam charged across the interstate and up the opposite exit ramp, engine protesting as she climbed the hill toward the overpass intersection.

As they approached the stop sign at the top of the hill, the UHaul truck drove right in front of them, heading west on the crossroad. "Sweet!" Brock exclaimed. "Now what?"

"Good question." Sam considered her options as she fell in behind the van, following at a good distance in order to avoid arousing the driver's suspicion.

They were in a rental car, which lacked the stopping power of a set of police lights. She considered pulling abreast of the driver's door and trying to flag the truck down, but it seemed a risky proposition. If the driver was hauling a moving truck full of frightened pink flesh, he probably wouldn't be inclined to stop for a friendly chat in the middle of nowhere with a random stranger wielding a badge of some sort.

Plus, if her suspicions were correct, and the truck contained enough people to account for all of the abandoned cars at the rest stop, it would undoubtedly take more than a couple of toughs to corral everyone. So she and Brock would likely be outnumbered.

And there was at least one shotgun in play, and at least one asshole with the willpower to use it in anger, if the bloody mess in the rest stop building was any indicator.

"I don't like the odds right now," Sam said. "I think we bide our time and look for an opportunity."

The noontime sun beat down on the Oklahoma prairie, and Sam felt the little car's air conditioner kick on, straining the undersized engine and causing a noticeable loss of acceleration power.

She followed the moving truck at a nonthreatening distance, lamenting the fact that she was forced to engage in a single-car tailing operation. In the counterespionage world, a single-car tail was an invitation to get caught, lose the mark, or both. In rougher parts of the world, it was a great way to get killed. The pros used teams of at least half a dozen cars, all connected via radio and cell phone, to keep tabs on a target vehicle without announcing their presence.

But you play the hand you're dealt, Sam thought. She suspected that the economic terrorist strike that had set off the financial meltdown was just a prelude to something else. It would be too easy to exploit the power vacuum and ensuing chaos, and even if the terrorists' original plan wasn't to take over the country, some enterprising asshole with means and an appropriate lack of scruples would certainly hatch a bright idea at some point.

So her suspicion of a deeper plot's existence sparked a keen interest in having a conversation with Mike Charles, the DoD muckety-muck who, before disappearing, had traveled to Fort Worth to watch a live demonstration of the beam-controller doohickey at Langston Marlin's factory, an event that was followed very closely by the theft of the same doohickey.

The thieves had made use of Charles' access badge and PIN, which suggested that Charles was either rolled and squeezed by the thieves for his access credentials, or that he provided those credentials willingly, and was part of the plot.

Sam suspected the latter, for the simple reason that Mike Charles had used his status as a senior DoD civilian executive to authorize a cargo aircraft to land at Langley Air Force Base, in Hampton, Virginia.

That was an interesting little tidbit to Sam, because the photon death rays, or whatever the hell the science geeks called them, appeared to have been sitting at Langley Air Force Base when they zapped several billion dollars' worth of communication satellites.

Right across the street from the four-star's headquarters building, to be precise. Sam's first impression of General Hajek wasn't favorable – a bit too heavy on the standard patrician chauvinist BS, and a bit too light on cooperation and forthrightness – so she found herself including Hajek in the universe of possible co-conspirators.

But the moving truck. That was a curveball.

Mike Charles might not even be one of the passengers herded like cattle into the back of the UHaul – if that's indeed what had happened to the owners of all of those abandoned cars at the rest stop – but Sam had no other leads regarding his whereabouts. Charles could easily have stopped momentarily at the rest stop, switched cars to throw off any investigators, and continued north on his merry way while the financial world continued to turn to molten slag around him.

That would suck for Sam, especially with no manpower back at DHS to work on an electronic trace of Charles' cell phone to provide clues to his location. Apparently, the on-call Homeland cyber investigation team had taken a powder due to all the chaos in DC.

So she was way out on a limb, possibly wasting hours of precious time, but she had little choice. She hoped that if back of the UHaul van *was* filled with hostages, Mike Charles would be among their ranks.

The UHaul passed an intersection with a dirt road, and Sam saw a police car turn in their direction and tuck in behind the truck. *Interesting. Should I try to flag down the cop?* That could certainly be useful. The van's driver was far more likely to pull over for a policeman than for a redhead in a Hyundai, big boobs notwithstanding.

She accelerated to catch up to the cop car, and dialed 911 to start coordinating with him through the local emergency dispatcher.

A recording told her that the wait time to speak with a 911 operator was fifty-four minutes. *Bastards. I'm going to stop paying taxes.*

She had nearly caught up to the police car when it suddenly pulled out to pass the UHaul. *Can't catch a break right now.* Oncoming traffic prevented her from following right away.

Brake lights. The moving truck was turning left, getting ready to head south down a dirt farm trail. *Decision time.* There was almost no plausible reason for a white Hyundai to follow a moving van down a dirt road in Nowhere, Oklahoma. If she followed, they would certainly make her.

Patience pays, Sam decided. She passed the intersection and continued west, noticing as she did so that the cop car had turned down the same dirt road. The cop now led the moving truck southbound over what looked like a poorly maintained jeep trail.

"The plot thickens," Brock said.

"You don't say. There's almost nothing out here. Why would the cop and the moving truck choose the same dirt trail?" She adjusted the rearview mirror to watch the cop car and moving van disappear over a low promontory, dust flying in their wake.

Once she was sure they were out of view, she whipped the steering wheel around, using both shoulders to flip a U-turn, and gunned the little engine to charge back to the previous intersection. Then she snuck her way southbound, driving slowly to kick up as little dust as possible as she followed the two vehicles down the dirt road.

There was nothing but tumbleweeds and prairie as far as the eye could see. She checked the gas gauge, and reckoned they had an hour before they'd need to stop to refuel using one of the reserve cans they'd finagled from the rental agency.

Her phone buzzed. Dan Gable. "Have they performed a cavity search on you yet?" she asked with a chuckle, the phone jostling with the car's bumps and jolts on the dirt road.

"Funny you should ask," Dan said. "My welcome is definitely wearing thin."

"It was only a matter of time," Sam said. "NSA isn't known for its interagency collegiality. What have you learned?"

"They're closing ranks here," Dan said. "Something's definitely up. They've sealed off the local server farm, and they're also not letting anyone leave the building at the moment."

"It does make a girl wonder what they're hiding."

"Doesn't it? Plus, there's a bit of an inquisition going on as well. I'd guess they've called in and interviewed a few hundred of the employees who didn't show up at the start of the workday, and workers are still trickling in."

"Sounds like great gossip fodder," Sam said.

"Right-o. They're starting to add two and two, piecing things together based on the interview questions."

"Which are…?"

Dan chuckled. "Amateurish. 'Have you ever inserted a USB device into your computer at work, or used any other unauthorized device?' That kind of thing."

"Smooth," Sam chuckled. "So smart money says the rumors are true, and the virus originated inside NSA."

Dan agreed. "Those implications are huge," he said. "Their servers are just two or three nodes removed from almost every personal computer in America, and maybe three or four nodes removed from every computer on the planet with an internet connection."

"My God. How?"

"Byproduct of all the spying they deny doing."

How could I have forgotten. NSA was busy hoovering every bit and byte of the US citizenry's telecommunications. Once you stole all zillion emails and phone conversations, you had to store them someplace, and the data center in the bowels of the Fort Meade fortress seemed like as good a place as any.

"So by virtue of their spying on us, they're in a great position to infect all of our computers with a virus?" Sam asked sarcastically.

Dan laughed. "Careful. What if they're listening now? But you're right. I did some bar napkin math earlier, and even using conservative propagation rate estimates, it's bound to be the fastest and most comprehensive malware penetration in evil geek history."

The dirt road angled to the southeast and rose to the top of a small hill, and Sam caught a glimpse of the cop car and moving truck a couple of miles in the distance, still kicking up a dust trail. She thought she could make out the top of a building further in the distance, but she wasn't sure.

She thought about the virus attack staged from within NSA. "So what's the point of the virus, anyway?"

"If I was going to try to hack my way into twelve Federal Reserve systems at roughly the same time, I'd probably want to recruit several hundred million computers to help me do it."

"So they've turned all those computers into an army of robot hackers?"

"That's my hunch. But the server farm is locked down tighter than a nun's nethers, so I have no way of confirming what happened."

Sam rounded a slight bend in the trail, undoubtedly carved to avoid a small copse of scraggly trees growing defiantly in the middle of the wasteland, and caught sight of a dilapidated barn and farmhouse in the distance. The UHaul and police cruiser appeared to have parked between the two buildings.

"Thanks, Dan. Gotta run. There's a thing happening here. Keep digging and keep me posted." She hung up without waiting for a reply.

She stopped the rental car, put it into reverse, and drove back around the bend, hoping the skinny trees would make their car more difficult to spot. Then she and Brock stepped out, snuck up to the edge of the promontory, and squinted against the sunlight to watch events unfold at the farmhouse.

A man got out of the cop car. Even from a distance, Sam could tell he wasn't wearing a police uniform. *Strange.* She was pretty sure there was some sort of a regulation that prohibited driving a government vehicle for personal business.

The man walked to the truck's side window and conversed briefly with the driver, then walked over to the barn. He wrestled to open a recalcitrant barn door, then got out of the way as the driver repositioned the moving van. It backed up to the barn entrance, and the driver got out. *Fatass,* Sam thought as she watched him spit in the dirt and waddle around to the back of the truck to open the loading door.

She couldn't see into the van, but she heard the harsh tones of barked commands, and saw Fatass gesticulating with his hands. She saw motion from within the barn, and thought she caught a glint of sunlight off of a shotgun barrel.

"Gun," Brock said quietly.

Sam nodded. *Looks like these are our boys.*

She squinted and used her hand to shade the sunlight from her eyes. "My God," she whispered. *Am I seeing what I think I'm seeing?* It looked as though the van's driver, the man from the cop car, and a third person were hustling more than two dozen shirtless people from the back of the moving van into the barn.

"Holy shit," Brock said. "They're herding those people like animals."

23

SABOT SLID THE MOUSE POINTER OVER A MINIMIZED window and clicked to bring it to the forefront. It was a computer script he had written in a little more than an hour, and it had been running for almost as long. It was still humming along nicely, so he made a copy of the output file, and opened the copy to examine its contents.

He smiled. A little over two thousand Bitcoin accounts had been created automatically since he'd set the script to work in earnest.

It wouldn't normally be a bright idea, creating thousands of new Bitcoin wallets from the same computer. It would certainly raise eyebrows, and would be a telltale sign in the event of an investigation of any sort.

So Sabot had hidden his tracks exceptionally well. He had programmed his computer script to use a particular tool, common among denizens of the Dark Web, the seedy underbelly of the internet where hackers, script kiddies, and hangers-on guarded their true identities and locations with a determined ferocity. The tool sampled the IP addresses of computers currently online, and masked a hacker's activity behind an IP address it selected randomly from among active users. The tool made it seem as if another computer's fingerprints were left at the scene of the crime.

Each of Sabot's new Bitcoin accounts thus appeared to belong to a different user. That was a key part of his plan. Sabot had learned that, contrary to popular belief and Justice Department misinformation, Bitcoin wasn't nearly as anonymous as cash. Every transaction was permanently recorded for posterity. So it was extremely important to cover your tracks, and extremely difficult to fence money in the Bitcoin world, and Sabot figured the best way to do obscure the thefts he was about to perpetrate would be to make it appear as if thousands of people were involved, rather than just a single person.

He double-checked that the passwords were being recorded properly. Each account would be completely useless without the correct password. The computer picked a thirty-digit random login credential for each new wallet it created, and logged the password into the script's output file.

Now for the really entertaining stuff, he thought. Satisfied that he had a solid plan to stash his spoils, Sabot got to work planning his electronic raid on unsuspecting Bitcoin owners all over the world.

Might as well start with the big guys, he figured, navigating to the world's second-largest Bitcoin exchange service, called BitChange. He clicked a button on his browser window, and the pretty pictures and clean edges of the well-designed web page disappeared, revealing the behind-the-scenes software code that made it work.

Websites were nothing more than database organization tools, designed to pull information from large repositories and display it in 256-color brilliance for users to manipulate. The website – the thing that people viewed in their browser windows – was little more than a skin, a pretty manifestation of the underlying facts, figures, and BS sales copy that formed the gristle, meat, and bones of the internet.

Sabot read each line of code carefully. While he hadn't been at the controls of a computer since his unpleasant experience as an FBI witness had begun, Sabot was anything but rusty. His FBI minders had brought him reams full of printed computer code, which he dutifully perused to ferret out illegal activity, and he was up to speed on all the latest tricks.

He only saw one vulnerability in BitChange's website code, one so obvious that it had to have been a trap. Time was of the essence – every hacker worth his salt was bound to be putting on a full-court press to swipe as many

Bitcoins as possible – but Sabot resisted the urge to take the bait. There was simply too much at stake.

Time to get social, he decided. Humans were the most vulnerable components of any computer network. People couldn't help themselves. There were simply too many faults in a human being's core operating system, residual byproducts of a hundred thousand years of evolution as a social animal, and Sabot had no doubt that he would be able to obtain the accesses he needed to begin filling his newly-created Bitcoin accounts with piles of virtual wealth.

His forte from back in the day used to be voice phishing, or "vishing," the art of calling people on the phone and tricking them into revealing their private account information. But there was no guarantee that the information he needed would belong to an English-speaking target, so his con man's phone skills might not prove useful.

No matter. Humans were still human, and they found all sorts of ways to do stupid things.

He wanted access to BitChange's succulent list of subscribers, along with any exploitable personal information that might also reside in the user database. He figured that BitChange's network administrators would have access to that information.

But who were BitChange's network administrators? *Probably the people who spent the most time on the site,* Sabot reasoned.

He clicked on an icon labeled Tor, which was an access portal to the most anonymous place on the internet, an entire sub-network of people using obscured IP addresses either to do bad things, or to hide from other people who were doing bad things.

He typed a lengthy and obscure web address into the Tor browser and waited impatiently while the spinning wheel whirred. His brief patience was rewarded when a website named StarSixtyNine popped open. Named after the old telephone trick that auto-dialed the last caller's phone number, the Dark Web version performed a similar function in the online world. For a nominal fee – 0.1 Bitcoin in this case – it was possible to download a list of all the computers that had visited a given website over the last twenty-four hours.

Sabot paid the fee, which was now the equivalent of just shy of $300. The dollar's free-fall into worthlessness had evidently continued unabated since the last time Sabot had checked the exchange rate.

Seconds later, he clicked open the report that had downloaded automatically onto his hard drive.

He skimmed the list of IP addresses, the virtual location codes that identified individual users who had visited the BitChange site. His thought was that the exchange's administrators, the people who likely had the credentials to see and manipulate user account information, were probably the site's most frequent users. So he chose the addresses of BitChanges' twelve heaviest users over the past day.

An IP address wasn't a terribly useful thing in and of itself, at least not for Sabot's purposes, so he navigated to another obscure site on the Tor network called "The Pirate's Chest." It featured a cheesy picture of a pirate, eye patch and all, and had a single input window.

The site was a repository for all sorts of stolen information. It was a surprising fact that most hackers didn't really care to use or exploit the information they stole. They simply enjoyed the process of stealing it. But there were other Dark Web users, ones who didn't love the painstakingly exacting work of discovering website vulnerabilities and exploiting them. Many of those users preferred just to use the stolen information to perpetrate other kinds of thefts, especially ones involving pilfered credit card information.

So The Pirate's Chest was created to serve both communities – hackers and thieves – and it contained millions of email addresses, along with their associated IP addresses, and a surprisingly large number of passwords, as well.

Sabot pasted the first IP address into the Pirate's Chest browser interface, clicked on the button helpfully marked "Aaaaaaarrghh!" and waited for the results.

He wasn't disappointed. Thorvald Jenssen's name appeared, along with a remarkably offensive email address and an even more offensive password.

Sabot navigated to the BitChange website, typed Thorvald Jenssen's email address and password into the login pane, and held his breath while he waited. He figured his odds were fifty-fifty. Even smart people were lazy, and tended to use the same password for multiple accounts. Perhaps Thorvald Jenssen would be one of the lazy ones.

"Welcome, Thorvald!" the BitChange site announced.

Sabot smiled. *Dumbass.*

He rummaged around the site for a while before stumbling across what he was looking for: the list of subscribers' account information. Six *thousand* accounts worth. User names, passwords, account balances, activity dates, and even their normal bank account numbers.

Sabot whistled. *Jackpot.* He saved the database onto his hard drive.

It took him another fifteen minutes to write and test another simple computer script. With a deep breath, Sabot set it loose on BitChange's six thousand unsuspecting users. The script logged into a user's BitChange account, then initiated a small, near-random payment from the user's account into one of Sabot's new Bitcoin accounts, created by his earlier script. And like the earlier script, Sabot made use of the IP masking technique to disassociate his computer from each individual theft, and point the virtual finger at another unsuspecting user somewhere out there in the wired universe.

Sabot kept the theft amounts small, always less than one Bitcoin. And he'd even thought to make the amounts "Benford-compliant," which was a concept he'd learned while working with a forensic accountant on a recent FBI case. Benford's Law – which was really just an observation that the digits one through nine didn't occur with equal frequency in natural, non-fraudulent numbers – had been used to catch and convict an impressive number thieves and embezzlers. So he made sure that the computer chose the nearly-random theft amounts in such a way that the transaction amounts wouldn't scream "fraud."

The script also initiated the transactions at random intervals. Site administrators would undoubtedly catch on if they saw regular, sequential activity in what was otherwise a messy and random world.

Sabot sat back and smiled, watching the Bitcoin transactions trickle in. *Pretty damn clean hack,* he decided. *Not bad for a high school dropout.* Watching the stolen bounty grow, he began thinking of the ways his life would change with his newfound affluence.

Maybe Angie could get that Subaru she'd been wanting.

Oh no. Angie. He suddenly looked at his watch. Noon. He hadn't spoken with her in over a day. He picked up the old phone from the wall receptacle and dialed her number. It went straight to voicemail. *Hope she's okay.* He thought of the chaos and looting Adkins had spoken about earlier, and of the shattered glass door at their apartment, and was suddenly very concerned about Angie's safety.

He navigated to a local news station's website, hoping for an update on conditions out in the suburbs, where Angie's mom lived.

As the page loaded, he was struck by its incongruous levity. Instead of pictures of the looting and rioting, as he'd expected to see, Sabot was greeted by a cartoon figure of an old man with a giant, white mustache, wearing a tuxedo and top hat. *What the hell?* Wasn't that the guy from that money game? Monopoly or something?

It appeared to be a video. Sabot clicked play, and turned up the speaker volume.

The Monopoly guy danced to cheesy music for a while, then stopped, pointed, and spoke. "You're free, but you don't believe it yet. That's why you're behaving so poorly. Yessiree. Free but ignorant. That's you. Most of you, anyway."

Then an exaggerated smile, complete with a cartoonish sparkle from one of his teeth. "But you've been pondering. You've thought about what I asked you last time. I can tell you've been thinking about it, because you're starting to make agreements with each other again. Not everywhere, mind you. But in some places, you're starting to get it figured out."

The cartoon figure hopped and clicked his heels. "Remember, those dirty dollars weren't things at all."

More dancing.

"Sure," he continued, spreading his arms, "the oligarchs might be a little angry that all their dollars have turned to dust."

His smile widened. "But not *you*." He pointed at the screen "*You* are about to realize that you have just been handed the biggest gift in modern history." The last word echoed dramatically, followed by more hopping and heel-clicking.

"Just remember," the cartoon said as it danced over to the side of the screen. "Money is just a symbol. The important thing is the agreement between us."

Then the cartoon's face turned serious, and he pointed a gloved finger at his listeners. "And for Pete's sake," he said gravely. "Be nice to each other."

Monopoly Man waved goodbye and disappeared.

"That shit is whacked," Sabot said aloud, shaking his head.

He stood up and headed for the snack bar, lamenting its dwindling supply of ramen noodles. *Maybe I need to make an agreement with somebody to restock this place. I'm about to starve to death.*

CARTER COUNTY, OKLAHOMA

SAM KILLED THE RENTED HYUNDAI'S ENGINE, CURSING the small cloud of haze and dust she had kicked up by repositioning the car a few hundred yards off of the dirt trail, hiding it behind a low berm. She didn't want the goons to discover they were being watched before she had a chance to formulate a plan.

She shut the car door, patted her Kimber .45 in its pancake holster, and walked in a low crouch back toward the small stand of trees, which sat roughly an eighth of a mile north of the run-down barn.

Sam sidled up next to Brock, who was lying prone on his stomach and surveilling the farmhouse. Together, they watched a man climb into the police cruiser and exit the farmhouse driveway onto the dirt road, driving back out toward the paved thoroughfare several miles to the north.

They flattened their bodies as the cruiser drove by, holding their breath, praying not to be seen, exhaling only after the cop car was well out of sight and nearly out of earshot.

"One fewer bastard to deal with," Sam said.

Brock nodded. "So we're going to rescue these people, then?"

Sam laughed. "We're not here to play bridge. And I sure as hell don't care to join them in the barn."

"So you have a plan?"

Sam shook her head. "Not at all. But something usually comes to mind."

"You never cease to amaze me," Brock said, giving her a peck on the cheek. "And you scare me a little bit, too."

Sam's response was interrupted by what she instantly recognized as a shotgun blast, coming from the barn.

Stalwart stood, legs unsteady and knees shaking, his feet sinking into the shit-filled hay inside the barn, holding his hands in a calming gesture. His ears were still ringing from the shotgun blast in closed quarters.

He took a deep breath to speak. The smell of animal waste, cordite, and blood hung heavy in the air, threatening to choke him. His voice quieted a wailing wife and the softly sobbing group of mourners that surrounded her.

Her husband's body lay crumpled in their midst, undoubtedly left as a grisly object lesson.

"Something horrible is happening here," Stalwart said. He spoke in low tones, both to avoid being overheard by the murderous dirtbags who had just left the barn, and because he knew that people listened more intently to a quiet, calm voice than a strident one.

"I think we all hoped for the best at the beginning of this ordeal. I think we all hoped that if we cooperated with them for a while, they would let us go."

Nods of assent. The victim's wife sobbed a little louder, then quieted as more fellow prisoners embraced her.

"Things have become dramatically worse," Stalwart continued, "and I think we need to put our heads together to come up with a plan."

"Damn straight." A young man in the back.

"But here is what we absolutely *must* do," Stalwart said, making eye contact with each of the male members of the group. "We must stop losing our cool. If we want to live, if we want to get out of this situation, then we have to use our heads."

"You wanna stand by and take this shit?" someone asked.

Stalwart shook his head. "You better believe that I'll be first in line to rip their throats out. But we need to be smart about this. Two guys let their emotions get the best of them, and we're now grieving their loss."

"They *raped* those girls!" an athletic-looking twenty-something said.

Stalwart nodded grimly. "Which is why I would love to kill them slowly and painfully," he said. "But we'll never get the chance unless we keep our wits and work together."

More nods of assent. "We've already proven that a one-man unarmed assault isn't the way to go," someone said.

"We have to be smart. This is a bad situation," Stalwart continued, "but it's not un-winnable. These guys aren't that bright, and this isn't the Hanoi Hilton. Let's figure something out."

Sam took a swig of water from their provisions and handed the bottle to Brock. It had been nearly half an hour since they'd watched two men in overalls, one fat, one skinny, both armed, exit the barn and shuffle onto the farmhouse porch. The men had perched themselves atop aging porch furniture and propped their shotguns across their laps.

"I think it's safe to assume that these guys know an awful lot about that corpse at the rest stop," Sam said.

Brock nodded. "No shit. I can't help wondering whether that was a warning shot we heard, or if it was…"

Sam grimaced. "Bad situation either way."

They heard the porch door creak open and saw a third man walk out from within the farmhouse, bottles of beer in his hand. He handed one out to each of his companions, then sat on the stoop.

"I'm not in favor of strolling up to the porch and striking up a conversation," Brock said.

Sam nodded. "The book says I have to attempt to read their Miranda rights to them. But I don't expect much cooperation. You okay with pulling the trigger on someone?"

"You forget that I'm a veteran of two wars. I've dropped a hundred tons of steel and tritonal on bad guys on two continents."

Sam smiled. "I know, tough guy, but this is a little bit different. This kind of stuff will stick with you."

"Tell me something I don't know. I watched you kill a guy with your bare hands once, remember? That would have scared off a lesser boyfriend, I think."

Sam smiled. "Reason number one zillion that I love your big dick. I think it makes you much less insecure than average."

He laughed. "It loves you right back."

Her face turned serious. "Here's what I'm thinking." She outlined her plan.

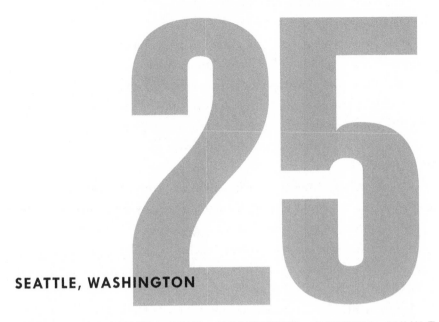

SEATTLE, WASHINGTON

SABOT WATCHED THE COMPUTER SCREEN WHILE munching a bag of chocolates, which represented the last food-like product in the converted warehouse where he'd spent the better part of the last twenty-four hours. He'd curled up on the floor for a brief nap, but was awakened after less than an hour by the ringing phone. It was Angie.

Everything was fine, she'd said, but the world was going to hell, and fast. There were starting to be roving blackouts in the suburbs, she'd said, something about the power plants running out of coal and not being able to buy more. And they were running out of food.

Sabot relayed the news about their compromised apartment, and filled her in on the strange turn of events with his employer.

Angie had been silent for a long time when he told her he'd been working at a computer since the afternoon prior. "Dingo, baby, if you go back to jail, I'm not waiting for you."

"Adkins' orders," he'd said. Which was true – his FBI handler had told him in no uncertain terms that he was to do as his new employers desired.

But Sabot was pretty sure Adkins had no idea they'd asked him to commit larceny on a spectacular scale. He irrationally hoped the subject never came up, but a part of him knew those were unlikely odds.

They made arrangements for Angie to come pick him up, and they planned to stay the night at her mom's house. Angie would arrive in a little over two hours, which made Sabot feel anxious. He had a lot to do.

He checked the running tally of stolen Bitcoins on his computer monitor, then did some quick math using the latest exchange rate. His automated scripts had swiped a little over $300,000 worth of Bitcoins. Not bad for a few hours' work.

Of course, he wasn't sure what $300,000 was worth anymore. Compared to just a day earlier, it took just shy of ten times as many dollars to buy a Euro, and a little more than eight times as many greenbacks to buy Yen. But all of them were in free-fall compared to the price of gold and silver. *I shoulda bought more bling.* And oil prices were through the roof – almost fifteen hundred dollars a barrel.

It was hard to wrap his mind around it all. He was accustomed to measuring the value of everything in terms of dollars. So it felt like a barrel of oil had suddenly become twenty times more valuable than it had been the day before, but he knew that wasn't right. A barrel of oil was a barrel of oil. It hadn't suddenly become twenty times more scarce in the last day.

So that's what happens when the money goes to shit. He thought of a picture he'd seen of a Zimbabwean trillion dollar bill. It bought a pack of gum or something, if he remembered the story correctly.

It reminded him of a snarky blog post title he'd read while researching Bitcoin earlier in the day: *Welcome to the Third World, America.* It was starting to look like the European blogger's gleeful and schadenfreude-filled prediction was more prescient than Sabot had originally thought.

He thought about his brilliant hack of the BitChange system, and all of the riches he was making for Balzzack011, whoever the hell that was, and he felt himself growing resentful of having to hand over nearly all of the spoils. It was *his* skill and savvy that had produced the bounty, after all, and he began to feel taken advantage of. *We'll have to see about all of that,* he thought.

But he was certain that Balzzack011 was watching him. It was inevitable. They wouldn't give a computer to one of the world's best hackers without protecting themselves by installing a key logger at minimum, and probably several other layers of spyware. If he was going to slice some of that Bitcoin pie for himself, he'd have to find a different computer to do it with.

His eyes were drawn back to the rising tally of stolen Bitcoins on his monitor. Swiping coins at the rate of a hundred an hour – safely and securely, no less – was an impressive accomplishment, but you couldn't eat a Bitcoin, and Sabot was hungry. So were Angie and her mom, from the sound of things.

Beaners gotta eat. Ain't like the farmer's market is open today.

But his years as a hacker had taught him that there was almost always a way to get what you wanted. And since digital currency seemed to be holding up much better than the paper stuff at the moment, he was pretty sure that if anyone had figured out how to turn digital currency in to tangible goods, it was probably the hackers.

Back to the Dark Web. He opened a browser window and typed a series of symbols into the address bar: J57—4—1u1z. The web address was a phrase written in a web dialect called "Leet," a name derived by bastardizing the word *elite*. Leet was a combination of slang words and homographic representations of letters. Leet users replaced letters with symbols or numbers that were similar in shape, to communicate the same words while avoiding chat room or website filters, and also to stymie neophytes lurking in the chatrooms.

Leet was second nature to Sabot, and his mind instantly thought of the symbols he had typed as "Just for Lulz." It was the name of a chat room frequented by power geeks.

"Lulz" was itself a bastardization of the popular expression "LOL," and a working transliteration of the chat room's title was "Just for giggles." It was a hangout for the bored and slightly malicious.

Sabot had been watching chat room activity for the last three years, but always from a distance, relegated to reading hard-copy printouts handed to him by FBI investigators. So he needed to create a new identity in order to participate. He called himself n008 1337, Leet for "Noob Elite."

A noob was a newcomer, subject under normal conditions to merciless ridicule and slander. But to call oneself "elite" was an outrageous boast and a horrific violation of unwritten hacker protocol. Sabot knew it would draw incredible amounts of vicious vitriol. That was exactly what he wanted – it would draw idle users in from the sidelines.

It didn't take long before nasty comments began to rack up, variations on the usual themes of maternal fornication, homosexuality, and bestiality, and Sabot made note of the usernames that contributed.

Then he searched the chat room's archives for previous posts made by those users, looking for references to Bitcoin and its uses in local real-goods economic transactions.

A particularly vociferous gentleman with the username "|>0gg`/ 57`/13," which Sabot recognized instantly as the words "Doggy Style," had written a string of posts in which he bragged about how easy it was to get almost anything you needed, just by using Bitcoins and the right connections. "Just gotta look around, man," one post read. "Ppl still wanna sell shit & ppl still wanna buy shit. I'm livin BIG yo."

Bingo.

Sabot got to work "doxing" the user named Doggy Style. Doxing was hacker slang for figuring out a person's real identity using online clues. Hackers who hung out in the Dark Web were generally ruthless, capricious, and merciless, and protecting one's real-life identity was paramount. Ruined relationships, lost jobs, and frozen bank accounts were frequent side-effects of failing to keep private information private.

But it was child's play for Sabot. He had risen to the top of the hacker dog pile for a good reason: he was damn good. It took a little bit less than an hour to dox Doggy Style and hack into his private computer, and Sabot was soon watching a webcam video feed of a lanky white kid just out of his teens, sitting in a small room with video game posters on the wall and action figures visible on a shelf in the background.

Sabot clicked a few keys, and watched gleefully as Doggy Style's eyes widened. *Damn, that never gets old!* He had just caused the video feed to pop open on Doggy Style's computer, and the kid had suddenly been confronted with an unexpected live camera view of himself. Sabot had just announced his arrival in grand fashion.

He saw Doggy Style's eyes flit about the screen, and watched as he typed at his keyboard. "Very funny, fkr," Doggy Style's chatroom entry said.

Sabot responded. "Fkg ownd." *I freaking owned you.*

"What do you want?"

"Pay ur respects, then we'll talk," Sabot typed. He watched the video feed. The kid dutifully took off his shoe and held it above his head, as if he were being stepped on like a bug. It was a hacker tradition, making the victim acknowledge his defeat and powerlessness.

"Good man," Sabot typed. "I got skillz, you got cnxnxs. Lets do biz."

"Whatchu need?" Doggy Style asked.

"Food," Sabot typed. "And chipzezz." Slang for a new computer. It was a risk. If Balzzack011 could decipher what Sabot had just asked for, there would be trouble. But Sabot was betting that Balzzack011 wasn't sufficiently well versed in hacker slang to catch the hidden meaning. If confronted, Sabot would claim he was asking for Doritos.

Sabot smiled as he read Doggy Style's response. "EZ. I gotchu bro."

CARTER COUNTY, OKLAHOMA

SAM AND BROCK KNELT LOW BETWEEN EMACIATED TREE trunks in the small thicket, shielding their eyes from the early afternoon sun as they watched the farmhouse.

But for a trip inside the house to fetch more beer, the three men hadn't moved from their positions on the porch. They passed what looked like a glass pipe and lighter between them, taking turns holding the flame beneath the pipe's bowl while sucking on its mouth, and laughter soon rolled up the small hill.

"Crack?" Brock asked.

Sam shook her head. "Too expensive and exotic for this area. That's probably a home chemistry experiment."

"Meth?"

Sam nodded. "The new rural business of choice, now that farming has consolidated."

"Doesn't it screw up their teeth?"

"Yep. Great job security for dentists, except nobody but the dealers can afford dental work."

She pointed to a low, uniform berm running north to south, on the west side of the farmhouse. "Irrigation ditch, looks like. We can approach using the berm for cover. I'm thinking it's the only way to get to the house without being spotted."

Brock agreed. They backed down the promontory, out of view of the farmhouse, and crossed the dirt road, being careful to stay clear of soft sand that would have left footprints. They stopped by their rental car, still hidden behind a low hill, and Sam collected a hit-and-run kit full of handy survival and first-aid items. "Just in case," she said, slinging the strap over her shoulder.

They low-crawled to the top of the irrigation ditch, being careful to keep their profile low as they crested the top of the stream's engineered banks.

The irrigation canal was designed to safely contain an Oklahoma-sized flash flood, but it had been a dry fall, and a feeble stream meandered at the floor of the canal, wandering from side to side within the ramrod-straight berms that extended for miles in either direction. Sam and Brock walked south toward the farmhouse, taking care to stay below the crest.

Stalwart surveyed the haggard hostages, wandering around the barn searching for anything that might be useful to help them escape from their predicament.

Their spirits were flagging, he noticed. The barn had been thoroughly sanitized of all of the normal farm accoutrements, and there were no tools or supplies laying around that might be useful as a weapon against their captors.

"What's up there?" someone asked, pointing to a hay loft above the far side of the barn floor.

"Ladder's been sawed off," someone else observed glumly. It looked like a city fire escape ladder, its last remaining rung suspended ten feet off of the barn floor, well out of reach.

A skinny teenager walked toward the ladder. "Can anyone give me a boost up there? I'll climb up and take a look around."

Moments later, Stalwart and another middle-aged man kneeled, then helped the kid stand on their shoulders, putting him within a few inches of the ladder's bottom rung. He hopped, grasped the ladder, and climbed up, soon scrambling onto the hay loft floor. "Stinks up here," he reported.

The group heard rummaging and an occasional curse from the kid as he searched the loft. "Old fishing pole and a bent-up tire rim," he finally said.

"Great," someone said sarcastically. "What are we going to do with that?"

Stalwart looked around the barn, and an idea struck. "Is there fishing line in the reel?"

Affirmative noises from the kid.

"Toss it all down," Stalwart said. "Believe it or not, I think those things will be helpful." As the kid struggled with the heavy tire rim, Stalwart explained his idea.

"Watch out for snakes," Brock admonished, inadvertently slipping into a patch of vegetation where the feeble stream neared the bank of the irrigation ditch.

"Rattlesnakes?"

"Water moccasins. Deadly bastards."

"Great," Sam said. "A poisonous snake bite would really round out the week."

They heard a peal of laughter coming from the farmhouse porch, now a quarter mile to the east of their position.

Sam peeked up over the irrigation berm to get her bearings. "Looks like we're getting close," she said. "I'll sneak up on the porch from the south side of the farmhouse, and you attack from the north."

"Simple as that?"

"How much more complicated would you like it to be?"

"I thought you'd have a few more words of wisdom."

"Be sure to click the safety off."

"Thanks." Brock shook his head, then kissed her. "If I haven't told you lately, I really love you in a grossly inconvenient, co-dependent kind of way. Don't get shot."

"Me too. And you either." She kissed him back, slipping him some tongue and pinching his ass. "Now let's go get those people out of the barn."

They fanned out, and on Sam's signal, they crested the berm and snuck toward the farmhouse.

Surreal, Sam thought. It seemed like eons ago that she had climbed atop Brock in his hospital bed in DC. Now she was sneaking up on a group of redneck deviants with a barn full of humans in the middle of Oklahoma. *Can't make this shit up.*

She instinctively drew into a crouch as they approached the run-down farmhouse, placing her footfalls slowly and carefully to avoid alerting the three men getting drunk and high on the porch on the opposite side of the house. She glanced to her left at Brock and noticed him moving stealthily as well, though he was visibly pained by the gunshot wound in his thigh.

Soon the house came between them. A large propane tank and a tangle of tall weeds climbing the wall forced Sam to step further away from the house than she'd otherwise have liked, making it harder for her to hide from the men on the porch. She drew her weapon and cocked the hammer, readying her piece for a lethally accurate single-action shot.

Sam reached the edge of the house. Heart pounding, she peered around the corner at the porch. One man on the stairs, one on a swing, and the third in a cheap lawn chair taking a hit from the meth pipe. She saw Brock peeking around the opposite wall on the far side of the porch. He winked. She smiled.

"Freeze, assholes!" she growled, stepping out from behind the wall, Kimber .45 trained on the nearest redneck. "Hands up!"

A shotgun swung around on her.

Pop pop. Two in the man's chest. He flew backwards down the steps.

Extremely dead, she assessed.

Another pistol report sounded from the opposite of the porch, and Sam saw the fat redneck spin wildly and fall to his knees. Brock had evidently shot him in the shoulder.

A skinny streak of blue jeans and elbows dashed into the house. *Sonuvabitch.* The scene just got messy.

Sam leapt over the porch rail and bounded onto the wooden floor, being careful to stay out of the line of sight of the door. Brock circled around the front of the porch. "Watch it!" Sam yelled. "One guy inside."

Brock nodded and snuck through the porch rail beyond the line of sight of the open doorway.

The fat guy with the wounded shoulder rolled over onto his side on the porch. "Stop moving!" Sam commanded.

He didn't stop. He stretched his arm out to reach for the shotgun that had fallen onto the porch several feet away.

Sam took aim at his elbow. She wanted to leave him with a painful memento that would stay with him for life. She squeezed the trigger, the Kimber barked, and the man howled like a little girl. The hollow-point bullet had cleared out most of his elbow joint.

"Ready for more?" she asked. The man shook his head.

"Then call your buddy out here to chat with us," Sam said.

"No way, bitch," he spat, rising to his knees and cradling his wrecked arm in his lap, rocking back and forth in pain.

She laughed, walked over to him, and slapped him across the face hard enough to make her hand hurt. It nearly toppled him over. "Who's the bitch now?" she taunted.

Brock chuckled, gun trained on the kneeling man.

Sam slapped him again. "Call your friend out here."

The kidnapper pursed his lips to spit at her, but she backhanded him across the chops again before he could follow through. "I've got all day," she said. "And you're not nearly as tough as your shotgun fooled you into believing. Now call your friend out here. *Now.*"

Crack! A loud rifle report seared through the air and echoed off of the large barn wall. Sam was vaguely aware of wood splintering on the porch railing. She and Brock instinctively flattened themselves on the porch, and rolled further out of the way of the door. "Came from inside!" Brock yelled. Sam nodded. *Hunting rifle.*

Motion caught Sam's eye. Fatass had lunged for his shotgun, his remaining good arm outstretched and closing around the gun's stock.

Sam took aim and fired. The round caught Fatass just above the ear. "Say goodnight, asshole," she said.

Another rifle shot sounded from within the house, and the slug passed clean through the slat-and-plaster wall near the doorway, just inches away from where Sam had taken shelter.

She looked at Brock, on the other side of the doorway opening. "Go around back," she told him, "and meet me on the other side by the propane tank."

Brock grinned. "I like the way you think."

Sam blew him a kiss and rolled off the side of the porch, ducking beneath the wooden rail. She crouch-walked back around to the side of the house and ducked behind the large propane canister, anchored on a small concrete pad beneath a window.

She unslung the hit-and-run kit from her shoulder and opened up the contents, fumbling around until she found a utility knife and a set of matches.

She heard the grass rustle off to her right, and instinctively trained her pistol in the direction of the sound. Brock rounded the corner. "Whoa, babe," he said. "Just me."

"Just in time," she said, handing him the knife. "Can you cut through the rubber hose leading from the propane tank into the house? Watch out for the window. I'll find a rock."

He gave her a quizzical look.

"Trust me," she said, walking toward a junk pile at the back of the house.

Brock sawed at the propane hose with the serrated edge of the survival knife, and the hiss of escaping gas grew louder to mark his progress.

Sam heard heavy footfalls from within the house. It sounded like Hunting Rifle was walking toward the back of the home. She quickened her pace, not eager to dodge deer slugs again.

It didn't take long to find what she was looking for, one half of a shattered cement cinder block, half-buried in the red clay. She worked it free, turning back toward the propane tank just in time to see Brock's final knife stroke sever the hose.

"Nice work. You're more than just a pretty face," Sam said, twisting the handle on the tank's flow valve until it was wide open and the hiss of escaping gas grew loud enough to hurt their ears. "Ready?" she asked.

Brock nodded.

Sam struck a match and tossed it into the dry grass near the house. She waited for the flame to grow, blackening and curling the dried vegetation, then she hurled the cinder block through the window.

Brock aimed the hissing propane hose toward the flames on the grass. The propane caught fire instantly, turning the hose into a flame thrower, which he aimed into the gaping hole in the window.

The drapes caught fire first, then the wall and ceiling, and before long, the heat from the burning interior had grown intense, forcing Sam and Brock to back away from the wall.

They left the flame thrower on the ground, pointed at the wooden substructure. Then they dashed behind the large UHaul truck for cover, peering around the engine block at the front door of the farmhouse.

Flames licked out the side of the house near the propane tank, and Sam watched through the open front door as the fire spread throughout the house. *Won't be long now.*

As if on cue, the third man ran out of the house, rifle in the air, and charged down the porch steps. "Drop it!" Sam yelled.

The skinny man looked around, confused about where the voice had come from, and uncertain about whether he should follow its instructions. "Drop it, asshole!" Sam repeated.

He didn't.

She shot him in the chest. "Thanks for making it easy," she muttered as she dashed to kick away the hunting rifle and check the man's pulse.

Not a man at all, she noticed as she got closer. *Punk kid.* Face like a rat.

She put her finger on his neck. Nothing. She amended her assessment: *Dead punk kid.*

"Holy shit, it's really burning now!" Brock exclaimed.

Sam looked up to see flames engulfing the side of the farmhouse, and she felt waves of heat blast her face. "Let's get those people out of that barn."

They dashed to the entrance of the barn. A long wooden beam held the doors shut, sealed in place by a steel strap and secured by a large padlock. *Nothing's ever easy.*

"Federal agent!" she yelled through the door. "Hang tight, we're going to get you out of there!"

She dashed to the dead kid and searched his pockets. No keys.

The other two dead rednecks were still on the porch, a couple of feet away from a wall of flames. Sam cursed, ran up the porch steps, and grabbed the fat corpse's booted foot, struggling to drag his heft toward the steps before the flames reached her. "Brock, help me drag them down!"

Brock ran to assist, grabbing Fatass's other boot and dragging him down the porch steps. The gaping wound in the dead man's skull left long, mottled streaks of blood and brains as his head bounced down the stairs.

Sam searched Fatass's pockets while Brock hauled the third man down the steps. She found hundreds of dollars in cash, undoubtedly stolen from the barn full of people, a condom (*those assholes were forcing sex or paying for it*, Sam thought), and three rings full of keys.

She cursed again, and started sifting through the keys one by one, searching for one that looked like it might fit a padlock.

Brock's voice interrupted her frustrated search. "Think I got it." He limped over to the barn door, inserted the key, and turned.

The lock yielded.

"Federal agent," Sam repeated. "We're here to set you free," she said as she and Brock hefted the large plank and tossed it aside.

They pulled the barn door open.

Two dozen scared, haggard faces, belonging to barefoot, shirtless hostages, stared back at them.

Sam held up her badge. "Sam Jameson, Homeland Security," she said.

A tall, athletic, distinguished-looking older gentleman at the front of the crowd met her gaze. "Ma'am, it's more than a pleasure."

"Mike?" Brock's voice behind her.

"Brock? What the…"

"Mr. Charles, I presume." Sam said.

Mike Charles, Co-Director of the DoD's Anti Satellite Weapon Program, extended his hand. "At your service, Sam," he said with a slight bow. "Brock's told me so much about you. We work together. Or rather, we did. Long story."

"Small world," Sam said, shaking Charles' hand and stepping inside the barn, Brock at her heels. "Everybody okay to move?" she asked, looking around the crowd of hostages, eyes adjusting to the darkness of the barn. "I'm afraid we'll need to be quick about getting out of here."

Then she heard a sound that made her heart sink. It came from behind her, outside the barn.

She turned to look, adrenaline slamming through her body.

Twelve-gauge. Black, pistol grip, extended magazine for extra capacity, undoubtedly full of buckshot.

Crowd pleaser, they called it.

Available only to cops.

In the hands of a cop.

Pointed at her.

A crooked, tobacco-stained grin crossed the patrolman's face. "Ya'll ain't goin' nowhere."

PART IIII

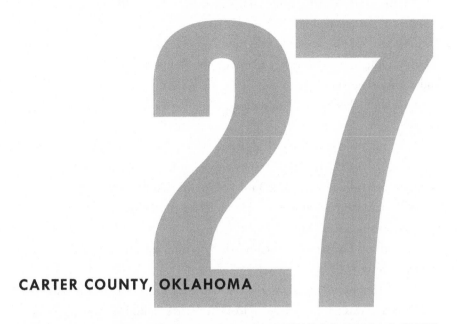

CARTER COUNTY, OKLAHOMA

COGNITIVE DISSONANCE. IT'S WHAT THE PSYCHOLOGISTS called it when two ideas clashed inside someone's head. For example, emblazoned on the cop's cruiser was the phrase "to serve and to protect." However, as Sam, Brock, and the crowd of shirtless and shoeless prisoners inside a barn in the middle of the Oklahoma prairie stared at the police officer standing before them, his black police-issue shotgun pointed menacingly, it was hard for them to conjure any notion of service or protection.

Sam took charge. "Federal agent," she said, holding up her Homeland badge. They weren't the two most popular words in any beat cop's vocabulary, but they generally sufficed to encourage cooperation.

But the cop didn't budge. He stood there, shotgun pointing at them, flickering light from the burning house across the yard dancing off of the shiny objects affixed to his uniform.

Sam cocked her head. "Please stand down, officer," she said. "I've got the scene under control."

She couldn't see his eyes through his sunglasses, but the cop appeared to hesitate for a moment, then make a decision.

Or maybe it was just her imagination. Tough to tell.

All the same, her finger moved instinctively from the trigger guard of her Kimber .45 and settled on the trigger itself.

"Ma'am, this is a volatile situation," he said in a slow drawl, the words taking far longer than necessary to mosey out. "So please set yer sidearm down and come on outside."

Sam shook her head. "Not on your life. Do you need a closer look at my badge?"

"No, ma'am, I can see yer badge fine. But this here's my scene."

What the hell? Cops didn't point weapons at federal agents. Or frightened civilians, rustled up and herded into a barn, for that matter.

Mike Charles caught her eye. He shook his head almost imperceptibly, a look of warning on his face.

"I'm afraid I won't ask ye again," the cop said, spitting tobacco juice, his jaw tightening.

Sam recognized the signs on the cop's face. Mouth drawn taut, jaw clenched. He was getting ready to do something stupid. He thought she was some sort of desk-bound bimbo out for a ride in the country, and he was going to show her what was what. *I don't have time for this.*

She saw his trigger hand move. It was all the confirmation she needed. She shot him in the kneecap. He toppled, hollering, shotgun falling beside him as he grasped his wounded leg. "Ye feckin' bitch!"

"It's him! He's one of them!" someone shouted from the darkness of the barn. "I swear it!"

Sam kicked the shotgun away from the cop's reach.

"That's a lie," the cop said through clenched teeth. "I was jes' called here to investigate a fire." Improbably, he struggled to stand, jostling an unusually large collection of keys and key chains attached to his belt.

"Stay on the ground," Sam ordered.

He disobeyed, struggling to his full height, weight on his good leg, hand on the barn door for support.

Sam debated where to shoot him next.

"You're a murderer." The powerful voice belonged to Mike Charles. Sam, Brock, and the wounded cop turned to look at him.

Charles nodded to someone off at the side of the barn door, positioned behind the cop, and Sam caught the motion of a pretty girl's arm yanking hard on something. Fishing line, maybe? Sam wanted to look closer, but something big, black, round, and heavy swung down in a wide arc from the barn rafters, gathering speed as it descended, slicing just in front of the barn door opening. A tire rim.

It impacted the cop's skull with a sickening crack. The impact left the tire rim ringing, and left the wounded cop in a comatose heap on the ground just inside the barn door.

"That's for my daddy," the girl said. She swung her foot, landing a vicious blow to the cop's balls. "And that's for me, you sick bastard."

She kicked him again, over and over, gathering steam, sobs escaping, flailing furiously until Mike Charles pulled her away and held her in a tight embrace. "It's okay," he said.

Sam rolled the comatose officer over onto his stomach and used the patrolman's own zip-ties to secure his hands behind his back.

Then she checked his pulse. "Huh. Dead." She shook her head, surprised.

"Basal skull fracture," someone said in the back.

"Must have been karma, kicking his ass," Sam said. "Thanks for not hitting me with that thing." She snapped the collection of keys from the dead cop's belt. "These belong to all of you, I imagine?"

Nods.

A burning ember from the flaming farmhouse next door landed in view of the barn door. "We need to get out of here," Brock said.

"I'm afraid the only way out of here is to pile back in that van," Sam said. "We're miles from civilization. Are any of you able to drive it back to the rest stop?"

Mike Charles was first to raise his hand.

Sam shook her head. "Afraid not, Mr. Charles." She grabbed his arm just above the elbow and walked him toward the cop car. "You and I have a date."

Sorting out the keys had taken some doing. The kidnappers had intermingled everyone's key chains with their own, and it took a solid ten minutes for Sam to find the right key to gain access to the cop car.

She commandeered it. Eminent domain, and all. She was pretty sure there was a court precedent for it somewhere. And she was also sure there weren't going to be any court cases of any sort for a long time to come, barring a social and economic miracle. So she wasn't nervous in the least about driving a dead Oklahoma cop's cruiser to Denver.

"Why Denver?" Mike Charles asked from his seat in back, behind the plexiglass window that separated cops from perps in the police cruiser. He wasn't cuffed, but neither was he free. He had no door handles and no vote.

"Homeland has an office there," Sam said. "They have skills in a particular area."

"Don't you have to do something about the murders?"

"Aside from killing all of the suspects?"

"I just thought there might be paperwork," Charles said.

Sam laughed. "I'm sure there will be. For somebody else to fill out. And something tells me it'll be a while before the bureaucrats get back to shuffling files around. But my job is to prevent whatever shitty thing is supposed to happen next from actually happening. That's where you come in." She used the rearview mirror to look at Charles. His expression was impassive.

"You don't look like you're in a helpful mood, Mike."

No response.

"I'm having trouble figuring out what an East Coast DoD heavy might have been doing in Oklahoma, and where you might have been going."

He stared blankly out the window.

Sam glanced at Brock. He looked a bit uncomfortable. He didn't report directly to Mike Charles, but to Charles' co-lead, Major General Charlie Landers, whom Brock hated. She knew Brock favored Mike Charles, and by all accounts, Charles was a good man and a good boss. All of that was probably what made it uncomfortable for Brock to witness Sam going to work on the shoeless, shirtless middle-aged man in the backseat.

And work on him she did.

"So let me tell you what I think I know, Mike. Mind if I call you Mike?"

Charles shook his head. He didn't mind.

Good. Any response is a start, Sam thought.

"So here are my puzzle pieces," Sam said. "Mike Charles, member of the Senior Executive Service, the civilian equivalent of a two-star general, signed a paper authorizing an airplane to land at an Air Force base two hundred miles away from the Pentagon."

She saw a little bit of surprise on Charles' face. She smiled. *We're not all blundering idiots.*

"Then, the same Mike Charles took a last-minute trip to Fort Worth, to witness a demonstration of a very expensive gizmo."

Charles finally spoke. "At the request of the Vice President," he said.

"The same gizmo that ended up stolen just two hours later," Sam continued. "And a few hours after *that,* the *very same* device ended up strapped in the cargo hold of the *very same* airplane that our hero authorized to land at Langley Air Force Base."

She looked at him in the rearview mirror again. "You see how weird all of that sounds, Mike?"

Sam had long held that everyone wore basically the same expression the moment they knew they were cornered. There were individual variations on the theme, of course, but it was still ridiculously easy to tell when subjects realized they were done for. It was a combination of worry and exhaustion. Carrying secrets around was tiring work, and it took a toll over time. And revealing secrets usually caused problems, sometimes very big one, which accounted for the worry.

"You're thinking of your family now, aren't you, Mike," Sam said. Brock looked at her, his expression asking whether bringing Charles' family into it was really necessary. She nodded at him, a tinge of sadness in her expression. She rarely enjoyed pulling people apart at the seams, but she was extremely good at it, and it tended to produce results.

"I'm sure people are going to be really pissed off about all of this, especially judging by the size of the mess you've made out of the entire world economy." She paused meaningfully, letting imagined consequences germinate, hatch, and flitter about in Charles' consciousness.

"And the espionage angle has an ugly optic, too," she added for effect, again pausing to let things marinate, watching his expression carefully for signs of the next big moment in the interrogation.

That moment didn't always come, but when it did, it was important not to miss it. It was the instant when a subject ceased to have sufficient control of his emotions to maintain his chosen resistance posture. It was a significant turning point, and Sam had learned to recognize the façade fading to reveal the subject's inner turmoil. It usually happened when the imagined consequences, invariably dire, started to feel inevitable.

"Don't you have a daughter in college?" Sam asked.

She thought she saw the turning point in Mike Charles' eyes. They misted, and his breath fluttered just a bit.

But then his eyes focused a long way out the window, his jaw clenched, and she saw resolve return.

Time to help the inner demons a little bit.

"So here's the score, Mike. I have you for espionage. I have you for accessory to grand larceny. And conspiracy. And I don't know if they've invented a legal term for bending over the entire world, but I'm sure the Attorney General will be able to dream one up. When you play alphabet soup with all of that, it spells many times more years than you have left in your life."

Another glance at him in the rearview mirror. She saw worry and tiredness.

"And that's assuming the state of Texas doesn't find a way to get involved," Sam continued. "I bet they use the old felony-murder law. A few hundred people have died in the rioting, which was caused by your felony, which, blammo, makes you a murderer. Considering the death penalty record in Texas, I don't like your odds."

Clearly, this was an angle that Charles hadn't considered. He blinked several times involuntarily before regaining his composure.

"You're assuming there will be a government left to do all of this," he said after a long moment.

Sam smiled. "Excellent segue. You're like my straight man. I was just about to say that everything I mentioned, that's all ancient history, and it all falls squarely in the category of someone else's problem to figure out. Me? I look forward. I want to know what happens next."

She looked at him intently in the rearview mirror again.

"So tell me, Mike. What happens next?"

Steely eyes, jaw clenched, hands in fists, neck vein bulging a little bit. There was a struggle going on in the backseat, Sam could tell, but it didn't look like her side was winning.

"So that, what you just did right there? That's why we're going to Denver," Sam said. "There's a guy there who deals especially with situations like this one."

She looked at him again. She wanted to watch his reaction to what she had to say next. "It's not really true, what you read in the papers. The Executive Branch talks a big game to keep the ACLU off their asses, but the big boss is actually a big fan of what people call 'enhanced interrogations.'"

Charles blanched. So did Brock.

Sam smiled. "I know, right? Even the name sounds like something Stalin would be proud of."

Charles struggled to keep his composure.

"I'll do my best to save you from the assholes, Mike, but this is a two-way street here. So Denver's maybe, what, seven hours away? Lots of time for you to weigh your options."

A few more miles passed in silence. Sam occasionally glanced at Charles in the rearview mirror. He kept his eyes out the window, a faraway look on his face, but Sam could tell that he was wearing down.

"You know, Mike," she said after a while, "people talk a lot about how bad women have it during torture, and I can certainly attest to the truth of it." She shuddered, briefly recalling her horrific hours once spent at the mercy of a Venezuelan madman. *That* was a shitty weekend.

"But let me tell you," she went on, "I am really glad I don't have a sack full of testicles hanging down between my legs. I never really realized what a liability the ol' bean bag was, until I watched some interrogation footage a while back. Turns out, there are about a million and one different ways to make a guy's nuts hurt."

In the rearview mirror, she saw Charles' face turn a whiter shade of white. "Anyway, that's just me talking," she said, a small smile in her voice. "You enjoy the ride back there."

LOST MAN LAKE RANCH, COLORADO

"BUT IT ISN'T INHERENT VALUE THAT WE'RE TRADING when we pay modern currency to someone," Archive was saying, cigar waving in the cool mountain breeze. "We're trading *implicit* value."

It felt like old times, Protégé thought.

Almost.

The scotch, cigars, and subject matter were largely the same, but the atmosphere was quite different. He and the old man used to have these kinds of discussions in the tycoon's house-sized study, at the center of his DC mansion. With its ornately carved oak furniture and tiffany lamps, it was a far different setting than the rustic mountain retreat, Protégé thought as he watched the sun set over the east peak of Geissler Mountain.

This particular conversation was also unique because they were no longer just discussing theories and ideas. They were now talking about the global reality that their efforts had indelibly altered over the past twenty-four hours.

Surreal.

"But you could make the argument that even if people were trading gold

150

coins before yesterday, they'd just have been doing the same thing – trading symbols of something else."

Archive nodded. "From one standpoint, that's very true. After all, a gold coin won't fill your belly or keep the rain off your back. It's still very much a proxy for items of real value."

These discussions always made Protégé's brow furrow. None of the old man's ideas would ever fit within a typical MBA curriculum. Even Harvard's, with its famous case studies, which wove tales of inevitability between events that, in reality, occurred stochastically, the pompous old charlatans casting hindsight pearls before the poor swine charged with producing favorable future outcomes. Predicting the future was impossible, but it didn't stop people from searching for entropic alchemy, some holy heuristic to sidestep the inevitable arrow of time in a random universe. And it certainly didn't stop the gurus from claiming prescience, and charging an arm and a leg to spew forth B-school platitudes and other delusional dribble.

"But there's always the problem of fungibility," the old man continued. "Hence, currency."

Protégé nodded. "How many chickens is a house worth?"

Archive chuckled. "Right. Sounds like a koan."

"Answerable only with shiny objects, apparently," Protégé offered.

A belly laugh from the old man. "How true. We're silly beasts, at our core, just like magpies picking up glimmering shards to decorate their nests."

"So what now?" Protégé asked, face darkening, thinking of the chaos and turmoil and, in some places, bloodshed, brought on by what was, in retrospect, a remarkably arrogant gambit designed to suck the life blood out of the world's fiat economy.

Pretty damned successful gambit, Protégé thought, *judging by the gnashing of teeth.*

"Ride it out," Archive said, exhaling gray-blue Cuban cigar smoke into the crisp, cold mountain air. "People are smart."

Protégé snorted. "Not smart enough to avoid charging headlong off of a cliff. They let the currency bubble get completely out of control.

What makes you think the herd will be able to lift themselves out of the morass now?"

"Ah, the impetuous certainty of youth," Archive chided.

As usual, Protégé bristled at the old man's presumption and patronizing air. Also as usual, he let the annoyance pass, awaiting the inevitable lesson on the other side of it.

Archive didn't disappoint. "Simple, really. Given the way the world was arranged at the time, it was not in the best interest of any individual, public or private, to alter their behavior. Money was cheap, so people borrowed cheap money to acquire nice things. Easy. And, as a policy, cheap money was a great way to earn both reelection and outrageous corporate profits, so there was tremendous dis-incentive to make any changes. The system simply had to run its course. There really was no other way."

"You're saying that's different now?"

"I sure am," Archive said, suddenly animated. "If you weren't living here now, taking advantage of the painstaking preparations my team and I orchestrated, you would be awash in the welter, negotiating your time and talents for food and water, learning for the first time that *you* always held the power of the agreement, and that the little green pieces of paper *never* had the power."

Protégé smiled. "Now you sound like Monopoly Man."

Archive laughed. "Amazing coincidence, that."

He rose abruptly. "Speaking of, it's time to check in on our resident troglodyte."

Protégé followed him through the large glass doors leading from the giant deck, into the eco-lodge's cavernous great room, and down a spiral staircase leading to a finished basement carved into the side of the mountain.

Archive walked to a far wall and moved a painting aside to reveal a keypad, the kind that normally granted access to secret spaces in exchange for a demonstration of the right numerical knowledge. But Protégé could see no visible door.

Archive typed a surprisingly lengthy sequence of digits into the keypad, and Protégé heard the unmistakable clack of a lock receding into its receptacle. The sound seemed to come from the wall opposite the staircase.

Sure enough, a dark gap appeared at the ceiling and floor, widening with a hydraulic hiss, the entire wall sliding to create an opening several feet wide. "Secret doors in a secret hideaway," Protégé said. "How perfectly cliché."

Archive laughed. "Quite. But it usually pays to plan for the worst case. The remoteness helps, but doesn't grant us immunity from angry hordes, if things were to suddenly go unexpectedly sour."

"I think you mean *more* sour."

The old man shook his head as he walked down a lengthy hallway, his footfalls echoing in the close quarters, surrounded on all sides by concrete. "Things didn't go as neatly as we hoped," he said, "but neither have they turned out nearly as badly as the worst-case scenario in our planning."

"Admit it," Protégé said. "You're scared shitless that this is going to turn into hatchet wars and ethnic cleansing."

Archive laughed. "Yes. That thought does cross my mind with annoying regularity." He came to another keypad and typed in another code. The door opened, and Protégé felt the heat and hum of computers, and smelled the distinctive scent of ozone.

A short, vaguely ethnic hacker with the oversized nose and unkempt hair sat hunched in front of two screens. Protégé didn't know his given name, but Trojan was his handle. A large laptop computer, cords protruding from a crude hole drilled in the casing next to the keyboard, sat adjacent to the monitors. Protégé counted two towers, and a rack full of servers.

The place looked like the IT closet in his office building in DC, Protégé thought, full of GE Government Services Division employees. *Probably not full today,* he corrected himself. *And maybe not for a while.*

"You can make the lights dim in New York from here, can't you?"

Trojan smiled.

"Gotta be sucking a lot of juice," Protégé observed. "Dependent on grid power?"

Archive shook his head. "Not in the least. Lots of solar photovoltaics, as you know, and there's that Archimedean generator sitting in the stream at the low end of the lake. Not to mention those outrageously expensive batteries. Our man Trojan will be in business long after the power grids go offline." The old man looked at Trojan. "Which I suspect is already starting to happen, yes?"

Trojan nodded. "That's right. Looks like they're having trouble paying for coal." He smiled. "I managed to get us a ringside seat in the power management network," he explained to Protégé.

"We're not pulling any levers yet," Archive said. "But it appears that we would have that option, if it came down to it."

"Meaning, we've hacked into a critical global system for the third time in a day?" Protégé asked.

"Continental," Archive corrected with a smile. "Not quite global. But yes, computers are useful little tools, in the right hands."

"There have been some encouraging developments," Trojan said. "Some of the smaller regions have begun to figure out how to use a combination of surrogate currency and bartering to keep the coal moving to fire the plants. But those circumstances are rare, and seem to rely on a few enterprising individuals from within the coal plants who know how to reach out and get things done in a crisis like this. All the other plant operators appear to be waving their arms and making shrill noises."

Archive nodded. "Government agencies?"

"Among those still responding? Mostly noise," Trojan said. "Though it's obvious they recognize the link between power and the long-term survival rate, especially with winter coming on. But they can't throw enough dollars at foreign coal producers to make the ships move, and the domestic producers are demanding a less volatile form of payment."

"Speaking of alternative currencies," Archive said with a smile, "how are we looking?"

Trojan typed a key command, and the open windows on the laptop rearranged themselves. "Value-wise, just as expected. Our portfolio of metals and Bitcoins is now worth just shy of a trillion dollars."

Archive laughed aloud. "But what's a dollar worth these days?"

Trojan smiled. "I actually know the answer to that question," he said, calling up another screen. It showed a red line rising at an exponential rate. "We're about to blow through one thousand percent inflation."

Protégé did the math and grimaced. "Today's dollar is worth yesterday's penny."

"Tough to wrap your mind around, isn't it?" Archive asked.

Protégé nodded. "Nothing unusual at all about hearing some other country going through currency woes. But the Almighty Dollar?"

Archive smiled. "They said it was impossible."

"Like the Titanic was unsinkable."

"There's a problem, boss," Trojan said, his face suddenly concerned, his eyes squinting to read a series of red numbers on a spreadsheet.

"What am I looking at?" Archive asked.

"Bitcoin accounts. They appear to be falling."

"The value of the coins?"

"No," Trojan said. "The number of coins in our accounts. Someone appears to be siphoning them. That means they've hacked into our wallets."

"All of them?"

Trojan shook his head. "It appears just to be coming out of our exchange-traded accounts. Honestly, it's smart of them. If I wanted to steal a bunch of Bitcoins, I'd hack into the exchanges' servers."

Protégé whistled. "Those numbers are getting serious," he said. "What do we do?"

Trojan clicked on an icon on the desktop – a picture of a little robot – and a page full of computer code popped up. Then he clicked a green button marked "Run."

"Done," Trojan said. "The script will empty all of our exchange wallets and get them ready for cold storage. Should take no more than fifteen minutes for the transactions to be verified by the network, and then I'll store them securely offline."

"Total damage?" Archive asked.

"We caught it early. Just thirty or forty Bitcoins," Trojan said.

Protégé looked at the exchange rate. "That's a hundred and twenty grand!"

Archive laughed. "Even *our* minds are infected by dollars. But we'll all converse in a more meaningful measure of value before too long, I'm sure."

His expression suddenly turned serious. He looked at Trojan. "Can you trace the thefts?"

"Maybe. But does it matter? We stopped it in time to prevent serious damage."

"To our accounts, yes," Archive said. "But I've just had a disconcerting thought. What if this is a systematic, organized theft?"

Protégé considered. "A working currency is a hugely important thing in a situation like this. If someone is stealing a bunch of Bitcoins, they could end up in a very powerful position."

Archive nodded somberly. "Exactly my concern."

"I'll get to work," Trojan said.

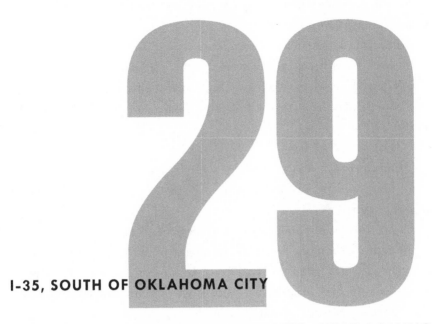

I-35, SOUTH OF OKLAHOMA CITY

SAM DROVE IN SILENCE. BROCK DOZED, HEAD LOLLING against the police cruiser's window, twitching occasionally. Her eyes drifted to his thigh, bandages visible beneath his khaki trousers, lingering remnant of the weekend spent in a cement cell, shot and abducted from their Alexandria home.

Disorienting, she thought, trying to put context to the frantic, crazed search and herculean effort that had ultimately saved him, but just barely. Seemed like an eon ago, rather than just two days ago.

Their current unlikely location, driving a commandeered police cruiser northbound on an abandoned interstate highway through the middle of nowhere in the post-sunset darkness of the Oklahoma plains, did nothing to ease the surreal feeling.

She glanced in the rearview mirror. Mike Charles rode silently in the suspect's section of the cruiser, staring tiredly out the window, eyes unfocused. *I gave him a lot to think about,* she thought with a smile. And his tiredness worked to her advantage, too. It took a lot of emotional energy to resist interrogation, and subjects tended to become exponentially worse at hiding information as their exhaustion grew. *Won't be long now, and we'll be in a talkative mood,* Sam surmised.

The phone buzzed in her pocket. Brock stirred, and Charles' eyes focused on the back of her head. She answered quietly. "Hi Dan."

"What do a math geek, a hacker, and three satellites have in common?"

"Sounds like the start of a bad joke," Sam said. "But don't forget the bureaucrat."

"The who?"

"Our illustrious and heretofore elusive friend, Mr. Charles," she said, giving him a wink in the rearview mirror. She thought she detected a resentful glare in return.

"Ahh. You nabbed him? Learn anything yet?"

Sam shook her head. "We're still coming in from the cold," she said with a pointed glance at Charles. "What have *you* learned?" she asked her deputy.

"Here's the deal," Dan said. "I was hanging around the water cooler at NSA, waving a warrant around like a Willie Wonka ticket, and—"

"You got a warrant?" Sam interrupted. "From whom? For what?"

"The only federal judge on duty today, I think, judging by how long it took me to find someone to answer the phone at Justice. Anyway, if you ever want to see a confused person, just show a court warrant to an NSA employee. Talk about divided loyalties."

Sam chuckled. She passed a car on the highway, watching warily for signs of trouble. If the barn incident was any indication, the sudden crisis had seemed to draw out society's nascent highwaymen. Like weed spores, waiting for the right conditions to sprout roots and raise their ugly heads.

"Are you listening?" Dan asked.

"Sorry. What?"

"I said, I learned that the NSA extended its little accountability exercise to a very small group of contractors it employs to do various things."

"Accountability exercise?"

"Yeah," Dan said. "They called everybody in to talk to them, despite all the craziness in the city. They extended the personnel recall to a short list of contractors. The list is so small, in fact, that there's only one company on it. Pro-Tek."

"Sounds like a jockstrap manufacturer," Sam said.

"Right? But no. Building full of nerds. They make algorithms."

Sam feigned confusion. "Hmm, if only we had a clue about which of its algorithms the NSA might be interested in hunting down at the moment," she said sarcastically.

"Exactly. These guys do decryption. Some pseudo-quantum thing they figured out. Simultaneous summing over numerous probability density distributions."

"You switched to another language there."

"It's a code-breaking algorithm. Makes 256-bit AES keys look like a kiddy puzzle."

"In English?" Sam asked, exasperation sneaking into her voice.

"Advanced Encryption Standard. The highest encryption system we have. Nuclear codes, top secret military hardware specs, war plans, you name it. No match for this little beauty."

Sam considered this for a moment. "And banking system passwords, too, I'd imagine."

"Right," Dan said. "So you see where I'm headed with this. NSA was pretty hush-hush, but like I said, the warrant generated enough confusion for a while that I was able to sneak out a little information."

"Do tell." Sometimes she had to hustle Dan along towards the point.

"Turns out that everyone but two guys at Pro-Tek showed up for work this morning. One of them was mugged, showed up late, kind of beat up."

"And the other?" Did she sound too impatient?

"Called in sick. But guess what? Not at home."

"Name?"

"Vaneesh Ramasomethingorother. I got his vitals from their HR department. They were pretty confused about why a Homeland guy called just minutes after the NSA goons left, but whatever."

"So you've followed up on the Vaneesh lead?"

"I'm one warrant away from seeing how he lives," Dan said.

Sam looked at her watch. Nine p.m. in Oklahoma meant ten p.m. in DC. "So they're burning the midnight oil at Justice?"

"Shit, no wonder they've been unresponsive."

159

Sam chuckled. "You should get some fresh air."

"I may smell smoke when I walk by Vaneesh's apartment later," Dan said.

Sam smiled. "I'm sure you'll do what any responsible citizen would do in a situation like that."

"Right," Dan said. "I'll keep you posted."

Sam hung up. She glanced in the mirror at Charles. He eyed her back, his expression neutral. "Know anyone named Vaneesh?" she asked.

He shook his head, his eyes cold and his expression implacable.

SEATTLE, WASHINGTON

SABOT TOOK A DEEP BREATH, FEELING THE TENSION IN his neck and shoulders, smelling the cigarette smoke wafting from around the back of the house, where Angie's mother enjoyed her sixty-ninth smoke of the day. He remained on the front porch, seated in a cheap but comfortable lawn chair situated in the shadows, and watched the street carefully.

He heard the water running inside the house, evidence that Angie's shower hadn't yet ended. The power was on, at least for the moment, and for that, Sabot was thankful.

He wasn't armed. As a convicted felon, legal gun ownership wasn't an option for him, and before the meltdown, he wasn't ballsy or stupid enough to risk the parole violation. But with Angie and her mom to protect, and roving gangs of looters breaking into houses and beating up residents, a gun suddenly seemed like an important item to get one's hands on. He would have to consider how best to go about that. Maybe the next delivery from Doggy Style, or whatever that goofy gringo's real name was.

He heard Angie's mom cough in the backyard and shook his head. She was beginning to wheeze, undoubtedly from all the cigarettes.

He liked Consuela well enough, and generally felt that she and Angie had a healthy relationship, but there was still some tension there. For one thing, Angie's mom didn't know that Sabot was a felon. So there was that. Plus, Connie was only ten years Sabot's senior. They'd nearly be contemporaries, really, under different circumstances. Also, the math betrayed thirty seconds of sweaty teenage bliss somewhere in Connie's past, which had resulted in Angie's arrival in the world, so Sabot suspected there was some residual Catholic shame that Connie hadn't quite gotten past.

Still, for all of that, they got along fine, though Sabot hoped Angie didn't have plans to stay indefinitely at Connie's place. A man had his limits.

Headlights. SUV. Escalade. *My man,* Sabot thought, feeling a zing of adrenaline. The first thirty seconds were critical. He remembered the feeling from his days as a punk kid in Queens, where he'd nearly become a street thug. But the lamentably low survival rate wasn't lost on him, and he'd decided instead to become a computer thug. Fewer sharp objects and firearms.

The truck pulled to a stop at the curb, facing the wrong way down the street, driver's side door near the sidewalk.

Sabot pulled his hands out of his pockets to make sure the driver could see them, and walked toward the Escalade, hoping he looked much more casual and collected than he felt. His heart was really pounding.

"Noob Elite?" a slightly squeaky male voice queried.

Sabot nodded.

"Doggy Style sez heya. Good lulz earlier. No hard feelins he sez."

Whigger. Sideways hat, big brim, neck tattoos, a shiny tooth, the whole nine. Strange combination for a hacker, Sabot thought, but it took all kinds. A bag of groceries emerged from the window, attached to a skinny arm by a skinny hand. "Thanks," Sabot said.

"He sez good one with the dox, yo. Straight up pawned him in like thirty minutes flat." The messenger extended his arm again, this time with a laptop case in his grip.

Sabot looked around guiltily. Parole violation. Might not be meaningful at the moment, with roving herds of white-bread accountants and middle-class clerks smashing in windows and looking for leftover food in people's refrigerators, but Sabot figured the time would come when a blackmail photo could have a seriously unhealthy impact on his future. He slung the laptop case over his shoulder nervously, and shifted the grocery bag into the crook of his arm.

"Tell him thanks, bro," Sabot said. "Doggy's super pro. Tell him there's lots of biz in our future." Positive reinforcement never hurt.

"Right on, man."

Sabot resisted the urge to ask the messenger's name. Unwritten rule, best not violated despite the social awkwardness it produced. He patted the top of the SUV and made his way inside.

He emptied the grocery bag. No perishables, per his instructions. He arrayed the food on the countertop, like a hunter displaying the day's quarry.

Then he made his way to the back room to find Angie. Perhaps it was a side-effect of the adrenaline rush the clandestine encounter had produced, but Sabot suddenly felt quite frisky. He walked into the bedroom, unwrapped the towel from around her trim, athletic body, and pulled her close. She knew instantly what was on his mind. Her smile told him that she found it more than agreeable.

Afterwards, he told her about the food, and about the way he planned to look after them. To be sure, there was a bit of risk, he said, but the greater risk was starving to death, or getting beat up by a hunger-crazed ambulance-chaser wielding a pipe wrench. Times like these, he reasoned, you really had to think on your feet and take advantage of the opportunities that came your way. Carefully, of course, but you definitely couldn't let things pass you by.

But he didn't feel any safer after having said the words, and he still felt that vague uneasiness, all too familiar from his pre-confession days as a hardcore hacktivist trying, with the hubris of youth, to lead a high-profile underground life while avoiding *too* high a profile, at least from a law enforcement perspective.

Right. Worked out about as well as one might expect, he thought as he made his way back to the kitchen.

He looked at the computer on the table, feeling the adrenaline begin to surge. *Time to fish or cut bait, esé.*

WESTERN KANSAS

SAM FELT THE COFFEE WEARING OFF, AND TURNED DOWN the temperature, hoping the cold air would keep her from ploughing into the ditch. There were no trees to speak of, and this stretch of I-70 was laser-beam straight for about a zillion miles, with not even a timid stream to interrupt its westward charge, all of which made for excruciatingly soporific driving conditions in the best of circumstances.

She looked at the clock on the dashboard. Midnight. Sunrise's reprieve was still a solid five-plus hours away.

More boredom ahead.

Which was not to say that the trip had been entirely uneventful. They'd been stopped twice by roadblocks, haphazard and poorly-organized affairs reminiscent of those pictures from Third World countries, complete with skinny kids perched atop cars, brandishing firearms.

One roadblock was set in the middle of nowhere several miles south of Oklahoma City, which Sam found a little confusing. The cop car and her shiny badge had done the trick. No resistance. "We've, uh, heard tell of some gang activity 'round here," the lackey had lied nervously.

"Right," Sam said. "Let me guess, you were just about to report the suspicious activity, weren't you?" She didn't wait for the answer.

The encounter had convinced Sam that where people were concerned, fewer would be better, and it would be far easier to approach Denver via Western Kansas and Eastern Colorado, where approximately seventeen people lived in a sixty-nine billion square mile area, than to drive north through Trinidad, Pueblo, and Colorado Springs. Those areas were sure to have all sorts of unsavories blocking traffic and demanding tributes in the form of gas, water, or sodomy. Nobody had time for that.

Their northern routing had gone well enough, until they skirted the western edge of Salina, Kansas. Just prior to getting on the interstate, they came upon another roadblock. This one appeared far more organized – undoubtedly the extra hours of practice had given the thugs a chance to dial in their technique – and Sam had actually chambered a round in her pistol and turned on the police lights to induce the right sort of behavior.

The combination proved compelling, probably more due to the social programming invoked by the flashing red and blue lights, and less by the image of a redhead with centerfold looks wielding a handgun, but Sam didn't spend much time pondering the sociology. She'd floored the accelerator as soon as the thugs had made an opening large enough for the police cruiser to fit through.

They'd also stopped once for gas, only to learn that there wasn't any. Fortunately, Sam had remembered to transfer all of the food, water, and gasoline from the rental car before they abandoned it in the field, next to the barn and burning house in southwestern Oklahoma.

Brock agreed with her assessment: they'd easily make Denver, but not much further.

She'd dialed the Denver field office number several times, hoping to make arrangements to deal with their passenger, a person of interest – which was to say, the prime suspect – in what was shaping up to be one humdinger of a crime/ espionage thing. Sam wasn't sure what to call it – espionage was a crime, after all, but this particular espionage episode happened to include all sorts of larceny, conspiracy, misappropriation of government resources, and other things.

She hadn't had any luck reaching the Denver guys, and, truth be told, she was hoping for a breakthrough with Mike Charles before any "enhanced" interrogation methods were required.

But it wasn't going well. Charles was snoozing in the backseat, wearing a ridiculous tropical shirt and a pair of neon yellow sneakers Sam had picked up for him at a small mom-and-pop truck stop along the way, to replace the shoes and shirt the kidnappers had stolen.

"You can have anything but gas," the old truck stop lady had said. "Ain't got none of that. And ya gotta pay cash." The old lady was apparently oblivious to the dollar's recent plummet. Sam paid her gratefully, without letting her in on the news.

One thousand percent inflation, one of the radio stations had observed, just before the giant Kansas nothingness had swallowed all the radio signals and the station went to static. *I'm no economist, but that sounds problematic.*

It made her think of those strange Monopoly Man videos. She'd noticed another one playing mutely in the background at the truck stop. "There he goes again," the lady said. "Tellin' us to make nice with each other. Well an' good to be Christian about it, I s'pose, but where'm I gonna get m'gas from?"

A good question, for which Sam, for one, had no immediate answer. She suspected that not many people did, despite the cartoon figure's suggestion that it was as simple as making another agreement with one another. *Whatever the hell that means.*

Brock awoke, groggy, and smiled at Sam. He laid his head across her thigh.

Random.

Beautiful.

Her phone buzzed. Dan Gable.

"What is it, 2 a.m. there?"

"Getting on toward three," Dan said. "I went home for a while to take care of Sara and the kiddos. A thought struck me around midnight, and I couldn't get back to sleep."

"Husband of the year."

"Right," Dan said. "Pretty sure Sara hates me. Anyway, I was thinking about those strange cartoon videos that keep popping up everywhere. You seen them?"

"Monopoly Man?"

"Right."

"Those have me confused. They fried a bunch of comm satellites, right?"

Dan laughed. "Three of them. That only leaves a hundred and forty of them remaining over the Western Hemisphere."

"Silly me. Nerd illiterate."

"I'm used to it by now," Dan said.

"So, anyway, you called your new NSA friends," Sam guessed, hoping to get Dan to the point.

"How'd you guess?"

Sam stroked Brock's cheek. "Magic."

"Anyway, the uplink signal has to be coming from somewhere."

"Monopoly Man himself being the existence proof," Sam said.

"Smartass. But yes. So I asked the signals guys at NSA to throw me a bone, in exchange for all of the discretion that I continue to display regarding what is shaping up to be the intelligence failure of the millennium."

"Did they balk?" Sam asked.

"Not at all. They came through in a big way. The uplink signal was broadcast to the satellites from dozens of locations each time. Different locations for each broadcast. The NSA guys were able to parse them in the time domain and do some serious multi-lateration math."

"Did you have any friends in high school?"

Dan ignored the barb. "They were able to measure the start time of each station's broadcast down to a silly degree of accuracy. The uplink dishes in the center of the US started transmitting microseconds earlier than the dishes on the coasts."

"So they got a source location by comparing the times?"

"Exactly."

"And?"

"There's a bit of uncertainty involved, and any kind of internal electronic delays at any of the relay dishes would totally screw up the math, but they think they have a large enough sample size to narrow the source location down."

"Which is where, exactly?"

"Denver."

"Seriously?"

"Well, sort of. Denver, plus or minus three hundred miles in any direction," Dan said.

"What?"

"The error ellipse of their triangulation math. A limitation of the number of samples they got and the measuring accuracy of the receiving equipment."

"That's a lot of territory," Sam said.

"Yeah, but it's narrowed down significantly from our prior search area, which encompassed the entire globe."

"Solid point. So Denver it is. Luck would have it, that's where we're headed already."

"Field office there?"

"Yep," Sam answered.

Dan connected the dots. "Mr. Charles in need of some extra persuasion?"

"Right. If you run across any dirt on him in your travels, that would be useful from a leverage standpoint. But I'm hoping he comes around."

"Count on it."

They ended the call.

Sam caressed Brock's face and neck. He smiled, turned, and kissed her hand. "You're quite a handful, Special Agent Jameson."

"So glad you don't seem to object."

"Object? I turned the world upside looking for you."

"Glad it wasn't just me." She stroked his cheek. "I happen to be excruciatingly fond of you."

"Thanks for inviting me along while you save the world."

"Thanks for making my life worth living." Ironic smile.

"We all do what we can."

BANFF, CANADA

THE FRIDAY MORNING SUN THREW SHEETS OF BLAZING orange across Lake Minnewanka, placid in the dawn stillness, bathing the opulent penthouse in the kind of light that made anything seem possible. At least, that was always the Facilitator's reaction to such moments, an optimism that was likely responsible, at least in part, for his rise to the top of what was arguably the world's most powerful organization.

It was certainly the world's most secretive organization – there were no written communications, no bank accounts, no disk drives full of incriminating evidence, no staff, no logos, and no mission statements. There wasn't any need for any of that. The Consultancy's mission was so obvious as to be unspoken: utter domination of the world's means of production.

Pragmatically, such an objective demanded dalliances of a political and military nature, which the Facilitator engineered with equal measures of careful circumspection and brutal precision. Anonymity was paramount. Shill corporations, politicians of all ilk and ideology, clandestine services, special operators, and now, apparently, convicted felons – all were useful arrows in a very impressive quiver.

But it had been a rough week. The Facilitator's innate optimism had been tested, forcing him to rely on his other three-sigma attribute: his ruthlessness. Sociopathic, some might say, and his isolated and insulated life would lend credence.

As would the ice-cold, nearly instantaneous decision to have his second-in-command, a fellow crusader with nearly three decades of loyal service under his belt, unceremoniously offed. Business was business. Leaks and loose ends were always fatal. It's how anonymous organizations remained anonymous.

For the Facilitator, it wasn't the having, but the *getting* that gave him a charge, a splash of what the hipster Québécois called *raison d'être*. Or maybe it was the French who said it. He was indifferent to the cultural nuances – he was an equal opportunity baron, and believed that all races were perfectly suitable sources of labor and capital.

At least, they had been, until the world had shifted beneath his feet on Tuesday morning.

But adaptation is the hallmark of the über-species, and the Facilitator considered himself among the über-elite. Not without cause – he had amassed one of the largest fortunes in history. He was, by his own reckoning, the richest anonymous man to ever walk the planet.

The phone on the mahogany desk made the peculiar, insistent buzz it always made when a supplicant awaited in the lobby. *On schedule.* Always a positive sign. The Facilitator buzzed him up.

A "normal" man of his wealth would have stewards, attendants, and fluffers of varying skill to tend to the more prosaic aspects of living, such as answering the door, but the aforementioned security considerations had robbed the Facilitator of the enjoyment endemic to his layer of the Upper Crust. He walked heavily across the large great room to the penthouse's front door, twisted the dead bolt, and held the door for the fat man on the other side.

"Good day." The Facilitator's greeting sounded stiff even to his own ears.

"Damn fine view!" And a damn fine comb-over, tossed over a slightly bulbous pate and greased into semi-permanent submission, yet failing to fully cover the big, shiny melon, leaving the characteristic monk stripe all the way around Bill Fredericks' head, and, in back, a beacon-red shape not unlike a monkey's ass.

The slovenly man's jocularity and lack of deference was testament to either his irrational indifference to the Facilitator's fear-inducing credentials and personal history, or his complete ignorance of them. Disagreeable either way, the Facilitator decided, motioning toward an oversized leather chair arranged in front of an equally outsized wall of windows.

The Facilitator sat heavily in an adjacent seat. "Ball Sack?"

"When in Rome," Fredericks said, by way of explanation. "Actually, Balzzack011. Apparently the numbers are important in the 'hacker' world." He made air quotes.

Balzzack011 was just one of his many monikers, each tailored to a particular situation. Bill Fredericks, Avery Martinson (to his wife and kids), Arturo Dibiaso, and a host of other identities checkered the man's past. Each had seemed like a bit of a new start, though he had dragged his disagreeable proclivities, characteristic irreverence, and body odor with him to each new stop along Alias Alley. An asshole by any other name, as his peers said behind his back, and sometimes to his face.

"News?"

"My trip was fine, thanks for asking."

"That's not what I was asking," the Facilitator said.

"That's what I was saying."

"Excuse me?"

"Certainly." Fredericks smiled.

The Facilitator was momentarily confounded. He had spent all of the decades in recent memory almost entirely insulated from people such as Fredericks, buffered by layers of far more refined, if somewhat sycophantic, executives and politicians. Insolence was rarely something he had to endure.

"Just having a bit of fun with you," Fredericks said by way of apology. "That guy was smoked, like you asked. At least I think it was you who asked, anyway. Really kind of tough to tell these days. Seems like there's a bit of what they call organizational change mismanagement, though I'm not pointing any fingers. Maybe we could call in one of those BS artists from one of those big consulting firms, you know, to use made-up words to misstate the obvious." Fredericks laughed at his own humor.

The Facilitator's eyes narrowed. He made it a rule never to show anger unless it was to his strategic advantage, and he wondered whether this might be a good moment to teach a lesson. "You are aware of whose audience you're now in?"

Fredericks smiled. "Not particularly. Though now that you mention it, it does kind of seem like we have different ideas about your importance. Maybe you can fill me in."

"Maybe not." A hard gaze.

Fredericks didn't blink, flinch, or otherwise wilt.

"What a difference a week makes," the Facilitator said. "I watched footage of your interrogation last weekend."

Fredericks responded with blinking, flinching, and if not wilting, certainly a close cousin to it.

A wicked smile grew on the Facilitator's face. "Eviscerated by a thirty-something pinup model. Redhead, no less. By your reaction, I can tell that you're appropriately ashamed."

Fredericks didn't answer. He was busy being appropriately ashamed, and thinking of the ways he would hurt Sam Jameson if the opportunity ever arose. Misplaced aggression, of course, because the vise that the Homeland bitch had squeezed him in was certainly of his own making. Details.

"But I compliment you on your taste in prostitutes," the Facilitator said, the pecking order now firmly established. "Relatively unspoiled, if memory serves."

Fredericks' blush deepened.

"I would imagine that this week's chaos wasn't entirely unwelcome to you," the Facilitator continued. "Spared you a few uncomfortable conversations, did it?"

Fredericks exhaled and nodded.

It was clear to the Facilitator that the fat case officer wasn't accustomed to the marionette's role. Fredericks clearly enjoyed the advantage in the vast majority of his leveraged conversations, and the Facilitator enjoyed watching embarrassment and annoyance do battle for a controlling interest in the Agency asshole's facial expression.

"I feel we're much better prepared to communicate meaningfully with each other now," the Facilitator said with a bemused smile, reaching for a glass of sparkling water. "You were just about to tell me about our dear friend Mr. Mondragon, the, as you say, *hacker*."

Fredericks nodded, visibly relieved by the change of subject. "Already off the reservation. He reached out to a supplier and asked for 'chipzezz.'"

"That's a meaningful request?"

"Geek slang for a new computer. Parole violation."

"Murky waters, given that his FBI handlers have sanctioned his computer use."

Fredericks nodded. "I'm not inclined to drop a dime to the Bureau stiffs. But he did make a copy of all the shit he built to steal all that fake money."

"Entrepreneurship?" the Facilitator asked.

"My guess is yes."

"Scale?"

Fredericks snorted. "He set you up on a global scale. What makes you think he did anything less for himself?"

"Is his setup repeatable?"

Fredericks shook his head. "Not easily. The guy is pretty special with computers. Like autistic or something. My guess? We'd have to recruit half a dozen people to replace him."

"Do so."

Fredericks narrowed his eyes. "I'm not squeamish, as you know, but are you sure it's necessary? I mean, he's not exactly wise to the big picture."

"The plan is self-evident by virtue of its execution. He was important in the beginning because of his unique skills, and we moved quickly to take advantage of the market chaos. But he's now a rival. You know what must be done."

Fredericks shrugged. "Suit yourself. Timeframe?"

"The monitoring software has provided you with the necessary account access information?"

"Pretty sure. I mean, it's geeky shit, and it's not my area of expertise, but there's a couple thousand account numbers and passwords stored up by now."

"Then he is your highest priority."

"Seems like an awful lot of brains just to splatter a wall with. Sure we can't use the kid for something else?"

"Loyalty above competency. Always."

"You expected loyalty from the kid?"

The Facilitator shook his head. "I had no such expectations. I'm merely reiterating what I hope are very clear priorities."

Fredericks' eyes narrowed and a knowing smile creased his lips. "They were right about you, old man. You're ice fuckin' cold."

With a flick of his finger, the Facilitator ended the conversation.

"I'll see myself out," Fredericks said.

The Facilitator watched him leave, observing that Fredericks' type always wanted the last word, always needed the illusion of control over something. They invariably became liabilities as a result.

Fredericks' time would certainly come, probably sooner rather than later.

But not right now. Right now, the Consultancy had use for him, disagreeable though he was.

LOST MAN LAKE RANCH, COLORADO

FRIDAY MORNING ARRIVED GENTLY FOR PROTÉGÉ. HE'D eased off on the scotch at just the right time during the evening's philosophical exchange with the growing crowd of illuminati that had been arriving steadily since the so-called "devolution event" four days earlier.

He hadn't been able to keep his eyes off of Allison, which he considered to be a good sign as they entered the second week of their whirlwind romance. She didn't seem at all put off by his amorous advances. If anything, he worried he couldn't keep up with her appetite.

Protégé heard her rhythmic breathing and rolled over to regard her. *Ridiculously gorgeous.* Dark brunette strands draped carelessly across her face, counterpoint to the perfect lines of her nose and cheeks, somehow parting to make way for those incredible lips. His eyes wandered down her length, following the line of her hips, bedcovers pulled low enough to cause tingling.

As if on cue, Allison's eyes opened, brilliant, piercing blue laser beams of intelligence and frank sensuality. "Caught me staring," Protégé said.

She smiled. "Lucky me." Her hand wandered.

"What a coincidence. It was dreaming about you."

"So I gathered." One thing led to another. They shared a loud, breathless orgasm, then laughed together about their lack of consideration for the neighbors asleep next door.

He caressed her cheek, amazed again that *she* had just given herself to *him*. "This kind of thing happens to me all the time," he teased. "Simulgasms with brainy Playboy models, I mean."

She laughed. "Color me flattered. I'm glad you didn't object to my advances. I'm a sucker for a nice ass in Armani."

"I don't even mind that you were paid to spy on me." It was a serious statement, but Protégé delivered it with a lighthearted smile.

Allison smiled in return. "I only agreed after they showed me your picture."

Protégé laughed. "We've never really talked about it. I figure our one-week anniversary is as good a time as any." He rolled over onto his back. "How long were you in on the whole take-over-the-world plot?"

"Months," she said. "I see things differently than most people, so it wasn't an ideological stretch for me."

"What would you have done if I got cold feet?"

"Cold feet regarding you and me?"

Protégé shook his head. "Not possible. I meant, what if I had decided not to steal the transmitter and drive it down to Langley?"

"My orders were to kill you. I thought maybe death by sexual overexertion."

He laughed out loud. "What a gorgeous way to go."

"Actually," she said, smiling, leg draped across his pelvis, "I was just supposed to let them know if you had second thoughts. I think they just wanted a heads up if you changed your mind."

"Are you glad I didn't?"

"I was agnostic, really." She rolled over on top of him and bit his neck. "I care much more about your libido than your politics."

Protégé finished his breakfast of fresh eggs, fried Colorado brook trout, and sliced tomatoes, plucked fresh from the aquaponic greenhouse in back of the ranch house, and marveled again that everything was produced sustainably and within a mile of where they sat. He glanced at Archive, sopping egg yolk with a slice of homemade bread, and inquired about the total investment the old man had sunk into constructing the ranch.

"Would a dollar figure be meaningful at this point?" Archive asked, amused.

Protégé shook his head. "It's difficult to recalibrate my sense of value. I'm still a dollar dude."

"I suppose you can be forgiven. We're only four days into the new world order." He smiled. "All told, I spent just north of fourteen million, including all the land and permits."

Protégé was surprised. "That's peanuts, actually."

"The Ranch and surrounding land produce almost everything to support a few dozen of us indefinitely. Tough to put a price on that."

"True wealth, I suppose," Allison said, gazing out the enormous picture window and across the mountain valley, marveling again at the scale of the peak on the other side of the lake.

A new voice joined the conversation. "I hate to interrupt the economics lesson," Trojan said, standing in the entryway to the enormous dining room, wearing the beginnings of a smile, "but I've discovered something important."

"What am I looking at?" Archive asked, squinting at the large screen on the wall, now containing a map of the Northwestern United States, spotted with hundreds of red dots.

"I made the assumption that the Bitcoin thefts we experienced were all pulled off by the same person or group of people," Trojan said. "Obviously, it might have been a false assumption, but I thought it would be a useful mental framework to approach the problem. It led me to plot the geographical distribution of IP addresses used in the thefts."

"I think I'm following," Archive said, "but I think it would be useful if you explained all of this to me as if I were a small child."

Trojan laughed. "I'll try. The Bitcoin network keeps track of every single transaction in the world, and the list of transactions becomes a permanent part of what the inventors of the protocol called a 'block chain.' The thieves hacked into some of our Bitcoin accounts using our account numbers and passwords, and in effect, transferred coins from our wallets to wallets of their own."

"But all of the thefts were permanently recorded," Protégé said.

Trojan nodded. "Exactly."

"Doesn't seem too smart," Allison said. "I thought those transactions were supposed to be anonymous."

"That's a common myth. They're not quite personalized, and it takes a little bit of savvy to associate a Bitcoin wallet with the computer that last accessed the account, but it can be done."

"So you looked up the IP addresses of the computers that accessed all those accounts?" Archive asked.

Trojan nodded. "I wrote a script to do it for me, but that's right. And each IP address can also be traced to a physical location."

Protégé pointed to the collection of red dots overlaid on the map of the US. "So those are all the computers that were involved in stealing Bitcoins from us?"

"Well, not quite," Trojan said. "If I were going to steal a bunch of Bitcoins from a bunch of different accounts, I would use an IP address masking program to make it look like someone else did it."

"Wouldn't you want to choose the fake account numbers randomly?"

The diminutive hacker shook his head. "You wouldn't want to use fake addresses, because the whole idea would be to create a long list of people for the authorities to have to investigate. Fake addresses wouldn't be associated with a real person, so there would be no false trail to waste investigation time."

"You have quite a devious mind," Archive said.

Trojan smiled. "Comes with the territory. Anyway, the idea is to find computer IP addresses belonging to real people, that are actually online at the time the theft was committed, in order to end up with a list of thousands of apparent suspects."

"They have programs that do that?" Protégé asked.

"Much easier than you might think. But there's a problem, something I think the thief didn't consider." He pointed to the dots on the map. "In order to steal online IP addresses, you first have to search for them, and you can't search the entire globe at the same time. The IP search program is a victim of the internet's architecture, in that it detects the nearest active IP addresses before it detects online computers that are further away."

"So the process isn't truly random?" Protégé asked.

"Exactly. The randomizer chooses randomly from among the list of active IP addresses, but it builds the list based on the active IP addresses nearest to it. So the effect, in aggregate, isn't really random at all."

"Producing a nice geographic distribution centered on the thief's actual location, I'm guessing," Archive said.

"Right, but only if you can put together a long enough list of theft transactions. But for safety reasons, our Bitcoin assets were distributed across hundreds of accounts." Trojan snapped his fingers. "So automatically, because we have so many wallets, we can build a nice map of the IP addresses they used."

"And the thieves are roughly in the center of that distribution?" Allison asked.

"Exactly," Trojan beamed. "In this case, Seattle."

"I'm glad you're on our side," Protégé said, shaking his head.

Trojan smiled demurely. "I don't know. We're up against some serious talent. Whoever put this theft operation together did a damn fine job. They have exquisite skills. Maybe only a handful of guys on the planet could have pulled it off. We just got lucky that we were paranoid enough to spread our assets out over so many accounts."

Archive laughed. "With apologies, I feel compelled to make the obvious observation that just because we're paranoid doesn't mean they aren't actually out to get us."

SEATTLE, WASHINGTON

SABOT SAT AT THE KITCHEN COUNTER IN CONNIE'S house as dawn broke, chancing a brief connection via the Almighty Interwebs to count his spoils.

It was an impressive number, becoming more so by the minute.

He wasn't quite sure how the money thing would ultimately shake out, but he liked Bitcoin's chances, given its lack of central control. Plenty of governments could mess with it, just like they could mess with guns and books and taxes, but he was relatively certain there would still be a market running in Bitcoins somewhere.

At least, he was convinced they would ultimately be worth more, in real terms, than whatever ended up replacing the greenback atop the fiat currency heap.

Something caught his eye. *What the hell?*

He got a sinking feeling in the pit of his stomach. The mouse cursor had moved. He was certain of it.

In a flash, he had opened a copy of Wireshark, a program that let him view the messages his computer was sending and receiving over the modem. It took less than a minute to confirm his suspicions.

Spyware.

Someone had installed a key logger on the new computer he'd just purchased the night before from Doggy Style. It was broadcasting messages back to different computer addresses at a rate of about one report every four and a half minutes.

They don't play around. He'd broken the plastic seal around the computer himself just hours before, and had ensured it was clean of spyware. *These aren't teenage script kiddies.* He figured a state security apparatus, or the remnants of one, or some other group with deep talent and resources to burn.

Like maybe the organization that Balzzack011 worked for, whatever the hell it was.

They know. He'd set up another Bitcoin operation for his own benefit, a clone of the one he'd created for Balzzack011. The spyware had born silent witness, then reported Sabot's dalliance to his masters.

His heart pounded in his chest. He had known that something like this was a possibility, but he wasn't truly prepared for it. He fought panic.

Get your shit together, bro!

Sabot watched the message traffic until the spyware made its next report. Then he started his stopwatch. *Four and a half minutes, vato. Don't screw it up!*

His fingers flew into frenzied action, floating over the keyboard, working desperately to sneak his fortune out from under the bastards' noses before the spyware made its next report.

He bought server space through Tor, the anonymizing network, paying in Bitcoins. One minute gone.

He paid for exclusive use of an entire server, which was not a small investment even in normal times. Another minute later, he had his Bitcoin theft program up and running on the remote server, the ones and zeroes piling inside a computer in a server farm probably located in an old mine shaft, disused auto manufacturing plant, or other industrial relic that was sufficiently uninteresting to the layman.

A brief eternity later, Sabot saw confirmation that the remote machine had begun adding to his growing stack of pilfered riches.

Ninety seconds left. *Faster!*

He used Excel's randomizing function to create a one-time cipher, still the most secure encryption method available, then pasted the encoded list of Bitcoin accounts and passwords onto his new server. He copied the cipher – the code that would unlock what was rapidly becoming a fortune of global proportions, and without which Sabot would be just as penniless as the next poor schmuck – onto a zip drive disguised as a tube of lip balm.

The fortune of a lifetime, sitting in the palm of his hands.

Thirty seconds. *One more failsafe.*

He grabbed a new thumb drive, this one hidden inside a heart pendant. He pasted the encoded account list to the portable data drive and unplugged it, just as his stopwatch crossed four minutes and fifteen seconds.

Then he ripped out the power cord, pried the laptop's battery loose, and smashed the computer on the floor.

Too close, esé!

Had he made it?

The question was academic. Knowing the answer wouldn't have changed anything.

He picked through the shards of shattered computer parts until he found the hard drive, putting it into his pocket just as Angie made her way into the kitchen, pulling her robe around her shoulders, sleepy and concerned. "Dingo, what's going on?"

He rose to face her.

Her face changed.

She knows.

He saw her eyes fall, tears forming. "You promised," she whispered.

"Baby, I kept that promise. I provided for us. I made a life for us. It's time for you to trust me."

She shook her head, tears falling freely. "No, Dingo, I can't be part of this."

He grabbed her arms and looked in her eyes. "Angie, they came for me. I didn't start this. Do you understand? *They* found *me*, okay? I did what had to be done."

He saw fear and anger in her eyes. "Because of your past." It was more accusation than question.

Sabot snorted. "Of course, because of my past! And because of my job.

182

My damned FBI job, Angie, the one I go to every day! These people know what they're doing."

The tears intensified, her shoulders shaking as she cried, Sabot's embrace tightening around her.

The crying stopped, and Angie pulled away. Sabot saw her eyes fall to the groceries on the counter, and to the destroyed computer on the floor, weighing one against the other. She shook her head. "I knew this was going to happen."

"Bullshit!" Sabot was suddenly irate, the tension and exhaustion finally getting the better of him. "You knew the world would go to shit? You knew they would kidnap me and threaten me and make me steal for them? You knew that?"

Connie appeared in the doorway, cigarette in hand, scowl on her face, displeased by the early-morning commotion, instantly taking Angie's side out of an entirely predictable maternal bias, but one for which Sabot had no tolerance at the moment.

"Angie," he said, still talking too loudly for the scant distance between their faces, "these people turned on us, just like their kind always do. I took precautions, okay? I took care of you."

He looked at Connie, still glaring at him from the doorway. "And I took care of you too! That food you ate last night? Where do you think it came from? *I* did that." He pounded his finger into his own chest. "Me. And there's much more out there where that came from. There's a whole economy rising up, and I'm in the middle of it. I know how it works. And I'm really *good* at it."

Connie nodded slowly.

Angie looked at him for a long moment.

"Okay, Dingo," she finally said, eyes softening. "What now?"

Sabot slammed Connie's car trunk shut, their hastily-packed bags barely fitting inside the large white import. Just for a few days, he had lied, knowing that Angie's over-packing penchant was undoubtedly genetic.

"Can I see your phone, babe?" Angie handed her handset to him. He composed a text message to Doggy Style: "Dinosaurs?" Slang for gasoline.

The reply was almost instantaneous. "WTHAY?" Who the hell are you? Angie's cell number was unfamiliar to the young black-market entrepreneur.

Sabot identified himself, and Doggy Style's tone changed instantly. A devastating hacking victory, such as the one Sabot had attained over the skinny white kid with all of the handy barter-economy connections, went a long way toward creating a conducive atmosphere for business. "My man! For you? Brontosaurs! But ching ching." Lots of gas, but it would be pricey.

"Can you dlvr 10 gals in 30 min?" Half an hour wasn't a lot of time for the kid to work his connections, Sabot knew, but time wasn't on their side.

He had another thought. "Throw in a burner and a gun, too?"

Long pause. "10 BTC," Doggy Style replied.

Sabot laughed aloud. "4get who ur talkin to?" It was an outrageous sum. "Make me an offer."

They came to terms – two Bitcoins, equivalent at the moment to six thousand dollars, but climbing rapidly – and agreed on a meeting location.

Sabot asked Angie to drive, then thought of something important. "We gotta leave behind all our cell phones." There was gnashing of teeth, which escalated to an uncomfortable pitch when he mentioned that the girls' e-readers had to stay behind, as well. "Yeah, it sucks," he finally said. "But it beats getting a knife between the vertebrae."

Moments later, with their personal electronic devices reluctantly abandoned, Angie merged onto northbound traffic on the highway. "Canada," Sabot said when Angie asked about their destination, which had thrown Connie into something between a mild conniption and transpolar orbit.

But he didn't relent. He wasn't sure who was pulling Balzzack011's strings – or the Bureau's strings, for that matter – but he didn't plan to leave any advantage on the table, even if the concept of national sovereignty appeared to be in the throes of a serious test at the moment. Best to put as many barriers as possible – real and virtual – between himself and his employers.

EAST OF DENVER, COLORADO

IT LOOKED LIKE THE ROCKY MOUNTAINS HAD ENDURED an early winter snowstorm. A fresh blanket of white reflected the bright Colorado sun, a little painful on the eyes, maybe more potent than at lower elevations because of the thin atmosphere, Sam supposed.

Her eyes were red and irritated, a byproduct of having driven through the night to reach Denver with minimal interruption by the nouveau barbarians and highway robbers who had come out of the woodwork since society's strictures had suddenly gone slack a few days earlier.

Brock dozed in the passenger's seat, but Mike Charles was wide awake in the rear, behind the plexiglass shield, staring absently, his face tinged with a bit of a maudlin look, Sam thought. *Let him stew.*

She felt her cell phone buzz, and found herself squinting to make out the words on the text message. *I need to get my eyes checked.* A little bit of sleep probably wouldn't kill anyone, either.

The text was from Dan Gable. "Mike Charles has a daughter." There was a video attached to the text. *I'm glad the cell phone companies haven't gone belly up just yet,* Sam found herself thinking.

She clicked on the video. A pretty young girl lay on a mattress in what looked like a shelter or youth hostel of some sort. A group of people stood in a semicircle around the girl, talking in concerned tones. She was trembling visibly, mumbling something about missing her shot. Drug addict?

"Type 1 diabetic," Dan's next missive explained. *She's run out of her insulin,* Sam realized.

Leverage came in all sorts of forms, some of them alarming, but there was only one rule in Sam's line of work: use it while you had it. She held the phone up against the plexiglass divider that locked Mike Charles into his mobile prison in the backseat. She played the video.

She watched his face carefully in the mirror. It was more instinct than habit by now, after years of reading volumes in slightly arched eyebrows and almost imperceptibly oscillating pupils.

No clairvoyance was required in this case, however, and Sam watched as any remaining façade melted instantly away from the smart and charismatic senior executive's face at the sight of his sick daughter. His eyes misted over, and he seemed to deflate.

She let a few seconds pass, to let the first reverberations gang up on him, then started gently to work. "Type one. My grandmother had that. That's where the body attacks its own insulin-producing cells, right?"

He nodded.

Brock stirred, awakened by the conversation.

"What's her name?" Sam asked, a subtle twist of the knife, emphasizing the familial connection.

"Jenny." Charles struggled for composure, forcing himself to look away, squinting out the window through the harsh reflections of the morning sun.

"My grandmother was a sufferer. It was tough as she got older. She kept forgetting whether she'd taken her meds. Lost feeling in her extremities, and ended up on dialysis. I'm no doctor, but it looks like Jenny's gone too long between shots."

She saw Charles' jaw clench. "I told her to stock up." His voice was almost inaudible.

"There were fires in certain neighborhoods, and some gang activity, from what I hear. Maybe she had trouble getting home to take her shot."

She watched him steel himself.

Brock caught her eye, with that look he sometimes got, asking wordlessly whether working a man's family angle like that was really necessary. She gave him a small, sad smile and a nod in answer.

"It can get serious, though, if the blood sugar builds up too high, right?"

Charles gave her a hard look, aware of what she was doing, annoyed by how well it was working on him. "Life-threatening. As you know. Who took the video?"

Sam shook her head. "I don't know."

She let a few more miles pass in silence. "I've been thinking about something you said, Mike. About how you told your daughter to stock up on her medications." She turned to look at him, adding emphasis to her question: "Why?"

"A diabetic must always have an emergency supply of insulin." The reply was terse, and a little unfriendly.

"But you said, 'stock up.' As if in preparation for something catastrophic."

He snorted. "Semantics?"

"They only matter when they do. Which means a girl has to pay attention." She eyed him, staring him down. "You knew this was coming. This meltdown. Didn't you." It didn't feel to Sam like a question, more like an expression of the preverbal knowing that she'd formed over the past couple of days.

She saw Charles' jaw clench, but he steeled himself against his anger and helplessness, and it was as if a veil had descended over his face. His expression was implacable. *That's right, Mike. Get that feeling like you're back in control. Perfect preamble to the coup de grace.*

"NIH and Homeland work closely together, Mike. It's not common knowledge, because the medicaid crowd would come after them in droves demanding handouts, but there are drug stockpiles in every major city."

Charles tried to remain impassive, but his eyes gave him away. The gears were clearly turning.

"I'm sure a word or two in the right ears could go a long way." Dramatic pause. "Given that this is a national security situation, of course, and you're a guy with a lot of relevant knowledge at the moment."

Anger flashed. Charles sat forward, losing his cool in what Sam surmised was an exceptionally rare apoplectic episode. "How dare you toy with my daughter's life!"

Sam laughed derisively. "But kneeing the global economy in the stones wasn't out of bounds?" *Surely, he had to have thought of this.* It didn't take anything more than average human predictive power to conjecture that someone would eventually find some sort of uncomfortable situation in Mr. Charles' personal life that was suitable for exploitation. After all, more than a few people were certain to go looking for a little enlightenment regarding the most outrageous conspiracy in memory, the little to-do from which no country on the planet appeared to be immune at present.

"You're a federal agent!" Charles said. "It's criminal to knowingly withhold lifesaving medicine from someone who needs it."

Sam shook her head. "I'm not withholding anything, Mike. Jenny has just as much right to help as any of the millions of other diabetics in the same boat right about now. You and I were merely discussing what might make me feel compelled to spend a little effort trying to move her closer to the front of the line, particularly in light of the national security situation that you seem to be directly involved with."

He stewed in silence.

"And let's not forget," she pressed, "who kicked this whole thing off. As far as the blame game goes, my money's on the guy who stole the beam director and authorized its delivery to Langley."

It was a theory she'd paraded in front of Charles before. The effect had been muted, at best, and Charles had clearly prepared well to resist interrogation efforts.

But it was different with a daughter in trouble, Sam figured, which was why she decided to take a gamble. "I'm going to figure this out one way or the other, Mike. It's too big, and you weren't careful enough, and even a lumbering government employee like me could eventually fit the pieces together."

She watched his eyes carefully. He blinked a few times, more rapidly than average, she thought, a sign that the idea of an inevitable revelation of his culpability was at least rattling around his brain, its sharp and spiky consequences pricking all sorts of precious things in his life.

"Difference is," Sam continued, "people might be inclined to cut you some slack if you help us stop what's next."

Charles sat up and leaned forward. "What makes you think there's anything else coming?"

Was that a trap slamming shut? She smiled, with unabashed smugness. Charles' outburst was delivered far too quickly. "It's always the same with you alpha males," she said. "You can never bear to lose a battle, even to win the war."

Sam saw him blush, and she laughed a bit harshly. "Too much foreskin and too little forehead, I think."

Brock chuckled in the passenger's seat, despite his efforts to remain as unobtrusive an observer as possible, captive audience that he was.

"Like I said," Sam went on, "this will all end up out in the open. Too big and messy, which means there are too many loose ends to button down. I give it two days, max. A week, at worst. And honestly, even accounting for the reduced workforce due to all the mayhem, we'll have more than half of you clowns in the bag by sundown."

She turned her head to look at him again, her face serious, her eyes hard. "So twelve hours, max. That's what you'll gain in exchange for your daughter's life."

Sam let him mull, watching him through the mirror as he did so, wondering what was going on inside his head.

Ideologue? It was possible. They came in all sorts of flavors, even the otherwise level-headed type.

But she didn't think that was what made Mike Charles tick. Disgruntled and disillusioned, maybe, but that was a very long way from conspiring against the free world. Plus, he just wasn't that riled up about all the trouble that he'd caused. He wasn't pleading a case or preaching, as an ideologue might. So the zealot angle wasn't really working for her.

He had even taken his misfortune largely in stride. Being rescued from the buck-toothed animals at the rest stop, by the very same federal agent who was sent to bring him to justice, was terrifically shitty luck. But he'd seemed to roll with the punches remarkably well.

Until the video of his daughter. Maybe the family angle was something

Charles had considered, and maybe he had even tried to prepare himself for it. But it certainly wasn't anything he was on top of. He was clearly rattled, and he'd even lost his cool.

That's why she wasn't surprised when Charles began to speak. "We'll need to get gas in Denver," he said. "I think you'll be interested in something a bit further west."

PITKIN COUNTY AIRPORT, ASPEN, COLORADO

BROCK OPENED THE CAR DOOR AND HOBBLED INSIDE the terminal building to inquire after Dan Gable's arrival time. The high-priority case had apparently shaken loose some federal resources that were otherwise reserved for the upper crust, even in the nation's 'hour of need,' and Dan had finagled private jet service to Aspen from DC, nonstop, with no ear-piercing badgering or livestock treatment at the hands of the bargain-basement airlines.

Sam stayed with Mike Charles, who was still imprisoned in the backseat of the Oklahoma police cruiser. The mood in the car had become strangely affable since Charles had begun opening up about the conspiracy.

He had done much more than merely cooperate with Sam's investigation, it turned out. He'd even arranged for a few of his co-conspirators to meet them at the airport. Sam thought his gratitude at her arranging insulin treatments for Jenny might have worked against his own best legal interests, but she certainly didn't stop the effusion of juicy tidbits. He'd revealed enough to keep a grand jury busy for years, Sam thought.

If there's still such a thing as a grand jury these days.

The radio reports had been a bit grim, though admittedly, not nearly as grim as she would have anticipated. People seemed to be figuring things out. That annoying Monopoly Man, with his smug pith, was more insightful than Sam cared to admit. They'd listened in silence to yet another intrusive message during a lull in the conversation, the bygone-era cartoon voice speaking again about currency as nothing more than a symbol of a social agreement.

She resisted the thought as a consequence of its source, but a quieter, slightly niggling voice in her head, to which she was not yet prepared to grant prominence, seemed to have a different sense of things. She'd have to revisit the idea, she decided, when she had a little more mental bandwidth.

Something else was on her mind at the moment. She was replaying the conversation she'd had two nights earlier with the asshole-esque old coot who ran the show at Langley Air Force Base, General Mark Hajek. He was too smart to be as dumb as he sounded. "Mike, something's been bothering me," she said to Charles. "Was Hajek really in the dark? He said he knew nothing about what was going on at Langley. Which makes me think he knew everything that was going on at Langley."

Charles' eyes twinkled just a bit. "I don't know what COMACC knew."

"Why'd you sign the authorization for the cargo plane to land at his airstrip?"

The sparkle turned into a sardonic smile. "I'm the designated lightning rod."

Sam laughed. "How's that working out?"

"Would have been better not to have made the bathroom stop in Oklahoma, I think." Charles shook his head. "I suppose that's life in a random universe."

"Some might call it comeuppance."

Charles laughed. "The thought certainly crossed my mind. But I still think this is the least painful way to make the transition. Better we deal with the debt problem now, than to have to deal with it as part of a larger political or military conflict later on."

Sam pondered. "There's some wisdom there, I'm sure." She looked at him in the mirror, with a motherly expression aimed at a man who could be an uncle. "But a lot of folks are going to have a lot of things to say about it, and the old 'ends justify the means' thing probably won't float."

"In court?" Charles asked. "You've heard the radio reports, right?"

"Same radio you've been listening to. But it's hard to know what's credible. It's the news media, after all."

Charles shook his head. "Hard to fake burning courthouses and government buildings."

"It is definitely starting to feel like an uprising, I'll give you that."

"When you meet them, you'll recognize many of the players who were involved in engineering this event. It's not a collection of dunces and dullards, and there are some exceedingly accomplished individuals involved. I think we all hope that the public comes to see past the momentary inconvenience to grasp the big picture."

"Tall order," Sam said. "The public generally doesn't seem to see past much."

"Don't conflate the public with the news media's portrayal of us. They're vastly different things. The media serves the purpose of its owners."

Sam laughed. "You sound like me. But you're more of an idealistic curmudgeon than I've managed to become."

"Just a frog who happened to wake up to the uncomfortable temperature in the pot. Thankfully, it wasn't boiling quite yet."

Was that pride she saw, that impish wrinkle at the corner of Charles' eyes? "Thousands hacking at the branches of evil, all of that?" she asked.

He nodded, maybe with a trace of self-satisfaction. "I went after the root." *Always the ego that gets them,* Sam thought again.

"Winning hearts and minds will be an uphill battle, I think," Sam said.

Charles shook his head. "Honestly? I don't think so. I bet fewer than one person in ten honestly thought the old system was sustainable."

"That won't stop them from tarring and feathering you in the meantime."

"Thanks. I wasn't worried enough already."

Sam decided she liked Mike Charles, as far as one could like a perpetrator of such a megalomaniacal plot, anyway. No shortage of chutzpah. *Something admirable about having the gonads to change the tilt of the world,* she thought.

She watched a plane land. Dan Gable's, undoubtedly. The other rich people who could afford to retreat to their Aspen or Vail abodes had already done so, judging by the lack of empty space on the airport tarmac.

Her mind returned to gnawing on the pieces of the conspiracy. "So, Mike, back to Hajek. Involved?"

"No comment."

"So, yes?"

"Draw your own conclusions."

Sam smiled. "Hazardous, in my line of work, at least without a trail of truth stones to hop across. He had dumb answers but intelligent eyes, and I thought I might have detected a hint of annoyance at having to play the fool."

"I don't know him well," Charles said.

"But you chat at sewing circle?"

"His organization is a customer of the program I ran."

"I did happen to notice the past tense there," Sam said. "Optimism or fatalism?"

"Not much difference in my case." Charles' smile was wistful and a little inscrutable.

Sam turned to look at him again. "You lack the career bureaucrat's bovine eyes and non-statements. My guess is you weren't long for the job anyway. Either on your way up or on your way out."

"Out is up," Charles said. "Pay was way below scale for the aggravation."

"It'll read nicely in the Newspaper of Record," Sam said. "'Disgruntled government worker screw over the planet.' Should sell a few million copies, don't you think?"

Charles laughed. "But who's buying? Besides, you give us too much credit. The dam was going to break. I just did my part to help nudge it along before the water behind it became any deeper."

"Swell guy," Sam said. "You helped us keep from bludgeoning each other back to the stone age, is that it?"

"Actually, yes."

Sam smiled sardonically. "Forgive me if I'm a little less than thankful. I had a few days off coming to me that I was looking forward to enjoying."

"The best laid plans... I hadn't counted on the little Deliverance scene back in Oklahoma, either."

Sam chuckled, conjuring the Ned Beatty scene, "squeal like a pig" echoing in her head. Yes, she decided, there was some substance, some gravitas, humor, and intellect to Mike Charles. She'd have to remember to invite him over for dinner. Brock could undercook a few steaks, they could tell old flying stories using their hands, waving their big watches around.

If they don't hang him at dawn as a traitor, that is.

And, she found herself admitting reluctantly, the guy might even have a few valid points. If her politics were a bumper sticker, it might read Everyone is an Asshole, and she certainly harbored a good portion of learned distrust of authority. It had nothing to do with her decade spent working for one of the world's most powerful authorities, of course. And, upon reflection, she'd sort of had a sense of the fragility of the whole Big Brother edifice, probably borne of its utter disregard, in practice, for the people it was supposed to represent and protect. They were bound to get wise to it and sick of it eventually.

Sure, the slogans on the letterhead said something different, but Sam had seen some pretty draconian shit. That got her thinking, as she idly watched the government jet carrying Dan Gable taxi to a stop on the ramp in front of a private terminal building, about the reports of burning courthouses and government buildings. It wasn't hard to project motives into those events, to imagine that the populace had maybe, finally, wised up a bit to the perpetrations.

Sam found herself with mixed feelings on the subject. She'd watched the movers and shakers work their crooked magic for a lot of years, and she wasn't particularly enamored with the inner machinations of the world's self-proclaimed bastion of freedom and decency, but there were practical considerations. Like a paycheck. Those were still handy for Sam.

And there were bona-fide assholes in the world in need of removal from circulation.

One of them might be sitting in the backseat, she reminded herself, putting her game face back on.

Dan stepped off the airplane, walked down the steps, and shook Sam's hand. His hair was matted, and he had an upholstery line running across his face like a tectonic feature. "Good nap?" Sam asked.

Dan nodded. "How'd you know?"

She pointed to his face. "Bed burn. But don't worry. I don't begrudge you a few winks now and again."

"Boss of the year."

Brock hobbled over and shook Dan's hand. Sam looked at the two most important men in her life, her lover and her deputy, and laughed inwardly at the contrast. Brock was tall, rangy, athletic, and a bit more graceful than average. Dan was a bowling ball, short and squatty, with short hair and small feet, all muscle, steroids Sam would have guessed, except he always passed the random drug tests at Homeland.

"Where are the reinforcements?" Sam asked.

"What am I, chopped liver?" Dan asked with mock indignation. "Actually, all the policy wonks and lobbyists have proven to be surprisingly feisty, and Homeland's up to its eyeballs keeping the district locked down."

Sam frowned. "Lockdown?"

"'Martial law' is the term. Didn't you hear the president's address?"

"We must have been singing road songs at the time," Sam said. "Why would they lock things down? Seems like they'd want to get food and supplies into the cities."

Dan nodded. "They do. But more than that, they want to *control* the movement of supplies into the cities. Government 101: if in doubt, seize control."

"*Nationwide* martial law?" Sam asked. Dan nodded.

"Holy shit," Brock said, shaking his head. "This is getting serious."

Dan shrugged. "Maybe we should revolt," he said with a laugh.

"Anyway, how's progress with our favorite perp?" Dan motioned toward the backseat of the cop car.

"Singing like a bird," Brock opined.

"Thanks again for the video of his daughter," Sam said. "Amazing how quickly stuff like that works."

"Too easy," Dan said. "I can't believe he left her as a loose end."

Sam nodded. "That's been bugging me too. I'm sure he probably couldn't tell her about his plans due to the security concerns, but it was a pretty damn exploitable situation. Something tells me they didn't plan for their conspiracy to stay secret for too long."

Brock laughed. "'Golly how truth will out'?"

"Something like that. So I'm wondering whether our conspirators aren't of a mind to try to co-opt us. Why else invite us to their little lair?"

"Because we were about ten seconds away from finding it ourselves, anyway," Dan said.

Sam nodded. "Good point. Not quite a forced confession, but not exactly an act of conscience, either."

"I don't know shit from shingle," Brock said, "but is it really a great idea to follow the bear back to the den? I mean, who knows, maybe they're going to carve us up and eat us."

"Distinct possibility," Sam said. "Which is why I'm a big fan of human shields. Speaking of which." She nodded in the direction of an arriving limousine.

The vehicle was perfectly polished, a bit incongruously so amidst what had become an almost universal weeklong dilapidation. Who had time to polish a limousine when the world had stopped? Someone with resources to spare, obviously.

The limo driver got out, nodded toward Sam's entourage, and opened the door. A thickset man of medium height emerged, with a slightly flamboyant shock of white hair, impeccably trimmed goatee, and a walking stick with a silver handle, tarnished just enough so people knew it was real silver.

He beamed. As soon as he smiled, Sam recognized him instantly as one of the richest men in America, a media-friendly industrialist, banker, and philanthropist who always seemed to be photographed with an approving, grandfatherly smile on his face. "Jesus," Sam said. "Never saw that coming."

"Jack Anderson," he said, extending his hand as his labored gait brought him within a social distance.

"Pleasure," Sam said.

"Where we're going, you'll hear people refer to me as 'Archive.' A bit of silliness, really, but we felt it necessary. Before the big event, of course. Now, however…"

"Cat's out of the bag a little bit, isn't it?" Brock said.

Archive smiled. "Quite so. And in grand fashion, if I may say so myself." Was pride really appropriate? Too soon, Sam decided.

Sam noticed a younger man sidle up. He introduced himself as Robert Johnston. "'Protégé,' in this crowd," he explained.

"Do you have secret passwords, too?" Sam didn't regret the note of condescension in her voice. Best not to be too chummy with a group of people with the demonstrated willingness to zap satellites in geosynchronous orbit and decimate the worldwide banking and commerce system.

On the other hand, it was probably best not to be too unfriendly, either, with the full faith and credit of the United States Government not amounting to much at the moment, and with herself and her stocky deputy as the sole representatives of the vast federal law enforcement apparatus anywhere within a disturbingly wide radius. *Might be good to give peace a chance,* she thought.

Also good to exert a little control. It would set a good precedent. "Gentlemen, if you wouldn't mind joining your colleague in the backseat of our ride," she said, pointing to the Oklahoma police cruiser, "I'd enjoy a conversation with you during our trip to wherever we're going."

A knowing smile crossed the old man's face. "Of course. I suppose I would appreciate a little insurance myself, were roles reversed."

"That, too," Sam said, opening the door. "Watch your head."

Then, to Dan after she shut the door on the joyful reunion occurring between Mike Charles and the other two conspirators: "Mind riding in the limo? Token of my thanks for all of your hard work, in lieu of a paycheck this week?"

"Who'd say no to an offer like that?"

"Great. I say we go waltzing into the evil fortress of the lunatic oligarchs. You with me?"

Dan winked. "What could possibly go wrong?"

37

NORTHWEST WASHINGTON STATE, NEAR THE CANADIAN BORDER

SABOT'S HEART POUNDED IN HIS CHEST. HE HAD NO IDEA why he was suddenly paranoid about crossing the border to Canada. There was absolutely no reason to believe the federal authorities, and certainly not the Canadians, would have any pretext to stop them on their way north out of the States.

But there was also no reason to believe that Balzzack011's crowd lacked the kind of reach it would take to arrange a manhunt at the border. They had, after all, strong-armed the FBI into releasing him from their auspices, which was no mean feat. Especially considering his background.

Connie, his maybe-mother-in-law-to-be, rode in the backseat, her increasingly shrill protestations and accusations now thankfully silent for the first time since they'd left her home behind. Drugs, money laundering, even the mafia, had all made the list of Connie's paranoid fears about what she termed his "shady schemes," of which there never were any, though Sabot now knew precisely what Connie had thought of him all this time he'd been living with Angie. He regretted taking Connie along, but Angie would never have left Seattle otherwise.

And they'd left for good, he was now certain, though he hadn't told the two women anything of the sort. They'd never have gotten in the car if he had.

Perhaps it was the unregistered handgun in the glove compartment that had Sabot's heartbeat up. Illegal, maybe even an arrest offense. But completely necessary. He wasn't equipped for a showdown in meatspace, having long ago chosen cyberspace as the domain he was most interested in conquering, and he didn't know the first thing about trade craft and staying hidden. But he knew that he needed some sort of protection, and a gun seemed like a logical first step.

He was going to have to learn some survival skills quickly. Balzzack011's crowd had all kinds of pull, and they were liable to be a little upset about his entrepreneurship. They would undoubtedly view it as having come at their expense. There was enough money involved to induce violence, and that wasn't a game he was eager to play.

He momentarily thought that they might keep him around to administer the ongoing Bitcoin theft operation, but he quickly realized the naiveté of that idea. The sums involved were simply too large. With Bitcoin's value skyrocketing, replacing the dollar as the world's de facto base currency, the quantities he was swiping would establish their owner as a global force to be reckoned with.

They would view him as a rival, because his wealth would rapidly equal their own. And he'd already proven that he wasn't afraid to do a little moonlighting, which wouldn't engender much trust.

And now that he'd built a system that stole coins in staggering quantities, it wouldn't be all that hard to find a few hundred other hackers who had the skills to maintain the operation in his absence.

So, the grim upshot was this: they would extort the passwords for his mirror operation, the one he'd set up for himself just before leaving Seattle, then smoke him.

Which was a bitter irony. By the hour, Sabot was becoming one of the richest men on the planet. But would he ever enjoy any of that wealth?

He looked over at Angie. Her face was tense, and her jaw clenched occasionally. Her worry caused his chest to tighten. *I hope I haven't signed our death warrant.*

Sabot thought grimly of the old Russian proverb. With intrigue, it said, sometimes you can go forward. But you can never go back.

Ten miles to the Canadian border, a sign announced, sending another shot of adrenaline crashing uncomfortably in his stomach.

LOST MAN LAKE RANCH, COLORADO

THEIR ARRIVAL AT THE RANCH WAS UTTERLY ANTICLIMACTIC. There was no showdown, no drama, nothing but a peaceful mountain afternoon and a warm welcome, iced tea included.

Weird.

Sam had been expecting a much more sinister environment than the one in which she now found herself.

She was seated on the balcony of the vast ranch house, Brock next to her, the old man and his youngish fluffer on her other side. She marveled at the view of the lake, the valley, and the mountain beyond. A cool breeze, with a bit of a lingering bite at the end of it, as if to threaten of frost in the wings, ready to strike at a moment's notice, brought a full-body shiver. The old man waved to someone inside, and a steward appeared, jacket in hand. Sam donned it gratefully.

"So, the obvious question," Sam said, interrupting the babbling brook audible from the deck. "Why?"

Archive appraised her for a long moment, clearly pondering.

"You have the right to remain silent, of course," she nudged. "But circumstances as they are, you probably shouldn't."

The younger man, Protégé, blanched a bit. But the old man was unruffled. He donned a wistful smile. "Sometimes to save lives, you have to euthanize an idea."

"All right," Sam said. "I'll bite. You could kill a religious idea, and maybe stop a few million deaths every year. You could kill a political idea – neoconservatism or neoliberalism or force-fed democracy coming readily to mind – and maybe save a few zillion more lives."

Archive beamed at her.

She paused, taken aback. "What?" she asked.

His smile widened to improbably large proportions. "I find myself powerlessly captivated by the grip of your nascent question."

"And the home-run answer you're formulating, no doubt, but I'll pitch it right over the plate for you anyway. Why kill the economy? The *global* economy, no less."

The old man leaned his head back, eyes gleaming, looking off into the distance momentarily. Sam glanced at Protégé, and noticed a bit of a here-we-go-again look about him, as if he were bracing for a diatribe on a painfully familiar topic.

"I'll answer your question with a question," Archive said.

Sam held up her hand. "These kinds of games are fun," she said, "but my question wasn't really about the theory and the motives as much as it was about what comes next. So that's where I'm aiming with all of this, being someone who's supposed to uphold my sworn duty to stop global-scale disasters when the opportunity arises, and when it isn't too much bother."

Archive continued, unabated by Sam's attempt to focus him, holding up a solitary finger. "Just one question," he said, still smiling, a professorial air about him. "What is an economy?"

"I've been meaning to waste a few years on an MBA, but I haven't gotten around to it yet," Sam said. "But I'll play along. I'd guess that it's something involving banks, currency, and transactions between people, who are very likely to get pissed off when you pull the rug out from underneath the whole damn thing."

"Absolutely!" Archive clapped his hands, and Sam was sure she caught a little smile on Protégé's face, as well. "Except for the part about the banks, of course. They're not really a necessary participant, and, as the owner of a rather large banking concern, I can tell you that the world is a much worse place as a result of our activities."

"So you're a disillusioned rich guy," Sam said. "Couldn't you just start a charity, maybe some educational thing, or an orphanage, to burn down a bit of that guilt? Why pick on the whole planet?"

Archived wagged a finger. "No guilt here, madam. I was smart enough to know when I got lucky, and smart enough to take advantage of it. Nothing to feel guilty over."

"And now?"

"Difficult moments, but I'm hopeful our better nature will prevail, and we'll collectively recognize our new freedom."

"Freedom from what?" Brock asked, annoyed, sitting forward in his chair.

"Terrific question!" More pearly whites from the old man, Cheshire-cat style. "What made it all go? What was the life-blood of the whole thing?"

"The dollar." Dan wore his bad-cop scowl.

Archive clapped his hands. "Bingo!" He reminded Sam of the Monopoly Man cartoons.

"Now worth pennies, and on its way to nothing," Dan said, a little snarl on his lips.

"And good riddance!" Archive's joviality gave Sam the impression that he was a man deeply committed to his central delusion.

"Millions are suffering," she said, her low, even voice playing counterpoint to the escalating emotions floating over the conversation. "How do you figure you've spared anyone from anything?"

"Inflation," Protégé interjected. "The end of every fiat currency, the start of every revolution, the primary mechanism of wealth redistribution."

"You're well trained," Sam said.

He flushed. "Think I'm wrong?"

Sam shook her head. "I know you're not. But you'll still have to help me with the connection. You destroyed the world economy because you're mad about dogshit monetary policy?"

"We didn't destroy the economy," Archive said, pounding his walking stick into the deck floor for emphasis. "We *released* it."

"From?" Dan asked, still dubious.

Archive smiled. "Debt. Leveraged drowning. Unhealthy consolidation. The cancer of the twentieth century."

Sam shook her head. "I'm sorry. I'm not buying it."

Actually, she was. Economically, at least. She just wasn't sure what the old zealot had up his sleeve as an encore, and that was the rub. You didn't break things just let them lie broken. There was some consolidation plan, some way for a guy like this to get an even tighter grip on an even larger fortune. "And that was worse than what you've turned the world into?"

"Certainly, there's some momentary discomfort. But we've incited the transition from the debt economy, which was based on a toxic fiat currency to which the entire planet was deeply, deeply exposed."

"But here's the key." He waved his finger again, pounding the deck floor with the walking stick in his other hand. "We've done this without any harm to the *actual* elements of value. Houses, factories, crops, roads, bridges, intellectual property, professional skills, the trades – they're *all still intact*," cane pounding again, "and in better shape than ever, just waiting for people to realize they're free, *finally* free, to put all that glorious personal and public capital to work for themselves."

Sam nodded slowly, then narrowed her eyes. "For the moment. But you're going to lasso them, corral them for yourself, aren't you? That's what's next, isn't it?"

A tinge of sadness crossed the old man's face. "That's certainly the automatic, implicit assumption, and I don't blame you for it. Your line of work doesn't condition you to see anything else, at least not without a great deal of effort."

He sat back in his seat, both hands resting atop the silver eagle's head on the end of his cane. "Clearly, I am an ambitious man, as is obvious from my portfolio. And some of my colleagues in this endeavor surpass me tenfold. But we own our capital outright, and we don't lust after more." Archive took a breath, a wistful look on his face. "This is our gift to the people of our time. They were enslaved. Now, they are not."

Sam could tell it was a heartfelt statement, a little embarrassingly so. Her discomfort wasn't assuaged in the least by her sense that the old man might have just revealed the complete loss of his marbles.

Either that, or he was balls-on right. Tough to tell which.

She sighed. "Not sure what to make of all of that, to be honest with you. People are dying. And you've made a few billion people murderously angry. I don't think you'll ever convince them that you saved them from anything, and there's a pretty strong case that you've made things horrifically worse. I don't know how this ends for you, honestly."

Archive smiled. "That's certainly an interpretation that some people will choose."

Sam arched her eyebrows, silently piercing the pregnant pause with the obvious question, *But?*

"But over ninety-eight percent of the world was enslaved in a debt they had no say in creating. How might they feel, when the insight dawns that they are no longer beholden?"

Helluva point.

Sam nodded slowly, the beginnings of a smile on her face. She noticed gears turning in Dan and Brock's heads, too. And the young guy with the stupid name, Protégé, seemed to wear a bit of a smug smirk.

"Hero of the commoner," Sam said. "Cue the trumpets. But a little devil's advocacy here. What about the people to whom those debts are owed?"

"Yes, the famous One Percent. Really, the one-tenth of one percent these days. If they weren't smart enough to stay away from paper assets, they're bound to be exceptionally worse off than they were on Monday. Some will surely contemplate murder. But a few of them will call me up to thank me."

"How do you figure?" Brock asked. "You zeroed out their net worth."

"Every episode of class upheaval in the last two centuries has involved some variation on the French Revolution theme."

"Off with their heads?" Sam asked.

"Exactly. The rich are rarely rehabilitatable, at least to the angry proletariat on the rise. France, Russia, Germany, China, Cambodia, Vietnam, half of Latin America, and every almost-nation in the Sahel on a bi-annual basis. And I'm sure I'm missing a few. They slaughter the fat cats. Well, I'm betting that a few of our wiser fat cats will recognize that they escaped *this* little revolution with their lives and families intact. Besides, if they haven't bothered to tuck a little wealth away, I have no sympathy for them."

"But you robbed them of their wealth," Dan said, evidently still in bad-cop mode, which made little sense to Sam given the conspirators' talkativeness.

"The crux of the matter, young man," Archive said, causing Sam to cringe at the avuncular condescension she knew Dan wouldn't take kindly to, "is that painted paper is rarely a suitable proxy for wealth."

"Yet painted paper is the way we signify ownership of everything valuable," Dan argued.

Archive beamed again. "Ahh, yes! Absolutely! You've uncovered the very heart of the thing, haven't you?"

Another pregnant pause.

Get to the point, please, Sam nearly said.

"The agreements between us only work until they don't. And then they need to be reviewed, renewed, or removed."

"You've been waiting a long time to use that line, haven't you?" Sam asked.

Archive chuckled. "I am perhaps unduly proud of a well-turned phrase."

Brock laughed. "Time to shoot a new Monopoly Man video?"

"Brilliant idea."

"And you're saying that the dollar was a social agreement gone wrong," Sam summarized.

"Horribly so." Archive gazed off into the distance. "My comrades and I overlaid history's template on the future. Global-scale upheaval was inevitable, and the turmoil would have been disastrous for the true capital in the world, the infrastructure, production, and natural resources that sustain our lives and societies. We sought to kill the disease before it killed the host. Before it killed us."

Five minds chewed on that little gem, picturing wars, fires, hangings, and other atrocities, stark contrast to the mountain serenity surrounding them at the moment.

Before Sam reached any conclusions, the sliding glass door opened, and she turned to see a short, skinny man with a disproportionately large nose.

"May I introduce one of the world's foremost computer scientists," Archive beamed. "We call him Trojan."

"Sounds more like a prophylactic," Brock said, aiming to keep the comment beneath is breath, but missing.

The hacker ignored the barb. "There's a development, boss," Trojan said. He looked at the crowd and hesitated.

"We're friends," Archive said. "All in this together now."

Sam wasn't so sure about that. Things were about one hair's width from turning completely megalomaniacal. Or, maybe the mania had already run its course, and the old man was simply seeking a little retrospective validation. Either way, there was some serious bat-shit craziness in the recent past, and probably more on the way, and she had no idea whether the slightly patronizing old tycoon was part of the solution or part of the problem. So she certainly wasn't ready to declare allegiances and start waving flags.

But she was grateful for the peek at some of the group's dirty laundry, which the computer geek with the big nose had already begun airing. "I plotted the geo's of all the Bitcoin transactions over the last seven days."

"On the earth?" Protégé asked, incredulous.

Trojan nodded. "Worldwide. Really, the computer did it for me. Wasn't that hard."

Dan looked impressed, Sam noticed. *Maybe Dan and the other geek can get together later and compare their slide rules.*

"I presume there's a pattern of interest?" Archive's eyebrows arched.

Trojan nodded. "Still centered on the Northwest. No discernible pattern until Tuesday. Then, wham, a giant flood of transactions, randomly appearing, but all of them clustered within a thousand miles of Seattle."

"Translation, please," Sam said.

Trojan, Archive, and Protégé filled them in on the Bitcoin thefts they'd discovered, and explained the way the IP masking program had trouble getting a truly random sample of victim IP addresses. "Nobody has time to detect every active computer on the earth," Trojan said, stretching his arms out wide, "so the IP addresses they used, attempting to make it look like someone else's computer had done the stealing, ended up creating a beautiful Gaussian distribution centered on Seattle."

Brock frowned. "You're going to have to say it much dumber than that, please."

Trojan smiled. "I put a red dot at the location of every computer that received a Bitcoin transaction. A shitload of red dots ended up centered around Seattle."

Protégé translated further. "The upshot is that someone in Seattle is stealing massive quantities of Bitcoins."

"So this operation is as large as we feared?" Archive asked, worry in his voice.

"Larger," Trojan said. "If I use the volume and size of the thefts against our accounts as a scaling factor, and multiply it by the number of transactions I think are likely thefts committed by the Seattle people, we're looking at tens of thousands of Bitcoins already stolen. Dozens every minute."

Protégé whistled. Dan shook his head in amazement. Sam had no idea what the hell they were talking about. Brock looked as confused as she felt.

"Plus, as of this morning," Trojan went on, "there's another locus of activity on the East Coast. Looks like it's near a server farm I'm familiar with in upstate New York."

Archive looked serious, grave even. "This, I had not foreseen. Not even remotely."

Sam shook her head and held up her hand, confused and a little exasperated. "Listen, poindexters, you're going to have to help this criminology major understand what the hell is going on here. We're concerned about this, *why*, exactly?"

"Miss Jameson, perhaps your earlier worries about consolidation were well-founded," Archive said. "It is certainly not of our doing, but it appears that the other shoe has indeed dropped. By this time next week, if left unabated, the thieves will have amassed a fortune larger than all the private holdings on the European continent."

SEATTLE, WASHINGTON

IT WAS A FEATURE OF THE BRAVE NEW WORLD THAT, unless you lived in an RV in the middle of the desert, your face was captured on video nearly continuously. One camera kept watch over every ten citizens in the United States.

Benevolent watch, the camera owners were quick to add. But that was before the US Federal government co-opted their hardware, rendering their intentions irrelevant. It was in this way that Bill Fredericks discovered that one Domingo Mondragon, aka Sabot, had it in his mind to fly the coop.

Fredericks liked it when they fled. It triggered his pursuit instinct. He was fat, bald, and recently castrated, from a career perspective, but he still fancied himself a hunter, an alpha male. He ran field agents, and he wasn't really a field agent himself any longer, but changing times brought their own demands.

His quarry had taken along two boat anchors, in the form of a girlfriend and her mother, which made his job roughly three times easier. It was hard to travel light and unnoticed in a gaggle, particularly when nobody in the gaggle had the slightest notion of how to stay under the radar.

Fredericks had been to the warehouse where Sabot had set up the Bitcoin operation. He had been to the looted apartment where Sabot lived. He'd even been to the old lady's place, where Fredericks had correctly diagnosed the problem with the spyware. It hadn't sent a report in half a day, and Fredericks discovered that the virus' host had died a violent death, evidenced by the trash can full of crushed laptop parts in Connie Fuentes' garage.

So, in this case, Fredericks figured that two and two likely summed to four, and he had promptly enlisted the help of a computer-savvy agent who he knew would be utterly unruffled by the current economic kerfuffle. He knew this was the case, because the unwashed, unkempt recluse of an agent rarely emerged from his three-bedroom apartment, which he shared with two and a half bedrooms full of computer equipment and a powerful funk. The agent generally avoided opening the door, except to accept delivery of food, prostitutes, or computer gear, and he didn't care much who paid him for services rendered.

All of that made him pretty much the ideal asset.

Two Bitcoins and thirty minutes later, Fredericks hopped back in his car and pulled away from Connie Fuentes' residence, heading north, geo coordinates in hand, Canada his destination for the second time in as many days.

LOST MAN LAKE RANCH, COLORADO

"SO HERE'S WHAT I'M THINKING," DAN SAID. SAM recognized the facial expression – furrowed brow, one eye slightly squinted – that invariably warned of serious geekery to follow. She wasn't wrong. "We should run a recursive statistical refinement as the number of transactions increases."

Trojan shook his head. "We'll run smack into the noise floor of all the legitimate transactions going on in the world. It'll smear the solution accuracy."

"Unless we subtract out the noise floor," Dan said.

"How?" Protégé seemed to be following along.

"Continuous false alarm rate logic," Dan said. "Invented for radars, used to separate aircraft skin returns from the background noise. Pretty easy, actually."

"Suppose you get the noise thing figured out," Sam ventured. "How closely will you be able to locate the source?"

Dan looked at Trojan. Both shrugged. "Within a radius of a couple of city blocks, I would imagine. Hard to say for sure."

"That could leave us with a few hundred addresses to search."

Dan shook his head. "Not really. We'll narrow the search down beforehand by analyzing the modem traffic from the computers inside that radius. The people stealing all those coins are going to have a pretty high continuous data transfer rate over the past several days. Should leave us with a manageable search list."

"I was going to suggest that," Brock joked.

Sam walked out of the basement computer stronghold in the ranch, leaving the eggheads behind to work their black magic and summon the appropriate voodoo spirits to ferret out the location of the Bitcoin theft operation. She was glad that such hardcore computer wizards existed, but she had no desire to watch them work.

And she had her own preparations to make, which she hoped the old man could help with.

Every nutcase with a mountain stronghold had to have an armory, Sam figured. It was one of the immutable laws of the universe, like gravity, free healthcare, and other entitlements.

The stereotype held true. Archive's professed distaste for violence notwithstanding, he possessed a handsome collection of assault gear. While he may have been hoping for the rosier shades of human nature to emerge after his "bloodless devolution event," as he described it, he had evidently prepared for the opposite.

Panther Arms was a favorite supplier, apparently, which agreed with Sam's tastes. She chose several DPMS models, each capable of firing 5.56 or 2.23 rounds interchangeably, and each fitted with a holographic scope. "Sighted in?" she asked Mike Charles, whom she had learned was called Stalwart by the rest of the crackpot coterie.

He nodded. "Fifty yards."

"They'll do nicely, I think. You guys will donate for the cause?"

"Of course."

"Night scopes?"

He pointed to a large drawer in the armory, and Sam added them to the provisions, along with ballistic vests. It took her several trips to get everything out to the trunk of the Oklahoma police cruiser she'd commandeered two days earlier.

If the news reports were to be believed, the unrest in the cities had been largely quelled. But Sam was well aware that the government had a vested interest in appearing to be in complete control of the situation, and was certainly not above adding a little spin. Or completely falsifying things, for that matter. So she had reverted to her default stance – trust no one – and prepared for the worst. Her plan was to speak softly and carry a machine gun.

She finished packing the gear about the time that Dan and Trojan emerged from their basement Geekapalooza, a short list of Seattle addresses in hand. "We ride," Dan said.

"We'll need wheels," Sam observed.

"Taken care of," Stalwart offered. "Archive is cozy with the four-star in charge of Northern Command. Took a bit of convincing, but they'll have a six-pack truck waiting for you at the airport in Seattle."

"You're not going?"

Stalwart shook his head. "A man's got to know his limits," he said, extending his hand with a smile. "Thank you – you're not all bad, for a Fed."

"Thanks. You're okay, too, for an evil zealot."

With that, Dan, Brock, and Trojan piled into the cruiser, and Sam took the wheel.

An hour later, they climbed the stairs into the government VIP transport plane on the ramp at the Aspen airport. They lifted off and arced west, toward the falling sun.

WAREHOUSE DISTRICT, SEATTLE, WASHINGTON

SODO, OR SOUTH OF DOWNTOWN, A SEATTLE PLAY ON New York's more famous gentrified warehouse district, Soho, didn't quite live up to its East Coast rhyming partner's glory. Development dollars hadn't quite resurrected the desuetude left by failing physical goods businesses, yet there had been just enough investment to keep things respectable, maybe even a little hip, in a retro-grunge sort of way.

But Sam was much more interested in what might lay *inside* the quasi-dilapidated infrastructure, and, so far, they'd struck out.

Two addresses on Dan's short list, which was assembled based on larger-than-average internet usage, turned out to be buildings that simply employed internet-based security camera systems. They beamed hours of video footage to a server in a data center, accounting for the heavy internet traffic. Strikes one and two.

A third facility was indeed full of Bitcoin activity, but it was of the honest variety. Someone had assembled a gigantic array of Swedish mining hardware. Dan and Trojan each had a little geek hard-on, admiring the endless arrays of whirring fans and waves of heat thrown off by over-clocked processors crunching away on hundreds of billions of calculations per second, harvesting

Bitcoins for their efforts. The internet bandwidth usage was attributable to each of these mining rigs communicating with the worldwide network that kept the books on each Bitcoin transaction.

"Getting warmer, at least," Brock observed.

Sam nodded, gritting her teeth a bit. The sun was just about to set, and she was losing her patience. There were two more places on their list, and she sincerely hoped one of them panned out. Plus, the assault gear was uncomfortable and heavy, and she was ready to slip into something a little more relaxed.

They pulled into an empty parking lot at the next address, belonging to another nondescript and slightly run-down warehouse. They announced themselves, tried the door, and were surprised to find it unlocked.

Sam sighed. The cavernous space was completely empty.

Then she noticed a collection of offices, drywalled off from the rest of the warehouse, tucked into the far corner. They advanced slowly. Dan and Brock flanked the entryway, assault rifles at the ready, while Sam tried the door.

Unlocked.

Two for two. Too easy. Getting ready to walk into a bullet?

Dim lights shone, but nobody was inside. There was evidence of recent activity – candy wrappers and styrofoam noodle bowls, mostly – and the place had a vague human stench, the kind that accumulated when someone spent too much time in an unventilated room.

A green light flashed on and off in a small adjacent room, its door ajar. "Bingo," Dan whispered. "Modem light."

They advanced, slowly clearing the dingy office space. When they had satisfied themselves that they were indeed alone, Dan and Trojan got to work on the computer in the closet-sized office. Sam watched and listened, while Brock stood guard at the entrance to the warehouse offices.

"256 encryption," Trojan announced after toying with the laptop's password protection. "Wanna see something cool?"

Dan nodded, a bit too eagerly in Sam's judgment, and Trojan inserted a small USB device into a port on the side of the laptop.

Seconds later, they were in. "Holy sweetness!" Dan exclaimed. "How'd you do that?"

"Friends in low places," Trojan responded.

"You're the one, aren't you?" Sam asked. "The decryption toy that crushed the banks and exchanges?"

Trojan blushed a little. "Partly. I assembled the delivery vector. Someone else perfected the algorithm."

"And dropped it in the server farm at NSA," Dan finished.

Trojan nodded. "Team effort."

"Best damned hack in history."

Sam was pretty sure that Dan was awestruck. "Want his autograph?" she teased.

"Actually…"

"So here's the deal," Trojan announced. "Looks like this machine is running the script that's generating the thefts. At least, some of them, anyway. Assets near a quarter of a million Bitcoins, looks like. They must have hacked into a number of different exchanges to find that many small-time users to rip off."

"Can you disable it?"

"Already did. I can dig around a little bit, maybe pull together a few more clues about who these people are."

Sam shook her head. "Not here. They'll be back. I can't believe they've left the thing unattended in the first place." She got a chill down her spine. "In fact, let's get the hell out of here, now."

"Not just yet," Dan said, eyeballing the phone on the wall. He lifted the receiver, clicked a few buttons on his own smart phone, and held the old-school wall phone up to his handset. Sam heard tones beeping back and forth between the two phones. "Mapping the phone number by reverse-lookup. We'll be able to get a call log that way."

"What would I do without you?" Sam asked.

"Catch a lot fewer assholes, I think."

"No argument. But hurry up. I have a bad feeling."

Trojan tucked the laptop and modem under his arm, and Dan hung the receiver back on the cradle. The foursome made their way out of the warehouse quickly but cautiously, and drove into the Seattle night, Dan and Trojan's faces illuminated in the backseat of the giant six-passenger pickup truck by the glow of the computer devices in their hands, fingers buzzing in a torrent of activity.

It didn't take long before the pair had found a destination to explore. The list of calls made to or from the phone on the wall in the dingy warehouse office included a cell phone belonging to one Angela Fuentes. Nobody answered, but the phone was on, and had been stationary for several hours. The address resolved to a residence belonging to Connie Fuentes, half an hour away.

"Now what?" Brock asked. The house was empty, with an abandoned look about it.

Sam's search had revealed no essential toiletries, evidence that the occupants didn't plan on returning any time soon. They'd also left their cell phones, which reinforced Sam's flight theory.

Dan discovered the destroyed laptop. "No idea what this is all about. But they took the hard drive, which leads me to believe that something went awry."

Sam nodded. "Internal strife, maybe. There's a boatload of money in play. People get funny."

She looked at her watch, still on Mountain time. Nine p.m. Eight in Seattle. Each case had a half-life, after which the odds of cracking it diminished dramatically. Her years of investigative work gave her a strong hunch that this particular case's half-life was probably measured in hours, rather than days. "Gotta figure this out now, boys. I don't think we're going to get another crack at it. Not if Archive is right about the sums involved."

"Who's next on the call list?"

FBI Special Agent Adkins, it turned out. Not at the office, but not that hard to find, given that he was in the Homeland database of federal law enforcement officers.

He answered his cell phone on the fourth ring.

It took a bit of explaining, along with Sam's badge number, to get Adkins in the right mood to talk. But talk he did, in clipped Fed staccato, equal parts cop and college, explaining that Domingo "Sabot" Mondragon was one of the world's foremost hackers. So talented, in fact, that he once shut down a government, which brought the kind of attention that could feed both an ego and an indictment. One thing led to another, Mondragon played ball, did some time in exchange for ratting out a few dozen hacker cronies, and now earned a living working cyber crimes for the Bureau.

Until Tuesday, Adkins amended, when people who only used their first names and threw tons of weight around had spirited Mondragon away. To do what, Adkins had no idea, but he knew that it involved an officially-sanctioned parole violation, namely using a semiconductor computing device.

"How do you feel about that?"

"I just work here. That shit rolled downhill with some serious snap. Regional director put his stamp on it, and some opinions don't count as much as others."

"I understand," Sam said. "Have you been in contact with Mondragon since Tuesday?"

"I drove him home a couple days ago. He'd spent something like twenty-four straight hours pounding away on that computer. Like a long lost love, I think."

"In the warehouse over in SoDo?" Sam asked.

"That's right. You've done some homework, I see."

"We're not the Bureau, but we try," Sam teased. "How about recent contact, over the last day or so."

"None. Haven't heard from him. I was actually going to give him a call tomorrow to see how he was doing. Everything okay?"

"I'm not sure."

"Is he in trouble?"

"He might be on vacation."

"Shit. I was afraid of that. Can I join your investigation?"

"More the merrier. Send me a picture of him, first, please."

Adkins complied. Dan fed the image of Mondragon's face into the national database, and submitted a search request, centered on the Northwestern US, with a Most Urgent tag on it.

Across the continent, four stories full of computer equipment in a downtown DC office building whirred to life, polling all of the public surveillance camera output streams, running a program called BIDSS, or Biometric Identification and Surveillance System. Big Brother had strong-armed Big Data, and the ensuing sweaty love knot had produced an Orwellian system that could spot anyone, anywhere, in near real-time.

Provided, of course, that they were unable to hide their faces from the ubiquitous surveillance cameras, posted at every American intersection, in every store, restaurant, and parking lot, and atop nearly every building of consequence. Staying hidden was no mean feat. You'd basically have to wear a ski mask and sunglasses around town, because the computers measured all manner of facial features, many of which were unaltered by even the best disguises.

Upshot: one Domingo "Sabot" Mondragon had crossed the Canadian border, without incident, it seemed, an hour and a half ago.

"Sonuvabitch," Sam said, running back out to the six-pack truck. "Back to the airport!"

In the backseat of the six-pack truck, Dan lifted fingerprints from the laptop they found at the abandoned warehouse, took a picture of the print sheet, and scanned it into the national database tool. Less than a minute later, he had a positive match: Domingo Mondragon. "He's our guy," Dan announced, getting to work on his second assignment.

Sam had a stroke of brilliance during their mad dash to the airport. "Any chance you can ferret out a Bitcoin account address for any jet charter services operating out of the Vancouver area?" she'd asked Trojan and Dan. Her thinking was that Sabot Mondragon had just stolen a giant pile of Bitcoins, which suddenly gave him much more power and mobility than the average joe currently enjoyed.

It didn't take long. Every Bitcoin transaction was visible in the block chain, and Trojan had earlier figured out how to plot the IP address – which also revealed the physical location – for the computers involved in any Bitcoin sale. It was relatively easy for him to correlate those computers with the businesses they served. "Blammo," he exclaimed. "Five of them just set up accounts since Tuesday."

"Major transactions?" Sam asked. "Like, enough crypto cash to haul three people to the South American destination of choice?"

"Just one," Trojan said. "Obsidian Air. Based out of Pitt Meadows Regional, near Vancouver. Someone paid them three Bitcoins, which is worth, like, seven gazillion dollars right now."

So Pitt Meadows it was.

Sam called ahead to the airport, the pilot had the plane ready, and they taxied and took off without delay.

Sam had given the Wonder Twins another assignment: figure out, for the sake of confirmation, whether the originating wallet, or wallets, that had paid Obsidian Air were in any way related to the thefts that had occurred over the past few days.

"In other words," she said, "tell me if it really is our Bitcoin thief who just booked passage to a life on the lam."

It was going to take some luck, Dan said, and no small amount of doing. Plus, even if they were successful, they would really only discover whether the money used to buy the plane tickets had come from somewhere within the collection of red dots that was centered around Seattle, the same density plot that Trojan had used to detect the wave of thefts initially. There was no guarantee that they would provide proof.

"I suppose that'll have to be good enough," Sam said.

But they got luckier than that. The thief had tried to launder the funds through a number of shill accounts and wallet-obscuring services, but that was an exercise in futility. It was an easy matter to follow the funds back to the originating wallets.

Several of those wallets had received stolen funds that had originated in several accounts belonging to Archive's group.

"Smoking gun," Trojan announced as the plane rotated skyward. "We caught a supremely lucky break. Turns out that part of the money the thief used to pay for his plane tickets was stolen from Archive."

"Holy shit. You figured all of that out?"

"I don't know why you Feds are so paranoid about Bitcoin as a laundering tool. It's a forensic accountant's wet dream. You just have to know what you're looking for."

Sam suddenly had a panicked feeling. *What if he's already gone?* She dashed forward to the cockpit, tapped the pilot on the shoulder, and asked, "Any way you can step on it? We need to be there as fast as possible."

Which wasn't fast enough for Sam's taste, and she spent the remainder of the twenty-minute flight in nervous anticipation, knees bouncing impatiently.

PITT MEADOWS REGIONAL AIRPORT,
BRITISH COLUMBIA, CANADA

DOMINGO MONDRAGON, SABOT TO FRIENDS AND enemies alike, had the ghost-white look of a man on borrowed time. Angie noticed, and so did Connie, and all of his denials, in various octaves across his vocal register, had failed to convince them that he was in anything but deep shit.

Which, by extension, meant that they were in deep shit. So there was a bit of nervous energy in the car as Sabot picked a parking spot in the Obsidian Air lot.

"Are you sure about this?" Angie asked, not for the first or even the fourth time.

"Sure as I'm gonna be, baby. I don't see better options."

They dragged their bags into the posh terminal, checked in with the desk clerk, and took seats in the waiting lounge.

Sabot sat down, exhaled, and allowed himself to relax just a little.

Then he noticed the large man seated in the corner, hidden behind a newspaper, large gut heaving with each breath. The man lowered the newspaper to reveal the kind of elaborate middle-aged hair arrangement that only denial could produce, with a part originating somewhere above

223

the left ear, and a gravity-defying flap of stringy, greased hair clinging improbably to his bulbous pate, cascading carelessly down the right side of his head, the whole thing threatening to unwind itself at the slightest tilt of the man's head.

He beamed a gigantic, jowly smile. "I heard you were heading a long way south. I was hoping I could catch a ride with you. There's a little bit of job trouble, if I'm being honest. Happy to pay my way, and then some. What do you say?"

Angie and Connie turned as one to look at him, affirmative looks on their faces. Misery loved company, evidently.

He shook his head slightly, almost imperceptibly, afraid of opening themselves up to unnecessary human interaction of any kind. He caught daggers from Angie, and ignored the ones from Connie. "Would it kill us to give a guy a break?" Angie said quietly, through a smile and clenched teeth.

Sabot mulled, inhaled, exhaled, and stewed some more. He glanced across at the fat guy thumbing a ride to Central America. The man looked like someone's porky, comical uncle. He still wore that silly, yokel-esque smile, a transparently uncomplicated expression on his wide face. He didn't look like he could fool anyone, Sabot figured, so it was probably good that the guy was trying to get out of town before anyone wised up to whatever scheme he'd perpetrated.

Sabot glanced again at Connie and Angie, who were still looking at him expectantly.

The guy looked harmless, Sabot decided, and he'd offered to pay his way. Maybe karma would remember a good deed, and someone would lend them a hand when they needed it.

Sabot nodded his assent.

"Great! Hey, thanks, buddy, you really helped me out of a jam," he said, a little bit of a conspiracy in his tone. "I really want to get out of here while the getting is still pretty good, you know?"

Sabot understood the desire very well.

The clerk entered the waiting lounge and summoned the passengers. It was time. Sabot found himself relaxing, believing, possibly for the first time all week, that he might emerge unscathed from a very dicey adventure.

As they made their way to the waiting aircraft, the fat man extended his hand. "Thanks again, buddy. By the way, the name's Fredericks. Bill Fredericks."

"Nice to meet you," Sabot said, following him up the stairway to the well-appointed cabin.

The door sealed behind them, the engines wound up, and, moments later, they taxied to the runway.

They made small talk, Sabot's innards unclenching a bit more. None of the passengers noticed that their takeoff was momentarily delayed by the arrival of an American government jet, which landed and barely slowed down before it exited the runway and charged toward the private charter ramp that Sabot and his family had just left behind.

Moments later, they lifted off, made a wide, arcing turn to the south, and sped skyward toward their entangled fate.

Sabot wasn't sure, but he thought he caught a smug smile on the fat guy's face. Probably just felt good to have made his escape from whatever trouble he was leaving behind, Sabot reasoned.

He knew the feeling.

He squeezed Angie's hand, reclined his seat, and drifted off to sleep.

"IT'S A GODDAMNED CLIFFHANGER!"

Yes, this novel just ended as a cliffhanger.

Yes, cliffhangers are a crime against humanity.

Lars followed some bad advice at the beginning of his career and he has regretted it ever since.

That's why he wants you to download the conclusion to this story with his compliments.

Or copy and paste:

https://dl.bookfunnel.com/wp3rw4adp4

A SAMPLE FROM INTERNATIONAL #1 BESTSELLER MINDSCREW

THE END OF THE MODERN WORLD BEGAN IN NEW JERSEY.

This proved a number of people right, who asserted that New Jersey sucked, a capacity which, it might well have been argued, grew very suddenly to encompass the entire globe.

At least, the portion of the globe whose lives were impacted directly by the whims and fancies of the US dollar, a population which included almost every human on the planet, minus a token tribe or two of hunter-gatherers.

The trouble was that almost nobody knew the world was ending. Not even the guy who had helped begin its ending.

Especially not him.

He just thought he was getting rich. Right guy, right place, right time. Right on.

The whole thing wasn't even his idea. He was kidnapped, coerced, and cajoled into using what was by any standard a rare skill set. His task: to reapportion ownership of certain virtual financial assets.

In short, he was made to steal things. Crypto-currency, to be precise, something he hadn't heard of until the time came to begin stealing it.

Domingo Mondragon was his name, but he was known far more

widely by his *nom de guerre*, Sabot. He was a hacker. He had Anonymous, Antisec, Lulzsec, and various other credits to his name. Arcane monikers notwithstanding, those were meaningful credits. He was damn good.

Equally meaningful was the fact that Sabot's real name – Domingo Mondragon – appeared on another list, one that contained the names of the Federal Bureau of Investigation's stool pigeons. He was a rat, and there were just shy of two dozen people who were Big House guests on his account.

He was also on a list of convicted felons.

And a list of FBI employees.

And, now, Sabot occupied the top slot in Special Agent Sam Jameson's Biggest Bastards list.

She knew the world was ending. Or, if "ending" was too dramatic a term for the kind of economic subjugation that was occurring second by second as a single server in a single cluster in a single data center — in New Jersey — steadily and inexorably redistributed a controlling percentage of the world's wealth, Sam at least recognized the magnitude of the problem.

Freaking huge.

It was the kind of wealth that would make the Queen blush. Maybe Louis the Fourteenth, too.

A little blinking light on a little box full of semiconductors, situated in a server farm in a dark cave that used to be the main dig in the Naughtright Mine, protected by millions of tons of rock, cooled by spring water piped in from the nearby stream, was a terrifically poor indication of the mayhem being unleashed in the digital domain within.

The machine didn't know Sabot, didn't know Sam, and didn't know anyone called Archive. It certainly didn't know the Facilitator. And it also didn't know that its simple script, which it repeated several hundred times per second, performed a task that tilted the entire socioeconomic world on its axis.

It just knew that its system diagnostics reported a clean bill of health. So it continued to work. Find new account, unlock new account, remove money, repeat.

The light blinked on, placid, content, oblivious to the destruction it wrought.

TERENCIO MANUEL ZELAYA ABSENTLY SWATTED A mosquito. The annoying buzz of parasitic wings had a lower pitch in the jungle, owing to a larger wingspan than city mosquitos, evidence of a larger supply of blood to suck. Zelaya had swatted thousands of mosquitoes, during thousands of hot, sweaty Central American evenings, on his way to thousands of jungle interrogations.

He was good at interrogations, and in spite of his deeply religious upbringing, or maybe because of it, he rather enjoyed them. A 1983 graduate of the United States Central Intelligence Agency's "Human Resources Exploitation Course," and an ex-member of the Honduran death squad known as Battalion 3-16 – the biblical reference wasn't lost on him – Zelaya had so much to hide that hiding was impossible, and intimidation was the only remaining defense mechanism in a society that increasingly frowned on the kinds of political murders that had been Zelaya's bread and butter for nearly four decades.

He was well beyond nightmares. The atrocities he had committed over his long but insufficiently lucrative career had woven themselves into the fabric of his persona, and were as much a part of his identity as his scowl, his scars, and his ghost-white head of cropped hair, unusual for a man of Honduran descent, but not unusual for an American product.

Zelaya was both. He'd only been to the States a few times, always to attend CIA training courses, during which he had applied his unusual memorization skills to chapter and verse of the KUBARK, a politically toxic tome that distilled the state of the art of coercive interrogation techniques. It existed to train generations of crusaders and ideologues in the arcane arts of pain and extortion. Zelaya was a star pupil.

Many of his compatriots enjoyed the sadism, and many more merely endured it for its utility, but Zelaya had the perfect combination of zeal and twisted proclivity to enjoy a long career as a pipe-swinging, throat-slitting, mind-screwing utility man.

The politics were complicated and ever-changing, of course, but there never seemed to be a shortage of *them* for *us* to fight. Near as Zelaya could tell, the Americans were interested in the region for what seemed like a silly reason: Honduras grew the shit out of some bananas. Bananas, as in the bright yellow phallic fruit, though the country had its share of the other kind of bananas, the kind of mental insularity and infirmity that produced civil and international strife lasting decades.

There was an even sillier reason that the gringos had come south, with their large words and their even larger impositions. This related to the uniquely gringo delusion that the entire world would be better off under a new religio-political system, called (drum roll, please) Democracy. Like Truth and Beauty, it was self-evidently, axiomatically, undeniably *good*. Better than everything else, even.

At least to the gringos.

Zelaya hadn't bothered to point out that if Democracy needed the same kinds of goons, assassins, spies, shills, and puppets that supported socialism, communism, dictatorships, and other lesser forms of government all over the globe, perhaps the idea wasn't really all it was cracked up to be.

Making such an observation would have been counterproductive, however. While the gringos were clearly naïve and misguided, they were also dizzyingly well-resourced. And their interests appeared to align more or less with his own, a happy coincidence which, together with the open-faced

American gullibility for anyone who murmured the right ideological pet phrases at the right time, formed the backbone of a long and symbiotic relationship.

But here he was, in his sixties, still traipsing through the Central American jungles on the way to a prisoner camp to inflict grievous emotional, psychological, and physical harm on yet another human being, one who was unfortunate enough to find himself positioned by fate on the wrong side of a social or conceptual divide.

Surreal.

Old.

But it was remarkably commonplace in Zelaya's world, where borders were short but bitterly contested, and seemingly drawn to ensure that political divisions bisected as many familial and historical alliances as possible. There were more beefs per square foot than even Europe at its most truculent.

Job security.

And even in the relatively peaceful times, such as the era after the cocaine wars, the Americans' need for politically palatable places to conduct "enhanced interrogations" kept Zelaya plenty busy. Most of his reluctant guests over the last few years had been religiously misaligned gentlemen of Middle Eastern descent. They usually had little knowledge or concern regarding any nascent terrorist networks upon their delivery to Zelaya's care, but that didn't stop him from performing the proper due diligence.

Zelaya had expected the sudden gringo money problem – the dollar seemed intent on implosion, and appeared to be on the verge of tumbling into an inflationary oblivion of Dinar, Drachma, and Weimar Deutschmark proportions – to have unfavorable cash flow implications for him, but that hadn't turned out to be the case. A dear old Agency compatriot had called just days after the global meltdown had begun, in need of short-notice service for three Americans, two of whom happened to be female.

It was work, and it was of the lucrative variety, due to the political sensitivities involved, and Zelaya rarely turned down an opportunity. He had his eye on a small villa befitting a man of his loyalty and service, but not quite fitting within his means at the moment, so Bill Fredericks' call had been most welcome.

Zelaya reached his destination, swatted another mosquito, and rapped three times on a tree trunk to announce his arrival. A hollow echo resounded with each rap, affirming that he had chosen the right tree trunk. It had been hollowed out and resealed with a plaster-coated door designed to replicate the gnarled bark it had replaced, providing a suitably clandestine entrance to a well-used but well-hidden underground facility.

The subterranean entranceway was even muggier and more uncomfortable than the stifling jungle air, lacking the benefit of an occasional breeze to wick sweat away and replace the sickly sweet smell of decomposing organic matter.

With the door safely closed and locked behind him, Zelaya descended an earthen stairway leading to a narrow passage. He swiped his hand in front of his face to find a dangling string, a yank upon which caused a feeble overhead bulb to glow, helping him avoid the gnarled roots protruding through the cavern floor. Tripping hazard. He would mention it to the lieutenant, who would undoubtedly take the hint.

He felt the familiar downslope begin to level off, meaning he had descended the full twenty feet below grade, and was now on the top floor of a two-story underground interrogation and detention facility built by American contractors in the Reagan era. Talk about bananas. An underground prison with a Tolkien-like entrance in a hollowed-out tree? Couldn't they have just put a wall around a cabin in the jungle? Zelaya shook his head for the hundredth time at the boundless gringo zeal.

But it was tough to argue with success – in the facility's lengthy existence, Zelaya was aware of no security breaches. Perhaps there was a method to their madness.

"Our guests arrived safely, I presume?" Zelaya asked, striding with nonchalant authority into the facility's control center, of which he was undisputed master.

"Si, Señor." Lieutenant Alvarez was bright, competent, and dedicated. But not mean enough, in Zelaya's judgment. "Mother, girl, and target. They thought they were on their way to Costa Rica," he said with a derisive laugh. "All in separate cells, currently undergoing preparations."

Zelaya nodded. Preparations, as they were euphemistically called, entailed various measures that were designed "to induce psychological regression in the subject by bringing a superior outside force to bear on his will to resist." It was as if a business school graduate had written the Agency's exploitation manual, except that the sentences in the KUBARK sometimes actually made sense.

A superior outside force. Zelaya had always liked that phrase. It was a fitting personal and organizational description, he fancied, as well as a goal worthy of continuous aspiration. Part of his DNA now. The CIA-recommended techniques were varied and voluminous, including prolonged constraint, prolonged exertion, extremes of heat, cold, and moisture, deprivation of food or sleep, solitary confinement, threats of pain, deprivation of sensory stimuli, hypnosis, and drugs.

In all, nature had provided a rich palette of available techniques to place the human psyche in an agreeably compliant condition.

He looked at his watch. Almost dawn. In a few hours, it would be time for an introductory visit with each of his new subjects.

TURBULENCE AWOKE SPECIAL AGENT SAM JAMESON. SHE
had the kind of nasty taste in her mouth that she always got when she
was awakened too early from too little slumber. She looked at her watch,
which confirmed that entirely too few minutes had passed while she was
unconscious. Just shy of an hour, to be exact.

Her watch was still set to Mountain time. It was a couple of steps behind.
Along with her compatriots, who together comprised the entire passenger
manifest of a US government VIP jet transport plane, she had left the Pitt
Meadows Regional Airport in British Columbia, Canada, and was hurtling
down the American Left Coast through the darkness toward Costa Rica.

It was a long story.

It involved what she had come to regard as a colossally bad idea, which
had spawned a shockingly successful conspiracy. One of the perpetrators
happened to occupy a seat on the airplane. He went by the unlikely name of
Trojan, and was busily pecking away at a laptop computer, trying to unscrew
what he had so well and truly screwed.

Trojan was part of a group of extremely competent, and in some cases,
extremely prominent, illuminati who had become of a mind, collectively, to

disable the US banking system. They were pissed off, near as Sam could tell, about the US socioeconomic system's steady descent into oligarchy, to be remedied only by the destruction of the oligarchy's lifeblood: the US dollar.

By all indications, they had pulled it off.

Their success had added the Mighty Greenback to a long list of failed or failing fiat currencies, a result that produced just the sort of economic and political upheaval that re-drew maps and invited newly-self-appointed Masters of the Universe to try their hand at wrestling society's reins from whoever used to hold them.

And *that*, in turn, was why Sam, a busty, beautiful, brash, and somewhat bombastic redheaded Homeland Security agent, found herself jetting toward a Central American country in the middle of the night.

Messy.

But what else would she have been doing, if she weren't saving the world from the bastards? Writing memos? Informing stakeholders? Adding value to a value-added team in some value chain somewhere? No, thanks.

She'd rather catch spies, despite the sleep deprivation it sometimes produced. And the near-death experiences. But those things kept life interesting, and she figured that they just came with the territory. After all, was the threat of a violent physical death really all that much worse than the certainty of a protracted and painful death caused by cubicle-induced boredom? Sam had given the matter plenty of thought, and she thought not.

She looked over at Brock James, the man whose bed she'd shared for what was entirely too short an episode in her life. He was, for lack of a better word, perfect. Not in the usual BS, starry-eyed sense, but in the sense that all of his jagged edges fit all of her jagged edges as though they were complementary pieces carved from the same sarcastic, intelligent, athletic, and doggedly determined block. Their relationship worked in the way that gravity worked. There was almost nothing they could do to *stop* it from working.

In addition to the economic meltdown of global proportions, the past week had seen a kidnapping, too. Brock's. Those were three of the worst days of her life. But Sam's bull-in-a-china-shop tenacity and her Kimber .45 had saved the day, and while his bedroom athleticism was temporarily diminished by a gunshot wound to the thigh, Brock had survived the ordeal.

Thank god for that. She loved that man and his bedroom athleticism.

She could go for a little of that right now, she thought, watching his beautiful face as he slept. *Alas.* She resolved to take advantage of him sometime when they weren't confined in the presence of subordinates, criminals, and other unsavory people.

Unfortunately, a cozy bed wasn't anywhere on the agenda. They weren't exactly headed to Costa Rica on vacation. It had taken convincing, cajoling, and even a little coercion, but Sam had eventually wrestled the destination of Domingo Mondragon's chartered jet from the Obsidian Air charter service's desk clerk. An American government badge didn't go far in Canada, but Sam had found an exploitable pressure point. Thanks to her above-average persuasion skills, they subsequently found themselves winging their way toward Juan Santamaria International Airport in the little banana republic's capital, San Jose.

She chuckled to herself at the absurdity of the situation. She was on a plane with her deputy, her lover, and an international criminal responsible for helping to castrate the world's banking and monetary system, flying to the Central American jungle to chase down a felon and FBI informant, turned FBI employee, turned rogue Bitcoin thief.

You can't make this shit up.

The sound of clicking computer keys interrupted her reverie, and she looked over to see Dan Gable's face illuminated in the blue-white glow of a laptop screen. Her deputy was built like a bodybuilder, though one who had perhaps enjoyed a few too many ho-ho's. His physique made his uncommon computer skills seem a bit incongruous. He was putting his geekery to good use, searching for digital clues left on a laptop in the warehouse they'd searched just a couple of hours earlier. By all indications, this was the very laptop that Mondragon had used to steal tens of thousands of Bitcoins.

Those were worth about seventy gazillion dollars, now that the dollar had inflated beyond recognition. This week's dollar, Sam reflected, was worth quite a bit less than last week's penny.

More clackety-clack, caused by Dan's meaty fingers typing excessively hard on the keyboard. He was, in her estimation, the sole trustworthy individual in the Department of Homeland Security. She loved him like a brother. Sometimes he was an annoying brother. But he was nothing if not effective.

Their relationship was extremely close, but always professional. He'd touched her naked body once, and had even put his hands on her bare chest, but that was in an attempt to restart her heart, which had stopped beating on account of her very recent death. Thankfully, death didn't take, and she returned to the realm of the living with a few scars and an outrageous story.

Dan noticed her looking over at him. "Found something, boss," he said, turning the laptop so she could read the screen.

Sam saw instant-message artifacts from several conversations that occurred between someone named Sabot – Mondragon, she assumed, since Sabot was his pre-incarceration hacker moniker – and a person who called himself Balzzack011. "So it looks like this wasn't really Sabot's idea," she summarized after reading the message traffic between them.

Dan nodded. "The reluctant genius, kept chained up in a warehouse, stealing a fortune in Bitcoins. But who's pulling the strings?"

Sam shook her head and scowled. "The fact that there's a master of any sort is a bit disconcerting. If Mondragon was just a random hacker with a bright idea about how to get over on the world, that would be much easier to deal with. But this sounds a bit like coerced theft, which means that someone understood the importance of Bitcoins after the dollar pancaked, but lacked the technical skills to actually steal any."

Dan assented silently.

Sam pondered. There was no shortage of megalomaniacal bastards in the world, it turned out. It was simple probability math. One in twenty-five denizens of Planet Earth had sociopathic tendencies. A fraction of those were also narcissistic. And a slice of that cohort had the intellect and social skill to manipulate their way to real power. The sudden rise of the Bitcoin market in the wake of the dollar's implosion was a juicy motivator, and Sam didn't doubt that it had brought the nut jobs out in force.

So she had no clue about who might have been running Sabot, the hacker-thief. "Any clues about why Mondragon ran?"

"Maybe," Dan said. "I found something in the ftp history."

"The history of what?"

"Are you completely computer illiterate?"

"No," Sam said. "I can program my vibrator."

Dan frowned and shook his head. "You can use the internet to transfer files directly between computers, without sending them in an email. It's called file transfer protocol, or ftp. It leaves less of a trail than email, which is the digital equivalent of petrified wood."

Sam nodded. She'd typed angry before, and had clicked send, which was how she had learned that email was forever.

"Our guy deleted the ftp history, which is a great indication that he's got something to hide. Porn, usually, but in this case, it turns out that Sabot transferred the scripts that were behind all the Bitcoin thefts to a server farm in New Jersey."

"How did you figure that out if he deleted the history?"

Dan smiled. "A few tricks of the trade."

"Constitutionally dubious, no doubt."

"No comment."

Sam smiled, shaking her head. "So he made a copy of his own program for his own use," she summarized. "I suppose that might be grounds for a falling out, given that this 'Ball Sack' guy seems to think that Mondragon works for him."

Dan nodded. "He must have been pretty scared. He took his girlfriend and her mother along with him."

"There's a ton of money in play. I can see why he was concerned. How about the list of Bitcoin accounts and passwords?"

"It's hidden behind 256 encryption," Dan said.

"Which will be child's play for the decryption bug that destroyed the Fed," Sam said, gesturing toward Trojan.

Dan nodded. "Exactly right. So I don't expect trouble hacking in."

"So we just un-steal the coins. Done. No more threat of world domination. Right?"

Dan nodded. "And we should be able to work the same magic on the mirror operation hidden on the New Jersey server." He smiled. "Makes me wonder why we're flying all the way to Costa Rica."

"Great point. Who ordered this expedition? She should be fired. But humor me, maybe, and un-steal a few zillion Bitcoins ASAPly, just to prove we can."

Dan opened the decryption program, briefly consulted with Trojan, the international computer criminal whose virus had brought down the banking industry and whose help they now enjoyed, and clicked a few more keys.

"Oh, shit."

Sam: "What's up?"

"I just opened the Bitcoin transaction ledger to get an idea of which private keys to go after."

"English, please."

Dan explained that a Bitcoin wasn't really a physical or digital object. Instead, it was an entry in a public record of private transactions. Each transaction involved a public key, which was otherwise known as the account name, and a private key, which was akin to its password. "I was looking for the right accounts to hack into."

"Should be easy, right? Aren't they using thousands of new accounts to receive the stolen Bitcoins?"

Dan nodded. "They are. But it looks like there's a parallel operation going on to disperse the cash through a bunch of different, new accounts, too." More clicking, and a low whistle. "Tens of thousands of accounts."

"Sounds inconvenient. But you can crack them all, right?"

"Fairly easily, if we use Trojan's network of slave computers. Disregarding the legal problem with using a network of virus-infected private computers to do federal government work, of course."

"I don't think Uncle Sugar has the luxury of splitting hairs at the moment," Sam said. "Besides, these guys are making a play for the kind of wealth that will buy any government they want. I think I can ask forgiveness."

"Let the record reflect that I am breaking the law on the suggestion of my immediate supervisor."

Dan squinted his eyes and examined a few new windows, a frown deepening on his brow. "Shit. This isn't going to work."

"What's not going to work?"

"It looks like they have their funds in continuous movement. In the time it will take us to decrypt an account's password, they will have easily established a new account and transferred all the Bitcoins out of the old one."

More clicking. "It's actually kind of brilliant," Dan continued. "They've found an elegant way to stay ahead of the tracing problem. Every Bitcoin transaction is public and traceable, so they're making every transaction utterly meaningless by keeping the money constantly in flux, establishing new accounts every second or two."

Sam frowned. "How wily of them. Any way we can maybe anticipate the account names, to get inside the time cycle?"

Dan shook his head. "Each account name has thirty-four random digits, each of which can contain letters or numbers."

"So looks like it's down to good old fashioned spy catching."

"Looks that way."

"I guess flying down to Costa Rica wasn't such a bad idea after all."

Dan smiled. "I hear it's pretty down there. And the cartel beheadings have slowed down a bit, too."

"See? It'll be fun."

READY FOR WHAT'S NEXT?

Get the latest book in the million-selling Sam Jameson
series, and catch up with USA Today Bestselling Author
Lars Emmerich, over at Lars' shiny new store:

store.ljemmerich.com

ABOUT THE AUTHOR

When Lars Emmerich was twelve, he went to an airshow. An F-16 flew over the crowd, low and fast and impossibly loud. Something stirred in his chest and tears formed in his eyes. It was love at first sight. Lars and the F-16 went on to enjoy fifteen incredible years together.

While Lars was a young lieutenant in Undergraduate Pilot Training, he read a Tom Clancy novel. It was his first exposure to the espionage and conspiracy thriller genre, and again it was love at first sight. "I will write stories like this one day," he vowed solemnly.

He's still trying to live up to that promise.

ABOUT SAM JAMESON

Sam Jameson catches spies for Homeland. Not a traditional female career path. But Sam's not really the traditional type.

She has great aim and a bad temper, and they don't always mix well. She also has the dubious distinction of having died once in the line of duty.

Sam is the star of the <u>Sam Jameson series</u>, which now boasts over 1,000,000 fans in 17 countries.

"This is the best writing in decades. Move over, Lee Child."
- Steve Harrell

WHY LARS 'FIRED' AMAZON

Once upon a time, Amazon decided not to pay Lars his royalties.

Lars was frightened and confused. Authors have children and must buy groceries, after all.

"Why, oh Amazon, have you done this thing?" Lars cried.

But the Amazon humans were too busy to answer, for Lars was not yet famous enough for their attention.

Only the robots took the time to reply... though the robots gave him no answers.

This taught Lars something important: **authors cannot rely on Amazon**.

So he learned how to connect directly with readers and fans, and it is the best decision he ever made.

Get the latest book in the million-selling Sam Jameson series, and catch up with USA Today Bestselling Author Lars Emmerich, over at Lars' shiny new store:

store.ljemmerich.com

ACKNOWLEDGMENTS

Lars wishes to thank the most important person in his business:

YOU.

Because of your enthusiasm, patronage, and support, Lars is blessed with the incredibly rare opportunity to pursue a lifelong dream.

Thank you.

Thank you.

Thank you again.

Made in the USA
Monee, IL
15 November 2021